Saving DEATH

Sometimes you can only find the light in the darkness...

Saving DEATH

R.L. ENDEAN

*This edition published in **2018** by*
OFTOMES PUBLISHING
UNITED KINGDOM

Cover design by Eight Little Pages
Interior book design by Red Umbrella Graphic Designs

For Tim and Lina.

Prologue

A burning sensation licks up his throat and he tries to swallow it back. He doesn't know I'm causing him this pain and he tries to focus on the girl. His whole demeanour is inviting as he pulls her towards him, but I know he won't kiss her. I know the real reason he is alluring her.

Hunger like he's never felt before makes every pore in his body throb with interminable agony. It's building inside him and as he reaches out, I know what's coming. I have to stop it but I can't stop the inevitable. His hand is already on her forehead. His chest expands and I can do nothing as her eyes flutter open in confusion.

It's over quickly. Her gaze quickly fades and becomes hollow, resembling glass and her body goes limp in his arms. I'm too late and I can't help but feel the rise of emotion in my chest. It's enough to make me scream—but he doesn't hear me over his own growl of fury.

His chest heaves, sending puffs of hot breath into the cold air, and his muscles contract angrily as he lets the girl's now lifeless body slide down his front before stepping over her and striding out into the orange glow of the street.

CHAPTER *One*

Time couldn't erase grief; it could only allow it to shrivel and wilt like a dead flower shedding its petals. That's what I'd learnt in the months following my mum's death. It made me wonder what I'd be left with afterwards. For now, I had to endure my inner deterioration without knowing what it would leave me with; perhaps a seed, or maybe just a husk.

I'd tried my best to deal with the poisonous concoction of numbness and excruciating pain grief brought, but I'd failed to find a way out. Most of the time, I felt nothing. I felt fine. I felt normal. That was the unbearable part. Then these pockets of pain would erupt from within me, beyond my control. It was comforting to know I felt something and frustrating to know I wasn't fine and probably wouldn't be for a long while. Getting better mentally would take longer than physically.

I'd spent the last three months in and out of hospital following traumatic injuries that should have killed me, but I was told by medical staff that someone up there didn't think it was my time yet. Fate, they said. I just hoped they were right and there really was a reason for all of this. A hope, which was probably stupid as I was being forced to move away from everyone and everything I'd known for the past seventeen years.

I was moving in with my dad on Willow Farm, in the far recesses of the west of England, where the undergrowth was as thick as the mist. My memories of Willow Farm were fond, but few and far between. I was never sure if my scant visits were reflective of a farmer's demanding work hours or my mum's damaged relationship with Dad. By all means, my parents had always been civil when they spoke, but there were always unsaid words drifting overhead. As far back as I could remember, they both made it their goal to avoid each other. A small part of me was looking forward to moving in with Dad and finally getting to spend some time with him. The only problem was I didn't like spending time with anybody anymore, preferring to curl up at home and avoid the outside world instead.

In the months after Mum died, I became attached to the cool interior of the spare bedroom in my aunt's house. Living with her had been a temporary solution whilst recovering, attending my mum's funeral and going to what seemed like endless hospital appointments. My dad had visited, but as I'd never particularly bonded with him, I may as well have been left alone. Most evenings were spent avoiding opening the bedroom door in favour of running over every tiny detail that my mind had saved for me from that night. When mum died, something inside me got ripped away and I knew, for certain, I wouldn't get it back. My world was lived in monotone now, and as I gazed out of the bus window and watched the scenery blur into one, I was curious to know if colour would return to me someday.

My head bumped against the dirty glass window, and I absently wondered if I'd have to work on the farm and whether the work would be hard enough to occupy my mind for the remaining days before I had to start college. Whatever the situation, I felt certain Dad would keep out of my way. Mum had left him when I was only four years old, and he'd not been able to look me in the face properly since. Everybody always said how much I looked like her. I guess he lived in his own realm of pain involving my mum.

The bus came to a brisk halt and I had to grab the seat in front to stop myself from hitting my head. The old lady beside me mumbled something in her thick country accent, but I couldn't bring myself to respond. She hobbled to the doors, which opened with a gust of wind, flicking my hair around my face and making me shiver. Pulling my hoody around me, I watched as the old woman mirrored me with her lilac trench-coat. Where had the summer gone? It had passed me in a frenzy of scattered emotions and well-meaning words from friends and strangers alike. I'd lived in a surreal reality. Even now, I felt like my mum's death hadn't entirely entered my conscious mind.

I felt numb and I felt guilty for not feeling more. Yet, the overriding emotion I felt in the quiet moments throughout every day was terror. I was utterly terrified because I couldn't remember a single thing about that life altering night. Had I forgotten possibly the most significant moment in my life?

I'd gathered I'd been in a near fatal car crash and that she'd been with me, but I'd failed to tell anyone that I had no memory of it. I'd decided it was something worth keeping to myself, even if it drove me mad.

My phone buzzed in my pocket, throwing me from my train of thought. I dug into my pocket for it.

Dad. *How's it going, love?*

New life was knocking at my door. I wanted to scream until my lungs burst; I wanted a few more months to wallow in the shadows of self-pity. Instead, I was being rushed into a new life, forcing me to leave the old one behind. The frustration I felt bubbling inside me was unbearable.

I typed a message back. *Nearly there.*

That was all I could manage. I stuffed my phone back in my pocket and rested my head back on the window. I hadn't even the energy to hold my own head up. I always felt so emotionally drained and it was beginning to get on my nerves. Would it never end? Grief was like having a constant unwavering weight around your neck, making it ever so slightly more difficult to breathe.

The bus rounded a corner and trundled up the country lane past a rickety old barn and a gate with a sheep dog barking behind it. At the end of a dirt track, the bus finally came to a stop and I suddenly felt sick. This was it. I sat for a moment and stared out into the darkening evening, building myself up to stepping into a new world. The bus driver's voice interrupted my reverie.

"This is your stop, love."

Feeling more than a little frustrated at the bus driver, I found the strength to shift my body off the grubby seat.

I really didn't want to be here, but then I didn't really want to be anywhere. Sighing in resignation, I grabbed my coat, pulled my backpack onto my back, and clicked open the handle on my suitcase to drag it across the bus floor. I hadn't seen my dad since the funeral and I had an irrational fear that he would want to talk to me about it. Climbing off the bus, I kept my eyes fixed on the ground until the last possible moment—that moment came all too soon.

"Ava," came the familiar voice of my dad. He looked the same as always in his green wellies and brown tweed coat with flecked greying hair, and I felt relieved. Something in my world had remained unchanged.

"Hi," was all I could muster. The cold nipped at me and I shivered.

"Where's your coat, love?"

I held up my bobbling woollen coat so I didn't have to talk, and after wedging my backpack between my knees, I pulled it on. I was thankful that it held out some of the biting cold.

"Here." My dad held out his hand for my suitcase. "Good trip?"

"Fine," I lied, hitching my backpack further onto my shoulder.

"Good."

My dad was a man of very few words and even fewer with me, so, as we wandered down the muddy path in silence, I felt no pressure to invent conversation. Instead, I allowed my mind to wander to what my bedroom might look like. Would it still have the single futon with the pink duvet cover like when I was little? I would probably have to make the room my own again somehow.

As we reached the front door of the farmhouse, Dad turned the key and gave the old oak door an extra budge with his boot. “Blasted door,” he grumbled as I followed him inside.

Despite not having stayed in a long while, the entrance room looked much the same as last time and a small sense of home flickered inside me. It had a log fire, which meant the room was nearly always warm, and as I took off my coat, I took in my surroundings.

A small flat screen TV was perched in the far-right corner next to the log burner and on the other side of the room there was the same long worn brown sofa with a red tweed blanket thrown over the back. Nearest the door, there was a blue winged grandad chair with an ottoman in front of it, and in the middle of the room, on top of the patterned rug, there was a short brown coffee table. I took a deep breath, trying to find the strength to accept my new home, but the smell of damp wood caught in my throat and I coughed.

“C’mon, I’ll help you up with this stuff,” said my dad. He lifted the suitcase by the handle and started heaving it up the stairs. I followed close behind and was surprised to discover that my bedroom was exactly the same, save the enormous iron bedframe topped with a double mattress and a fresh new bedspread. I raised my eyebrows.

“Thought you could do with a new bed,” he mumbled, leaning my suitcase against the wall and tucking his hands in his pockets.

The room felt familiar, yet new. It was as if I was

seeing a friend from long ago and I felt like I needed to get to know it again.

"Thanks."

He nodded simply, grunting something about a brew and wandering out of the room and down the stairs.

Dropping my rucksack on the floor, I tiptoed across the threadbare carpet to my bed and tested the mattress. The bed was comfortable and had an embroidered, cream coloured quilt. Dad must have bought it especially, I thought to myself, feeling a small ray of warmth inside me.

Behind me, there was also a small chest of drawers, which doubled as a bedside table. Relief spread through me when I saw the small silver lamp perched on top. I hated sleeping in the dark ever since she died. A deep-rooted feeling of unease always bloomed inside me when the lights went off, even though I'd never had a problem with the dark before. Now, it just sent waves of doom through me. I couldn't pin point exactly why, but I guessed this fear lived off the thing hidden inside me. Something in my subconscious was trying to make its way out. I hoped, in time, I could at least bring myself to turn off the lamp at night like a normal teenager.

Sighing and glancing around my old room, I saw that my desk was exactly the way I'd left it, right down to the pin board perched on top. I got up and walked to it, and I couldn't help but smile. There was a picture of me and Mum on a beach in Turkey from a family holiday when I was young. We were wearing swim suits and Mum was laughing; I had covered her feet in sand and modelled it into giant's feet complete with seashell toenails. Sadness twisted inside me at how happy I looked.

Tearing myself away to keep from crying, I wandered to the window and absently traced water droplets down the pane, gazing into the trees behind the house. It was getting dark. Darkness again—in the countryside night-time was especially dark too. My pulse quickened, my face became warm—I needed to think about something else. Yanking the curtains tight, I looked desperately for something to do, but it was too late. I could feel the panic rising inside me, making me want to bolt. A gentle knock interrupted and Dad came in, avoiding my eyes.

"Alright, love? Settled in?"

I nodded impatiently.

"Here," he said, holding out my favourite pink mug filled to the brim with milky tea. It wasn't my favourite anymore, though. I couldn't think straight. My throat began to constrict and my head began to spin.

"I have to get out of here," I breathed as I moved to the door and shoved past him, knocking the mug to the floor with a small ceramic thud. I heard him curse under his breath and I didn't know if it was at me, or the spilt tea. Not that I cared. I was already on the landing, flinging myself onto the stairs and racing for the door, but my body was taking over and my sweat drenched hands slipped on the wooden banister. There it was—that sense of looming dread again.

Launching myself through the front door and into the cool night air, I heard my dad's voice calling my name down the stairs, but I couldn't stop. I had to keep running, even if it was outside into the dark—the dreaded dark.

I ran to the back of the house and into the maze of

barns, through the noise of bleating sheep and the bitter smell of muck. I gasped for breath as I ran through several large barns full of sheep until I reached the last one. Being quite a distance from the house, I couldn't hear my dad calling my name anymore. Maybe he'd realised I needed some air.

Searching frantically, I finally found a quiet corner in the back barn where I slumped down in the hay. I couldn't get enough air into my lungs and I knew I needed to calm down, but there was no reasoning my way out of this feeling. I just needed to let go. Tears burned my eyes and this time, I let them flow. Huge sobs erupted from deep inside me and I gripped the straw until it dug into my hands. Pain made it easier to deal with. *Finally*, I was alone to let go and sink into my sadness and pain. A scream tore through the barn and I threw the straw from my grip and hit the floor.

"Why did you take her? I wasn't ready!" I screamed, anger ripping through me. Climbing to my feet, I turned on the iron, kicking it with all my might and felt the metal reverberate through my palms again and again until my emotions ran into nothing. Sinking to the floor with silent tears, the barn fell eerily quiet and still. Only the security light blinked on outside. It must be an animal, I thought to myself, but as I felt eyes on me, I knew I wasn't alone. Dad had followed me outside after all.

"Go away," I said without looking up from my self-indulgent misery.

"Couldn't if I tried," came an unfamiliar voice. I looked up, embarrassed.

"Sorry, I didn't know—" I started. A stranger stood in

the doorway to the barn. My vision was blurred with tears, but I could tell he was young. His arms hung into his pockets from broad shoulders, and he stood unnervingly still. I must look a mess, I thought, raising my sleeve to wipe at my face. I still couldn't see his face clearly, yet I could tell he was looking at me with curiosity.

He must be working for my dad, I thought. When he remained stone cold still, a feeling of unease settled in me. I knew I shouldn't be here with this stranger. I grappled from the floor and casually took a step toward the back of the barn. "I should head back," I said.

He laughed quietly and I felt a shiver run through me. I needed to get back to the safety of the farm house. My heel collided with a disregarded brick and I fell back just as a strong hand gripped my wrist to pull me up. His face came into the light and his black eyes pierced me, cold and unfeeling.

"Careful, city girl," he said.

I swiped his hand from my arm and backed away towards the other end of the barn, but I could still feel where he'd gripped my wrist. The light shone down on him, and I could see that his face was pallid and his jaw angular. He reached up and ruffled the wet out of his hair, but at no point did his eye contact waver, unnerving me.

"Who are you?" I managed, but something told me he wouldn't be forthcoming with introductions. I couldn't put my finger on it, but something inside me revelled in the unexpected sensation of risk that came with this stranger.

With a smirk, he cocked his head up, ignoring my

question. "You must be the prodigal daughter. *Ava* from the big smoke," he said.

I stared back and felt an impulsive sense of pride at having analysed this character so quickly—he wasn't going to tell me who he was. Two could play at that game.

"I'm here because my mum died." I wanted to embarrass him and I think it worked. He finally dropped his gaze and frowned. Feeling satisfied, I turned my back on him and began to stalk away—but his voice echoed through the barn.

"Have you remembered how she died yet?"

I froze, unblinking on the spot. It felt like my insides had turned to stone. "What?" I said, hearing the tremble in my own voice. Silence followed, so I faced the stranger.

He was leaning against the door of the barn with his hands tucked inside his pockets, satisfied.

"How do you… I have no idea what you're talking about," I said, knowing the quiver in my voice would give me away.

He grumbled a response, all the while assessing me, then without another word, he walked away. "See you around, amnesia."

Anxiety and anger rose in me like a tidal wave and I chased after him. There was no way he could make a comment like that and expect me to just accept it. "Hey—stop, will you?" I shouted, shivering as the cool air surrounded me.

He stopped, his gaze glinting as it dropped down my body and back up to my face. "You should go," was all he offered before continuing to march out into the fields.

I should have left it, but I wanted to know what he knew. I wanted to know *how* he knew. I ran out into the deserted fields after him, trying with all my strength to not let the darkness push in on me.

"Hey!" I shouted, slipping on the mud as he continued to stride into the distance. I strained my eyes into the expanse of the open field to see him, but my foot sunk into the sodden ground.

I whirled around, frustration bubbling over. I felt like crying as I yanked my ruined shoe out of the ground, cursing under my breath. I must have looked like a complete mess, but I didn't care. I just needed answers. Shoving my foot back into my dirty shoe, I stood upright—and found his cold unfeeling eyes. My eyes widened in response, but he tore his gaze away from mine and down at my ballet shoes.

"You should wear more appropriate clothes around here."

"Who are you?"

"Somebody it would do you good to avoid," he said with an air of arrogance. I prickled at this.

"Then you don't know me as well as you think you do," I fired back. Where a dull haze of moonlight lit up his features, I could see that his brows were black like his hair and his eyes. His eyes were so black they almost entirely concealed his pupils. I pulled my gaze away, but only managed as far as his lips.

He smirked and raised a hand towards my face, but I flinched. His hand froze, lingering a second in mid-air, before wiping a spot of mud from my cheek. All the frustration from before had melted from his expression. He laughed and leant in close enough that I could feel his breath on my neck. I didn't move an inch. I was like prey frozen to the spot before the kill, my heart thudding in my chest.

"I think you don't know *yourself* as well as you think you do," he whispered. I raised my eyes to him as he leant away from me. Squaring my shoulders, I tried not to let his words affect me in any way.

"Well I think you're an arrogant arse," I said curtly, tearing myself away from him. Yet, as I walked away, I couldn't ignore the gnawing feeling inside me that there was something calling me to this ominous stranger. He'd been in my life for all of two minutes, yet he was the only person to make me feel anything other than excruciating pain and I had to know why.

CHAPTER *Two*

Ambulance sirens pierced my mind and disinfectant burned the back of my nostrils as I entered the hospital. My mind was a blur of colour and my body a cocktail of nerves. Paramedics whipped past me in a flurry of activity and I became aware they were attending to my mum. I strained to see her through the throng of activity, but my heart stopped as my eyes settled on her lifeless body covered by a blue sheet. As they wheeled her down the corridor, her delicate hand slipped from under the sheet and hung off the side of the bed.

Panic gripped me. I didn't have a clue whether she was alive or dead. My legs felt like melting wax as they began to give way, but before I had time to give in to their weakness, I moved down the corridor towards the operating theatre. With every step, the sound of my shoes skidding on the lino floor reverberated inside my head; my pulse quickened until I thought I was going to be sick. The doors loomed up in front of me like two colossal tombstones, cold to the touch—then a hand gripped my shoulder.

"This way, please, Ava." The voice was caring but

professional. "Don't worry. They'll take good care of her."

All I could think was that it wasn't enough. I needed to be with her. I needed to see her. I *had* to know she was okay. Pushing the hand roughly off my shoulder, I turned back to the doors, but they were far out of reach. I ran towards them, but they seemed to creep away from me. I hurried on, but they only shrank away from me further as if they were at the end of a long tube being pulled in the opposite direction.

"Ava—" the voice came again. My heart was beating faster than it ever had and cold sweat trickled down my neck, but I was closing in on the door again. I could see the edges of the enormous operating lights through the window. My fingertips brushed the surface of the door—but the same hand held me back.

No! I turned to push the hand off, but nobody was there. Coldness swept through me like an autumn wind, and my insides twisted in discomfort as my hand dropped back by my side. I looked down at my shoulder, where I still felt the pressure of where someone had grasped me, and choked on my own scream. My shoulder was red with blood. Whose blood? Mine? Hers? I saw my palms were covered in blood, but my gaze was distracted and swept down my body. That's when I saw I was drenched in the sticky red substance. It soaked into my clothes in huge scarlet patches so that my hoody was sodden with it. It dripped from the end of my zip into a pool on the floor, onto my now red trainers. I gasped.

"No… get it off. Get it off me!" Sweat drenched my face as I tore at my clothes, then something cold clamped around my wrists.

"Ava!"

I opened my eyes and found myself on my bedroom floor with my dad holding my wrists. He stared down at me with concern, eyes puffy from sleep.

"Ava, you were just having a bad dream. You're safe, okay? You're safe now." He pulled me to my feet, gesturing for me to sit on the bed.

Climbing onto the bed, I clenched the bedsheets. They were cool under my hot palms, but it was the lingering feeling of blood soaked clothes that made me shiver. Why was there always so much blood? I swallowed hastily as my throat constricted with the bitter taste of bile. Had it been my blood or hers? Feeling the tears suddenly prick my eyes, I rubbed at my face to ward them off. Why did it always have the same effect on me?

"Was it the dream your Aunt Kate told me about?"

"She told you?" I asked, my hands dropping from my face. I looked at my dad in embarrassment, but was met by an earnest stare. My strength slipped immediately and I nodded silently.

I didn't bother to explain the dream to my dad, seeing as I had a hard-enough time attempting to explain it to myself. I tried to think myself out of feeling sick, but it was no use. It didn't help that the shakes had already started. Looking to my dad, I tried to gauge his reaction. He looked concerned—really concerned.

"Maybe I should find someone around here for you to talk to. You know, to help you deal with it all," he offered.

I thought back to my last weeks at school before the

holidays, after I'd finally come out of hospital. I'd been referred to the counsellor to *talk,* but I'm sure it had made everything worse. The pressure to talk was overwhelming and for a traumatised introvert like myself, it was torture. I'd ended up not engaging at all, and I half wondered if, somehow, I'd closed some gateway to my memories. I wished I could have blocked out the entire therapy experience as well…

I'd sat in her tiny beige office on the second floor of the science block. A stiflingly dry summer breeze blew in through the yellowing blinds, sweeping the smell of urine from the boys' toilets through the air. Miss Peters gazed at me curiously, her hands clasped neatly together on the top of her desk. I kept my eyes on my lap and felt nothing.

"You have to let it in, Ava." She had looked at me gravely through tortoise shell rimmed glasses. She was only a few years older than me—maybe in her twenties—and I wondered if she actually knew what she was talking about. I had wanted to ask her if she had ever lost anybody, but thought better of it. My head of year, Mr Furrows, had already spoken to me.

"We're all just trying to help you get back on your feet, Ava. You're a smart girl, and Miss Peters is trying her best to get you ready for your end of year exams—but you have to let her help. Just try, okay?"

I'd held my tongue since then and had become even more stubborn. During our last session, she'd sat back in her chair and sighed in resignation. "I know it's easy for me to say, but you need to do this, Ava. It's not something you can suppress. You can't lock it away and not deal with it." Her hazel gaze bored into mine, imploring me to share my grief with her, but she didn't know that I couldn't let it in because I couldn't remember what happened. To me, my only option *was* to lock it away and not think about it.

"Ava? You know—a counsellor or something? I know you didn't get on well with the one at your old school but..." I stared at my dad as he continued to prattle on about my experiences with the school counsellor. There was no way I was going through that again. "*Let it in, Ava!*" Why was everyone in such a rush for me to be "normal" again? I'd done the research myself; grieving was messy. I just needed to plod along and let it take its course. Maybe then, the incidents of that night would all come flooding back with clarity.

Thinking about it made me nervous and I pulled my legs into my chest, hugging them for security. Realising my dad had stopped talking and was now looking at me with something in between sympathy and irritation, I quickly sat up and gave him my best smile.

"No, I'm fine Dad—really I am."

He looked unconvinced and truth be told, so was I. I wondered if I would ever remember what happened. At this thought, a crushing darkness opened up inside me. What if I could *never* remember? Despite the feeling of dread, I felt glad that I hadn't told anybody about my amnesia. Sharing wouldn't help matters. But then, if I hadn't told anybody, how had *he* known? My mind was suddenly back in the barn, staring into those deep black eyes.

My dad coughed, bringing me back to the now. I

looked at him blankly.

"I just need to catch up on sleep, that's all," I said.

He gazed at me a moment longer before finally letting it go. "Okay," he said with a sigh. "Well, let me know if you change your mind."

I nodded, humouring him.

"I could do with an extra pair of hands on the farm tomorrow, though," he said, leaning over to kiss the top of my head, "So you best get some sleep."

"Yup," I muttered, watching him as he left my bedroom. As he closed the door behind him, my muscles relaxed and I fell back on my bed. What was wrong with me? Surely, other people dealt with losing someone better than this. How did they do it? Sighing to myself, I yanked the duvet up to my chin and settled onto my side, forcing myself into another uneasy sleep.

My head thumped in protest when I awoke the following morning. I wanted nothing more than to sink back under the duvet and forget today, but I knew I needed to show my dad I was okay. I had to do everything I could to get out of counselling sessions. There was no way I was going to sit in a stuffy office for an hour every week. Pressing my hand to my forehead, I forced myself up and out of bed and into some clothes.

I slipped on a pair of boy-cut jeans that had purple paint smeared down the legs. They were old jeans, but I found more and more excuses to wear them as Mum's painted hand print rested on my right knee. I smiled at the memory of repainting my bedroom with her. It had taken all Saturday and we'd ended up with more paint on our clothes than on the walls. Even my hair had been streaked with paint.

Gazing in the mirror, I had a shadow of a smile on my face at the memory. It was strange to see that smile. I hadn't seen it in so long. Brushing the thoughts away, I looked at myself properly. My complexion was grey with tiredness and my eyes were puffy and red as if I had been crying in my sleep. My hair was also as wild as ever, so I put it up in a loose bun. It's not like the pigs would mind what I looked like as long as I fed them.

Shrugging to myself, I grabbed my hoody from the end of my bed and made my way down for breakfast. As I reached the bottom of the stairs, I could hear Dad talking to someone in the kitchen. I stayed frozen on the stairs and strained to hear what was being said.

"…like he said, that was a bad crop," he said, chuckling to himself. A low laugh briefly joined in. There was someone else there, but I could only hear the noise of the tap running now. Forcing a smile onto my face, I continued down the stairs, turned into the kitchen, and came face to face with the stranger from the field. I almost gasped in surprise.

He was dressed in scruffy black jeans and a long-sleeved grey t-shirt, leaning casually on the kitchen worktop. He smirked wickedly at me, and I immediately regretted putting on the crappiest clothes I owned.

"Morning, love." My dad smiled at me and I forced a smile back, all too aware of the stranger's gaze. "Oh, Ava," he said, taking a bite of toast, "this is Sam. He's just moved to the area and he's giving me a hand on the farm."

Sam smirked down at the floor and slid his hands into his pockets. His sleeves were loose, but I could see that his forearms were muscular and his chest was broad; he was quite good looking. Then I realised he was watching me with raised eyebrows, as if he knew exactly what I was thinking. I flushed and looked away. What was I doing? It was only yesterday this same person had made me so angry that I screamed at him in the middle of a muddy field.

"Toast, Ava? You'll need it today." My dad was holding out a plate of steaming toast. I was starving, but butterflies lurched in my stomach.

"No, thanks," I murmured. Dad frowned, concerned by my sudden nerves. He probably thought I was going to run out again. "I'm just not hungry," I stammered, turning to leave, but Sam spoke first.

"You should eat something, Ava," he said, raising his eyebrows at me. "Trudging through all that mud really works up an appetite." He was actually enjoying winding me up. "Here, I'll even butter it for you," he said, taking a piece of toast and putting it on a plate.

Gritting my teeth, I begrudgingly sat down at the kitchen table. I felt like a child as Sam put the buttered toast in front of me, a daring glint in his black eyes as he sat across the table. I couldn't believe this guy. What was he trying to do to me? I gave him a suspicious look, but his amused expression gave nothing away. Lifting the toast to my mouth, I was very aware that he was watching me eat.

"Here you go, love. Sugar's on the table." A mug of tea was placed in front of me, and I absently noticed the pink mug was gone. It reminded me that I should apologise for having acted like such a brat last night. I didn't know what had gotten into me. It had all just happened at once and the only thing I could think was that I needed to run. Sometimes the darkness engulfed me and it was like I was ripped into oblivion.

Thinking about how I'd felt last night made me wish I was alone for a while before having to make small talk for the rest of the day with an obnoxious stranger, one who was so clearly comfortable in the house, it was as if he lived there. Sam's chair scraped out from under the table and in a moment of horror, I wondered if I'd said something out loud.

"Shall we make a start with clearing the barns? Ava could always meet us out there in five minutes," Sam suggested. My dad nodded and went to the porch to find his coat and boots, but Sam lingered in the doorway.

"I told you to avoid me," he said. I opened my mouth in exclamation, wanting to tell him that this was *my* house, but a dark smile crept onto his face. My stomach flipped in response, but I was unsure if this was a good or bad thing. He seemed to be enjoying my unease a bit too much, and despite his smile, something about him gave me the creeps. Shivering involuntarily, I turned back to my toast without replying. When no more smart remarks came, I glanced back curiously. He had gone and I felt relief mixed with a small stab of disappointment. At least I could finish my breakfast in peace before having to spend the rest of the day with him. I'd need to be ready with retorts, something I wasn't good at. Or perhaps, I didn't need retorts...

Stuffing the last piece of toast in my mouth, I ran upstairs to clean my teeth and brush my hair before finding myself a coat and some spare wellies. As I pulled them on, I readied myself for the onslaught outside, and prepared myself for the best act of confidence I'd ever put on. It might very well work in my favour to convince my dad I didn't need therapy, as well as proving to Sam I wasn't as pathetic as I first seemed. Two birds, one stone, I told myself as I wandered outside and into the yard.

My hands were slick with sweat by the time I discovered them both working near the back barn. Dad was moving the pigs and sweeping hay, whilst Sam heaved huge bales off of the trailer. Even the sight of him made me nervous and I felt my throat constrict as he stopped what he was doing and watched me. It was no lingering stare however, but something more predatory, and I began to wonder if the smile I'd seen earlier was just to lure me into trusting him.

In the barn, Dad was moving some of the piglets from one pen to another. "Alright, love?" he said.

"What do you want me to do?" I asked.

"You mind taking over here so I can take the quad up to the top field? I need to check on some calves."

"Sure," I mumbled, taking the broom from him and hoping I'd be able to avoid Sam once my dad was gone. At least the house wasn't far if I really wanted to get away from him.

After a half hour or so, I was relieved to have been undisturbed. I found that I was actually beginning to enjoy working outside on the farm, and as I put the last piglet back in the pen, I chucked my jacket over the barrier and leaned over the side.

The piglets were all fighting for space to suckle from their mother, but one of them began squealing over the others for space. He was the smallest by far and it made me wonder if he'd had any food at all. Leaning over the fence, I picked him up. "You need to eat more, little guy," I said, wrapping him in my jacket. He was so tiny and started snuffling against my jacket as I stroked his wiry head.

"You know he'll probably die."

I turned around to face Sam, who lowered a bale of hay down into the pen.

"Not if his mother lets him have some food," I said.

"Life doesn't work like that," said Sam, leaning on the barrier and looking down at the other piglets. "It has no mercy. It is what it is."

I continued to glower at Sam as he turned to face me, those black eyes calculating my every movement. I wanted to say something clever and slick, but just as I opened my mouth, Sam flinched as if pain had lanced through him. Raising a hand to pinch the bridge of his nose, he took a step back from me.

"I have to go," he muttered, almost stumbling into the fence as he turned away from me. I made to ask him if he was okay, but before I could, he was striding out of the barn and out into the yard. His shoulders were hunched over as he practically jogged away. In that moment, I knew I wasn't the only one with secrets.

CHAPTER *Three*

It was with mild surprise that I realised my first day at college had come so soon. New lessons and a new me, I thought as I looked out the car window. Hopefully, I could finally leave the old me behind, the one that everybody was expecting me to get back to. I wasn't the bright-eyed, carefree student I used to be. I was a different Ava now. I wasn't sure if this was the kind of Ava people would like, but I was done trying to please people. It was like me or leave me. Although, something inside me still screamed to please everyone.

As we pulled up outside Meadow Hill's gates in our dirty farm vehicle, I felt all eyes on me from outside. "Thanks, Dad. You really didn't need to drop me here. I could have got the bus."

"Just making sure you got here safely, love," he said, turning to face me in the cab. His mouth twitched into a wistful smile. "I've already lost one woman in my life." I stared at him and wondered what had brought him to make a comment like this. He never mentioned Mum—ever. I held my breath in anticipation of what he might say about her, but he shifted awkwardly in his seat, breaking eye contact with me, and I knew this was as far as it was going to go. Feeling deflated, I reached for the door handle.

"I know I don't talk a lot about your mum," he said. "She was the love of my life, Aves and,"—he stopped and took a deep breath—"and I regret losing her every day." He looked back up at me from furrowed brows, and I glimpsed raw emotional anguish before it was quickly veiled again. "So, I don't plan on losing you too," he finished.

I couldn't think of anything to say back. All I could do was sit and let his words sink in. He'd never spoken to me about Mum before and I didn't want to ruin the moment. Taking a steadying breath, I turned properly to face him. "You're not going to lose me, Dad." It was a shock to have anything like a conversation with my dad, let alone a heart-to-heart.

When I was growing up, it was hard for him to even look me in the eyes, which now I knew was because they were my mum's. Tears burned my eyes and I thought of something else quickly. If I directed my thoughts elsewhere, I wouldn't cry. It was something I'd become good at over the last few months. The last thing I needed were puffy eyes on my first day.

"I'll see you later, Dad," I muttered as I slid out of the cab onto the pavement. I could tell he was staring after me as I walked towards the gates, but I couldn't look back. I could already feel the nervous tension in my body, and I knew if I looked back, I'd want to go home. I had to get back to a normal life. Forcing myself along the path and through the gates, I looked to where I'd be spending most of my living hours for the next two years.

Meadow Hill Sixth Form College was a yellow brick building with a grassy common at the front. I knew it must open near the back, but the front of it looked tiny compared to where I had planned to go before I moved. A few students were milling about, laughing with friends, or heading to lessons, their heads bent against an early autumn wind. Pulling my own jacket around me, I made my way to what looked like the front office.

I pushed through a set of glass doors and the synthetic heat hit me in the face, causing a shiver to run down my spine. In front of me was a small sliding hatch that another girl was leaning through. She was talking to the secretary so quietly that I couldn't hear a word, even though I was standing directly behind her. When she finished, she pulled her scarf around her and smiled at me before heading out of the office. The girl was slight and looked about my age and I hoped she might be at least one person I could recognise in my new classes.

"Hello, love. How can I help?" A fair-haired woman in her early forties with a round, red cheeked face sat low in a swivel chair. As I moved to the hatch, she smiled at me kindly and I felt myself smile back—a reflex.

"Hi. I'm starting today," I said. The woman started moving the mouse across her desk. "My name's Ava Blume."

"Ava…Ah, yes. Ava Blume," she said, clicking something on the computer screen. "I'll just print off your timetable, Ava." I watched as she clicked a few more times and turned to collect my timetable from the printer.

"Here you go," she said, putting it on the counter between us and pointing at the first day with the end of her pen. "Your first lesson is in the English block, which is straight out this door," she said, pointing behind me, "then down the path to the right and into the building directly in front of you." She smiled at me once more as she handed me the timetable.

"Thanks," I muttered, taking the piece of paper and folding it in half.

English Lit was in a small block right at the back of the college. Reading the numbers on the doors, I finally found the classroom I was searching for. Other students were trickling in, so I joined the crowd, but they carried on past me and found seats next to friends, leaving me hovering near the front.

I looked over towards a desk where the teacher was shuffling papers and preparing for class. He was tall and slim and looked as if he was in his early thirties. I watched as he brushed a strand of blonde hair back from his forehead and acknowledged me with a smile.

"Ah, you must be Ava Blume," he said, moving towards me. "Come on in, Ava."

I smiled awkwardly and proceeded further into the class, but I was aware, despite the chatter, that most of the other students were throwing me inquiring glances. My teacher directed me towards a chair at the edge of the classroom and feeling relieved, I slid into the seat. I found myself next to a group of guys talking animatedly about a film they'd seen at the weekend. A few of them glanced towards me, but said nothing, and I began to feel on edge as I tried to ignore the burning sensation of all eyes on my back. I guessed most people already knew each other from school and had probably moved to the same college together. Tucking my rucksack under the table, I focused my attention towards the front as the teacher began talking.

"Right class, settle down, please. Books out, pens out, phones away!" He grinned and the boys next to me shuffled into their individual chairs, chucking bags under their tables. I felt the table move under my elbows as one of them threw himself into a chair next to me. I peeked through my hair and saw a boy with fair skin and a mess of blonde hair. When he caught me looking, he grinned.

"Hey, I'm Zac."

I smiled back nervously. "Hi. I'm Ava." I wasn't one for making small talk, and meeting new people always set my stomach into somersaults and left my hands feeling clammy. I was determined to fit in though, so I broached a friendly question. "So, what's he like?" I said, flicking my head towards the teacher who had his back to us, writing something on the board.

"Mr Jenson? He's cool," Zac replied. I couldn't help but notice he had blazing blue eyes. "Probably one of the better teachers here," he whispered, looking back to the front.

"Who can tell me what you read over the summer?" Mr Jenson held a book in one hand and a board pen in the other as he looked towards the class. Beside me, I saw that Zac had a copy of the text out in front of him. It dawned on me that I hadn't been into town to get any of the books from my reading list. It had completely slipped my mind. Feeling caught out, I looked up to find Mr Jenson pointing a hand in my direction. My heart rate quickened.

"We read the part where Gregor's mum calls him and he answers, but his voice is different," came a female voice from behind me. I breathed a sigh of relief. "…so, I think he must be changing into something—hence the title, *Metamorphosis*."

"Duh!" another boy near the back piped up and Mr Jenson gestured to settle down with his hand. I shifted awkwardly in my seat to look at the girl who answered. She was slender and dark skinned with a short, wavy, black bob. She smiled at me and I smiled back, hoping I'd made a friend. She seemed very sure of herself. I couldn't help but feel a little envious of her confidence.

"Great, Lou. Can anyone infer what might happen next?" Mr Jenson was pacing the room and his eyes lit up with excitement. "Come on, guys! What's the hidden subtext?" He was practically dancing on his tiptoes, and I avoided his eye contact. I hated answering questions in class and I hated it even more if I had no clue what was going on. The silence stretched out into the room and the tension was palpable. My chest tightened with every passing second.

Finally, someone raised their hand to answer, and the atmosphere breaking in the room was audible as a few people sighed with relief. In fact, I was so dizzy with relief myself that I missed the person's answer. Mr Jenson seemed pleased as he clapped a hand down on his thigh with a huge grin. "Excellent!" He moved towards his desk and perched on the edge as he opened his book to the next page. "Right, folks, we're going to read a few more pages, then we'll watch a clip from the DVD."

Thank God, I thought, as I felt an elbow nudge my own.

"Hey, you don't have a copy," Zac said with amusement. "Here," he pushed the book between us.

"Thanks," I mumbled. I leant over to look at Zac's

text and listened as several different people volunteered to read. I was not one of them and neither was Zac, but a freckled, brown haired boy next to him volunteered. He had a thick accent that reminded me a little of my dad's voice.

Once we reached the end of the chapter, Mr Jenson turned off the lights. Students near the windows leapt up to close the blinds, sending the classroom into sudden darkness. I froze and tried to regulate my breathing as the shadows threatened me, but then I heard Zac's whisper. His breath tickled my neck as I turned towards him.

"So, what's the story?" he asked. I chanced a glance in Mr Jenson's direction to make sure he wasn't watching.

"My dad lives here. I've moved in with him." Zac seemed friendly enough, but I didn't feel like explaining my whole story just yet. Not wanting to come across as rude and welcoming the distraction from the dark, I continued, pushing the focus back onto Zac. "Have you always lived here?"

He nodded. "Yeah. Well, kind of. My parents live over in Bath and I travel here every day."

"Why? Don't they have colleges in Bath?" I asked, raising an eyebrow.

Zac laughed. "They think this place is good. It's high in the results chart," he said, shrugging.

Taking another quick look in Mr Jenson's direction, I saw he was now sitting back in his chair watching the film too.

"Do they want you to be a doctor or something—is that it?" I teased, watching as Zac gave me a look that said *ha ha very funny.* "No? A surgeon then?" Zac laughed out loud this time and we both looked to the front. Thankfully nobody had noticed.

"A joker, huh?" He smiled at me through the dark. His grin practically gleamed, and it was obvious he was just as confident as the girl behind us. It made me wonder if anyone at this college was as socially awkward as me. Yet, something warmed inside me at the look on Zac's face, and I couldn't help but smile back. Perhaps it was the first genuine smile I'd had since my mum died.

"What about you?" he asked. "Your mum wants you to be the next Theresa May?" He laughed, but stopped abruptly when he saw my expression. It was if someone had thrust an ice-cold blade into my chest. "Sorry, have I said something wrong?"

I shook my head, but I could feel the darkness enclosing me. I needed a distraction, but as I swallowed against the grit in my throat, my vision began to blur.

"And I'm stopping it there—until next time," Mr Jenson's voice boomed through the darkness and I whipped my head up towards the front. Mr Jenson's eyes locked with mine and his face was full of concern. I groaned internally—it was happening all over again; I was becoming the odd girl whose mum had died. Tearing my eyes away before he could ask me if I was okay, I busied myself with writing on my notebook. Zac was still staring at me and I wanted to explain to him that I was okay, but the truth was—I wasn't okay. The bell sounded out and I ducked for my bag under the table, ready for my escape.

"You guys missed it all," quipped a confident female voice. The girl who had sat behind me was grinning at us. Leaning forwards to Zac with a pointed look, she said

"Don't expect me to help you with this essay, Zacharias. You're on your own this time!" He laughed and watched the girl turn to me.

"I'm Lou. You're Ava, right?"

"Hi. Yeah, Ava." My palms were already slick with sweat from the mention of my mum coupled with facing this girl.

"It'll be nice to have someone decent to talk to. I've been hanging around with these losers for too long," she said, nudging Zac. He poked her back and she laughed. I wondered if she'd been asked to befriend me. As I tried to think of something to say, she looped an arm through mine and dragged me towards the door, leaving Zac frowning after me. I gave him a small smile before being hauled out into the busy hallway.

"So, where you from? I'm guessing not from around here," Louisa said, pulling me towards a set of wooden double doors that had a plaque reading '*Study Room*'.

"No. I've moved here from Guildford," I said, trying my best to sound as confident as this girl. "I used to live there with my mum, but I had to move in with Dad." *Mum.* My heart constricted with sadness.

"Cool," grinned Louisa through long dark eyelashes. "So, what—they broke up? Parents are a nightmare!" She laughed quietly and walked over to a vending machine, putting a pound coin in the slot.

"Umm, no," I replied, trying to sound offhand, but Louisa caught the hesitation in my voice. Narrowing her eyes, she assessed me before opening her mouth in horror. It was obviously written all over my face as I watched her expression turn from confusion to embarrassment in a matter of seconds.

"Oh, my God, I'm so sorry. I've put my foot in it, haven't I?" she said.

I shrugged non-committedly.

"I'm so sorry, Ava. You don't have to tell me. It's fine." She waved a hand apologetically, but something about her made me want to tell her. Maybe I could chance it. Even at the thought of telling someone, my heart rate quickened.

"No, it's okay," I said, swallowing nervously and taking a deep breath. "Actually—my mum died." I watched as Louisa's eyes expanded even further. She was horrified that she'd been so casual.

"Oh, my—Ava, I'm sorry."

"It's okay. It happened a few months back. It was a car crash."

"You don't need to rehash it," she said, waving her hand in front of me and taking her can from the drinks machine.

"It's fine. It was going to come out at some point," I said, feeling like a weight had been lifted. Louisa smiled at me gratefully, wandering towards the edge of the room which was lined with comfy chairs. I followed her, slid my rucksack onto the floor and slumped into a chair next to her.

"So, are you single?" She grinned. It was a sudden change of conversation and I had to stop myself from gaping at her, but she was clearly trying to lighten the mood. "Zac's cute…" she said, nudging my elbow.

"No!" I cried out. "Well, yes, I am single," I muttered, embarrassed, "but I—"

"Then ask him out," she said, smirking.

My mouth actually dropped open this time. This girl

was definitely the most confident person I had ever met, but I liked it. Maybe Sam wouldn't be the only new person to make me feel something again. I needed to forget about him, but how could I? What he'd said about my mum had to be more than coincidence, and if it was, who the hell was he? A small seed of doubt spread its tiny roots and reminded me that my memory wasn't entirely cooperative at the moment. It made me wonder if, in fact, I did know him and I just couldn't remember.

"What, he's not your type?" Louisa said, bringing me back to the present. She was winding a strand of black hair between her fingers.

I smiled nervously and for a moment I thought she was talking about Sam. "Oh. No, I just—I don't really have a type…" I trailed off, embarrassed, hoping to end the conversation.

"Well, my BF's name is Blake and he has some seriously hot friends. So, if you're interested…" I looked at her in awe. She was trying to set me up with someone and I'd only just met her. I wondered if she'd be doing this if she knew how messed up I was. Laughing, she gave me another nudge in the elbow. "Come on, Ava! I could be your wing-girl. You know—like a wing-man…"

I laughed this time and stared at her with exasperated humour. "Are you serious?"

"Just wait and see. He's picking me up after lunch," she said, smiling. "You should come meet him." She looked at me over the top of her drink and raised an eyebrow. I knew she was daring me to—and for some reason, for the first time in a long time, I felt excited about something.

My maths lesson dragged and I watched every

second tick by until two o'clock finally came. As I clambered out of my chair and pulled my rucksack onto my shoulder, I felt eyes on me. Louisa was bobbing up and down in the corridor with excitement. She had a huge grin spread on her face, and even though I was about to meet more new people, I couldn't help but match her excitement. Laughing to myself, I headed out of the classroom.

"Hi," I mumbled a little awkwardly.

"C'mon," she said, taking my arm and practically dragging me down the corridor and out towards the college gates. I glanced at her with amusement. I already felt like I'd known Louisa for years rather than a matter of hours. I always marvelled at people like her and how they could fit into any situation, with anyone, with such ease. She was so bold and full of life, I imagined she could make me smile in the middle of an apocalypse.

"I'm thinking wing-girl thoughts," she said as we approached the tall gates opening onto the main street.

"Right… great," I replied, nervous. *What* was I doing?

Louisa was grinning at someone ahead of us. Looking in the same direction, I noticed two guys standing around a black car. One of them was leaning against the driver's door. He was stocky and had tattoos on his neck, which I could see over a snug black t-shirt. He looked as if he was in his early twenties.

Louisa ran gracefully over to him and into his arms, which snaked around her, pulling her into a full blown passionate kiss. Averting my eyes, I stood awkwardly on the side-lines and made myself busy by inspecting something on my jacket.

"Blake, this is Ava," Louisa piped up, pushing her boyfriend playfully in the chest. He continued to stare at her and didn't look at me. I shuffled uncomfortably on the spot, beginning to wish I hadn't followed Louisa out here.

"She started college today," Louisa said as she ran a hand up Blake's chest. "She's single…" she said suggestively, raising her eyebrows at Blake. Blake smirked as he caught onto what she was suggesting.

I thought I might faint my heart was pounding against my ribs so hard; I was in shock. I couldn't quite believe she had just come out and said it. My face reddened and all I could do was look down at my trainers.

"That's great, baby," I heard Blake say. "Hey, Ava…"

I looked up at Blake and smiled. "Hey."

"So, you're new around here?"

I nodded and chewed my lip. Beyond Blake and Louisa, Blake's friend was standing on the other side of the car. He was olive skinned with short wavy brown hair and as I caught his eye, he nodded. I smiled half-heartedly and let my eyes wander into the car. Slouched in the front passenger seat of the car was a muscular, short blonde-haired guy, flicking through something on his phone. It was only as Blake pulled Louisa into another kiss, however, that I saw him—and my heart froze.

Sam was sitting in the driver's seat, one hand casually hanging over the steering wheel and his black hair swept back. When I met his eyes, an easy smirk appeared on his face.

"Ava," Louisa giggled, pushing Blake off of her. "I didn't introduce you to the others." She pointed a long, pedicured finger over the car to the curly haired guy, who blanched slightly at the sudden attention. "That's Franco. He's the shy one," she said, leaving him looking a little bewildered. She bent and rested her arms on the open window ledge of the car, right next to Sam. My stomach twisted malevolently as she leant over him and pointed into the car at the guy with short blonde hair. "That's Jules and this," she said, leaning back, "is Sam."

Sam's gaze hadn't moved from mine. "Ava," he said, inclining his head.

Feeling light headed, I hitched my bag onto my shoulder and turned to Louisa. "Cool. Look, I've got to head off now, but thanks for introducing me."

"Sure," she said, giving me a brief hug. "It was great to meet you, Ava." She looked more than a little bewildered. "I'll see you tomorrow?"

I nodded and started walking down the path as quickly as I could, all too aware of eyes on my back—deep, black eyes.

CHAPTER *four*

September. It had been exactly five months since she'd died and I still hadn't remembered anything. What was wrong with me? With the familiar twinge of guilt, I slumped down on the sofa in resignation. My studying could wait. As much as I liked to get things done, I knew there was no point in trying to do work when my mind was elsewhere. Besides, I had the whole weekend. In fact, I couldn't believe how fast my first few weeks of college had gone. I'd ended up with an almost identical timetable to Zac and I shared English with Louisa who, I had worked out, was loved by everyone. She wasn't the kind of person to try to fit in, but somehow that meant she did. She was energetic and a lot of fun. On the other end of the scale, Zac was so laid back he was practically horizontal.

As I picked up the remote, I wondered whether their presence in my life would continue to be a positive influence on my mood. For the past week, I'd felt almost like a normal teenager again, apart from the recurrent nightmares. Thankfully, I'd been saved the trouble of explaining my mute moment in English to Zac. He'd sidestepped it completely and acted as if nothing had happened. Maybe Louisa had told him about my mum. Either way I loved Zac's company. I felt so relaxed around him. This was one of the reasons I liked being friends with boys—they avoided talking about emotional issues.

Flicking absently through the TV channels, I realised I wasn't taking the slightest bit of notice of any of it so I turned it off and grabbed my phone. I started scrolling through my online profile, more out of habit than actual interest, but paused on my main picture. I was smiling and leaning against a friend with long blonde hair whom I hadn't spoken to or seen in over six months. Clicking on the image to enlarge it, I stared at my own face. There was a small flicker of someone I recognised there, but I knew I had changed since the picture had been taken. My own image was a stranger. That girl didn't exist anymore.

My stomach clenched with the ghost of sadness, and I hastily closed my phone when a familiar ping erupted from my hand. A frown creased my forehead as I stared down at my phone and opened the screen again to find a request. Opening it dubiously, I found that Louisa had tracked me down online. Smiling, I accepted her friend request and another message came through.

Ava! PLEASE be online!

I laughed. *I'm online. What's up?*

Blake hasn't messaged me back all evening! Smoke is beginning to blow out of my ears...

Smiling at the neurotic message, I began typing and

retyping a message. I was useless at giving boy advice, especially to someone like Louisa. In fact, she was so good at flirting, she'd spent the majority of English sending messages back and forth. I'd heard her phone vibrating for practically the whole lesson as the rest of us watched the remainder of the DVD. Even Zac had turned around at one point and told her to "*Get a room, loser.*" She'd just smirked back, making us both snigger in the dark classroom. I was sure Mr Jenson knew we weren't paying the slightest attention to the film, but for some reason, he let it go. Maybe he was afraid I might have some kind of mental breakdown in his class.

Looking back to the message, I thought hard. *Ever heard of the phrase, 'treat them mean, keep them keen?'*

I waited as the message blinked indicating that she was typing back.

Yes! You are TOTALLY right... I'm being such a loser. I need to get a grip! In fact... I'm putting my phone away this instant. I might even throw it in the pond to stop myself from being ploughed down by the pathetic train!

I raised my eyebrows in amusement, closed her message, and started flicking through old posts on my profile when another message pinged through.

I have a plan! We're going out... without men. Just me and you. Cinema?

I hadn't been to the cinema in so long and the prospect of going out was an appealing one. I had no idea what was showing at the moment, though, so opening a new message, I began typing back only to be beaten to it.

Delirious II. 7.30 outside the noodle bar. Get the 21A

bus.

I stared at the title for a moment with a sinking feeling inside my chest. That sounded like a horror movie. Entering it into my internet browser confirmed my suspicions. The cover poster was a picture of a close up dilated pupil and the tag line read "*An unmissable thriller-horror hybrid. Finger nails will be bitten to stumps!*" Most reviewers had also given it at least four stars, but all that meant to me was that this movie was guaranteed to scare.

Opening Louisa's message again, I typed back. *Sure. That's a horror film, right?*

Yes! I've wanted to see it for ages. It's supposed to be scary so bring a change of underwear! Kidding! Sorry, I tell bad jokes when I'm uptight…

I read her reply and blew out a deep breath. I could do this, I told myself. If I didn't do it now, it would be another time. "Face your fears," I said to myself, feeling the thud of my pulse already pumping adrenaline into my bloodstream.

Yoshi Noodle Bar was filled with the hustle and bustle of any exciting new restaurant in town. The sweet smells of Japanese food filled your nose as you entered, making your mouth water, and the various sized red and black lanterns filled so much of the space overhead that it gave the impression of being in a cave. Customers sat at small round tables or tall red stools at a counter where you could watch several chefs working through the orders in the kitchen.

Taking our places on two stools at the end of the bar, which had just been vacated, I pulled myself up and hung my bag on the peg underneath the bench. As I took in my surroundings, I noticed that we were seated right next to a large gold and red cat statue. It held one paw in the air as if to high five us.

"Maneki neko."

I looked at Louisa blankly.

"Maneki neko," she repeated. "It's a lucky cat. It's supposed to bring good luck to the owner."

"Huh, I guess it's working, then," I said. All the customers in the restaurant were happily chatting away and even the chefs and servers looked cheerful, despite the fact the tiny noodle bar was crammed to breaking point.

"Looks like we made it just in time," I said, as another large group came through the door looking for seats.

"Yep. It's always packed, so I thought we should get here early, even though we'll be *way* too early for the film."

At the mention of the film, my heart skipped a beat, but I pushed it away and grabbed a menu to distract myself. I wasn't a fussy eater, but it always took me ages to decide what to order.

"I already know what I'm having," Louisa grinned. "I looked at the menu before I came, though I always end up having the same thing."

"What are you having?" I asked, hoping to make my choice a whole lot easier.

"Miso soup with prawn dumplings and vegetable gyoza on the side."

"Sounds good," I said, wondering what gyoza was, but not wanting to come across as stupid by asking. Though, I knew Louisa would never judge me; she wasn't that type of person.

"I think I'm going to have the noodles with beef and ginger," I said, setting the menu down. Feeling achingly hungry, I couldn't remember the last time my appetite had been so ravenous, and I was actually looking forward to eating. For the past five months eating had just become another process I had to go through each day.

Once the server had taken our orders, I turned my attention to the chef behind the counter flinging greens into the air from his wok. As I watched, my mind wandered to the prospect of sitting in a dark, crowded room full of people. The fact the film was horror was an added bonus.

"Earth to Ava…"

I shifted and looked at Louisa. "Sorry, I was—watching the chef."

"We can go home if you like. We don't have to watch the film," she said, concerned.

"No, I'm fine. I'm just tired."

Louisa eyed me intently and I felt compelled to confess. I imagined this was what it was like to have an older sister.

"I just… I have a thing about the dark. I have dreams

sometimes," I mumbled, fiddling with the chopsticks in my place setting, "…about my mum."

"Okay…"

"They're kind of weird. I always wake up and…"

"And what?"

Should I tell her about the blood? "And sometimes there's—"

"Ah!" Louisa jumped in her seat and clapped a hand to her thigh. Digging her hand into her pocket, she pulled out her phone and immediately her face lightened. Leaning over slightly, I could see Blake's name blinking on her screen.

"Answer it," I said, prodding her in the arm with my chopstick. She looked at me hesitantly. "It's fine. Answer it," I said again, fixing my eyes on the kitchen so that she couldn't argue any further. I watched the chef at the back slicing through raw pink fish, but I couldn't help but overhear Louisa's side of the conversation.

"What? *Now*?"

I turned slightly in my seat as a smile crept onto Louisa's face and her eyes brightened.

"But, I didn't tell you," she muttered, narrowing her eyes in suspicion. "How did you—" She tucked her hair behind her ear and caught me looking, so she leant in my direction. "They're here," she whispered, smiling.

"What—Blake?" I asked as she put the phone back to her ear, but the word "they" hung in the forefront of my mind.

"We're in Yoshi at the moment so we're not… u-huh… sure. Okay," she said, flinging a thumbs-up between us. "Bye!" She closed her phone, slammed it down on the table and sighed through her teeth. "So, Blake phoned me…" she said coyly and giggled.

"I guessed," I deadpanned.

"Please don't be mad…"

"Why would I be mad?" I asked, already dreading her answer.

"Because he's coming to the cinema too. But don't worry, you won't be a third wheel or anything. He knows it's supposed to be a girls' night out, so he brought the guys with him too."

I was afraid of that. "The guys? As in—?"

"You met them last week. Franco, Jules and Sam," she said, observing as my face dropped. I swallowed hard against the shards in my throat. "Oh, God, you don't like them, do you?"

"N-no," I stammered against a thick windpipe. "I just…they're a lot older," I lied.

"Oh, well, don't worry, they're all really lovely."

All I could do was force a smile onto my face and try not to think about how I would likely make a fool out of myself in front of Sam again. Not that I should care.

Our meals came out soon after and Louisa was keen to eat fast, even though we were already early for the film. She was already cheerful, but now that she knew she was seeing Blake, her mood had improved considerably.

When we left Yoshi, it was busier than when we arrived. As we squeezed through the people huddled near the doorway in thick coats, I pulled my own around me as the cold wind blasted in my face. Louisa handed me a small red foil packet.

"Here. It's a fortune cookie," she said, opening her packet. "I always take one when I leave, mostly for fun, but sometimes they turn out to be true." She shrugged and crunched the cookie in her gloved hand, stopping to pull out the small curve of paper. "*People learn little from success, but much from failure*." She looked at me dubiously. "That can't be good," she said.

I hoped I'd have something a little more uplifting as I crushed my own cookie. Pulling out the slip of paper, I read my fortune. "Mine says, '*Do the thing you fear and death of fear is certain.*'" A cool shiver ran down my spine as I reread the words on the tiny piece of paper. I knew that it was positive, but was I ready to face my fears?

"I guess that's a good thing…" Louisa said sympathetically, looping her arm through mine. I shoved the cookie into my jacket pocket as we walked along the high street, but I wondered which fear it was referring to.

Old fashioned, stone buildings rose up on either side of us in the twilight and I could see that Christmas lights had already been put in place, though it was only the start of October. I couldn't believe it was nearing Christmas already. It brought back memories of the year before when my mum was still alive. She'd always worn her Christmas apron with the holly leaves on Christmas Eve, and although she normally hated cooking, she'd loved to make all sorts of pastries and party nibbles on this night. The memory made me smile and sad all at once, and I was glad when I felt Louisa pull me along.

"We're here," she breathed, looking ahead.

Following her gaze, I could make out Blake standing slightly apart from the others. He was facing us, a lazy smirk on his face. Louisa broke away from me and skipped the last few feet into his arms. He caught her, slid his hands around her waist, and pulled her towards him for another session of passionate snogging.

I stood silently on the side and picked at my fingernails to make myself look busy, but a scrape of shoes on the ground grabbed my attention. Someone was standing in front of me. When I looked up, I was met with that already too familiar, arrogant expression.

"I thought I made myself clear, Blume," he said, his eyes fixing on mine as I searched them. He was wearing a black zip up hoody with a grey t-shirt underneath that just allowed me to see the angle of his collarbone, which was covered in the black lines of tattoos, just like Blake's.

"What do you want, Sam?" I said, surprised at how level my voice sounded.

"I want *you…*" he said, moving closer to me with a strange predatory grace, "to leave." I stared hard at him. He wanted me to leave, and he was leaning in even closer. I took a step back, away from that glare—

"Ow!" I turned quickly and found Louisa blocking my way, her foot under my own.

"Sorry," I said, jumping away.

"Don't worry," she muttered, her cheeks flushed and I knew she was embarrassed for being so full on with Blake. "Come on." She took my arm and headed towards the doors of the complex. My hands were shaking as I held the door open for a couple behind me. "Ava, what's wrong? Are you mad?" Louisa's voice sounded small and wounded.

"No." I shook my head and swallowed back the sting of tears. I wasn't sure why I felt so shaken up. What was his problem? "Nothing's wrong. I'm fine," I muttered, my heart still pounding in my chest as I slotted a ten-pound note into the ticket machine.

"You just seem on edge…" she said. That was it. I was annoyed with myself for not demanding to know what Sam's problem was. My hands were still shaking. Why did I let him wind me up so much? Why did he *hate* me so much?

"Ava?"

"I'm fine," I muttered, taking my ticket from the machine and glancing over my shoulder. Sam was standing with the others, his expression hardened as he stared at nothing in particular. Why did *he* look angry?

Louisa looked in the same direction. "Do you like Sam?" She asked.

"What?" I said, giving her my most exasperated glare, but I knew it was a lie. I couldn't ignore how uneasy he made me feel every time he was near—and it wasn't always the horrible type of unease. Trust me to get a crush on the guy who hated me.

"You, *do*!" she teased, smiling mischievously.

"No—I really don't." Swallowing hard against the cocktail of emotions I was holding back, I tucked my purse back in my bag.

"Then why do you keep staring at him?" she said,

grinning and glancing back.

"I am not staring at him," I said, walking away from the ticket machine towards the escalators without a glance in Sam's direction, but feeling all the more aware of his presence.

Louisa followed close behind. "Well, he's staring at you."

I breathed through the burning temptation to look round. "Yes, because he hates me," I said, wondering if he really was staring at me.

"What are you talking about? You only met the other day. How could he possibly—wait…" Louisa came to a halt at the top of the escalators and tugged me towards her. "You *know* him?"

"No, not exactly," I mumbled, avoiding her eye contact. "I just met him at my dad's. He helps on the farm."

"And you didn't think to mention it until now?"

"Well, no. It seemed unimportant," I said, shrugging. It was unimportant because regardless of the increasing number of butterflies he produced in me, he still hated my guts. "He seems to enjoy making my skin crawl," I said. "He always tells me to leave him alone."

Louisa frowned at this new information. "That's weird," she said, "because he definitely doesn't hate you." She gave me a pointed look.

"I suppose you're going to tell me that if a boy likes you, he's mean to you, right?" I said, smiling wryly.

"I'm not saying that," she said, taking my arm and walking down the corridor towards our screen. "I'm just saying that whatever he's *said*, it doesn't seem to fit with the way he's acting."

I cocked my head sideways at Louisa. What was she talking about? I wanted to ask what she meant, but I never got the chance because she marched away up the steps as soon as we entered the screening room. She led me further and further to the back, but it was only as we reached the top step that I noticed we were in the couple zone. I groaned internally as she located four seats on the back wall, separated by a bald guy and his blonde girlfriend, who smiled at me and moved her bag from the chair to the floor.

"It's okay, I'll sit here," I mumbled, spotting two seats on the row below, but Louisa grabbed my arm and planted me in the seat next to the blonde woman.

"Sit!" she hissed at me, her eyes alarmingly wide.

I frowned at her. What was that all that about? Dropping my bag on the floor, I sat back in the chair. Making their way up the steps were Franco, Jules and Sam. The two seats remained vacant on the row below me and one seat was still empty beside me.

I leant forwards and narrowed my eyes at Louisa through the dimmed lights, but she simply mouthed, "*You're welcome*" before turning back to the front with Blake's arm around her. I couldn't believe she had done this. A sick feeling in my stomach arose as I wondered if Louisa was right about Sam. At the mere possibility of it being true, my heart started beating hard in my chest.

Jules sidled into the seat just below me, and as Franco eyed me briefly, he came to the same decision.

Sam didn't say a word as he reached the top of the steps and casually slumped into the seat to my right.

I felt myself tense as I sat back and stared at the screen ahead of me. How could Louisa do this to me? Gripping the armrest, I tried hard to push away any stray thoughts about Sam. At least when I thought he hated me, I was less nervous. Now, I was a mess.

When the lights faded, I realised I'd missed all the trailers and had not given myself time to prepare for how scary this film might truly be. Before I could calm my nerves, I felt Sam's leg come to rest against mine. I stiffened at his touch and my head swam as I held my breath. I wanted to ask him what he was doing, but thought he might not know he was doing it. Instead, I focused on the film's opening credits, but I could feel the contact between us as if it were an electrical current.

Once the expectant silence filled the room, I chanced a peek at Sam's face from behind my hair and could just make out a glint in his eye. I was sure it wasn't the film producing this effect, yet neither did I think it was my effect on him. I supposed it must be my complete and utter awkwardness at being out with older guys. He must have known I was out of my depth, and he was winding me up, enjoying every moment of it. He'd probably go as far as trying to tell me off about it later, demanding to know why I hadn't avoided him.

Feeling the sting of irritation, I pulled my leg away from him, but something inside my chest twanged like a rubber band had snapped inside me. It was a reaction I hadn't expected, and when he shifted uncomfortably in his seat, I wondered if Sam had felt it too.

The sensation stayed with me for the remainder of the film. I had no idea what was going on as I gazed blankly at the screen and watched the scruffy protagonist enter an old town house. I'd spent most of the evening obsessing over Sam. So much from pushing away all thought of him. I needed to focus on the film, I told myself. I stared hard at the screen, determined to watch the last few minutes.

I watched the protagonist creep through the dark hallway. "*Lucy? You home?*" he called out. There was no reply, so he continued deeper into the house, his shoes making the floorboards creak nosily in the empty expanse of the hallway. I swallowed nervously as he stopped. The basement door was ajar and a light was blinking through the gap. Taking two tentative steps towards the door, his hand grasped the edge of the frame—that's when she appeared, eyes wide, dilated and violet. Her hair was wild and unruly and her nails clogged with dirt as she grabbed at his shirt. Her grimy teeth were bared at him as a long, howling shriek issued from her throat—she stabbed him hard in the chest with an ivory handled knife.

He remained frozen from her touch; only the sound of cracking bones and the gentle drip of his blood on the polished oak floor echoed into the hallway. As I watched the blood pool on the floor, it became a river and the river grew, flowing down the hallway towards me, faster and deeper until it started to flow over the edge of the screen into the crowds of people in the seats below. I stared in shock, as people began to scream and clamber over the high-backed cinema chairs to the safety of the stairs. The cinema was in chaos.

"Ava." His voice was rich and gravelly, and when I finally looked to him, his eyes shone with raw fury. I was confused as time seemed to stretch out like elastic between us. "Ava," he repeated, teeth gritted, edging ever so slightly closer to me.

"What?" I asked, my breath catching as I returned from my dreamlike state. My heart was hammering in my chest.

"My hand," he said, his brow furrowing as something akin to fear flickered in his face before it was hidden just as fast.

I felt something twitch under my fingertips and was mortified to see my hand firmly clasped over his. I dropped it as if it were poisonous. Before I could even mutter an embarrassed apology, Sam was on his feet and making his way out of the cinema.

CHAPTER *five*

My body ached with spent nervous energy as we reappeared on the street, hugging our jackets around us to keep warm. It was past eleven and the street was alive with people as they wandered around carelessly, buzzing with alcohol. Sam was nowhere to be seen, but the others didn't seem perturbed, so I tried to push it from my thoughts.

I couldn't just ignore what had just happened though. Had Sam just freaked out because I'd touched his hand? Did he hate me that much? I tried not to feel too hurt by his reaction. Only I already did and I couldn't get my head around why he would dislike me so much; or was Louisa right? There *had* been something alight in his eyes when we were in the cinema. Even those times he'd told me I should avoid him or to leave him alone, it always appeared that there was a part of him that enjoyed talking to me. I'd noticed that much, even if I hadn't noticed what Louisa had.

The gentle thud of music filled the chilly air as we passed the doorways of various bars and clubs and I wondered if he'd slinked away into one of these somewhere. He seemed old enough and was definitely safe from me, if that's who he was avoiding. Each was flanked by two or three burly men dressed in black jackets with yellow or orange identity bands on their upper arms. I watched as one of them grasped a younger man's arm and pulled him to the side to talk to him in a low voice. The younger man clearly wasn't listening and I thought it was a wonder he was even standing up. Maybe Sam's plan was to get as wasted as him.

"I can't wait until I'm eighteen," Louisa piped up excitedly, hugging Blake's arm for warmth. Blake made no comment, and instead leant over and muttered something to Jules, he smirked and look over at me. I felt my face go red. They probably knew why Sam had bolted.

Pushing my hands in my pockets, I walked ahead of them, but pain shot through my shoulder as a drunk guy rammed into me. The collision sent me stumbling off the curb and into the path of an oncoming car. Just as suddenly, a strong hand grasped my upper arm and pulled me back with a jolt.

"You could at least make my job a *bit* harder," grumbled Sam, dropping my arm and striding ahead of me towards the others. What did that mean? What job? I watched as he fell into step beside Franco, and I wondered if they were talking about me. Feeling dizzy with nerves, I decided it would be best to leave as soon as possible. Louisa was too polite to say so, but she probably wanted to spend some time with Blake anyway, and now that Sam had returned, there was another reason to leave. He clearly didn't want to talk to me. Maybe my leaving would improve his mood, and my own for that matter.

Fumbling in my pocket for my phone, I searched for bus times as I wandered behind the others. It was as much to make me look busy so I didn't have to make small talk with anyone. I was just thankful that I hadn't had a complete breakdown in the cinema. In fact, tonight, I'd seemed like the sane one.

When I looked up, everyone had come to a stop next to a black motorbike, where Blake was fumbling with the ignition.

"You coming, babe?" he drawled to Louisa as he slid a hand around her waist.

She looked at me. "Ava—do you have to be back home soon?"

I shrugged self-consciously. Obviously, nobody else had a curfew set by their parents, and as I hesitated, I was sure Blake was hoping I'd leave. On the other hand, Dad would kill me if he knew I'd got a bus back on my own this late at night. I was torn, but before I could come to a reasonable conclusion, Blake's voice barked out impatiently.

"Ava! My house?" Blake was staring at me with cold, dark eyes.

"Sure," I heard myself say, more out of reflex than anything else. I watched Blake pass Louisa a helmet and wondered how on earth I was supposed to get to Blake's house. As if he knew exactly what I was thinking, he paused half way onto the motorcycle and looked past me.

"Sam?" I froze as I felt Sam's gaze on my back.

"Sure," grumbled Sam. He was right behind me. I

knew he wanted to be in a car with me about as much as I wanted to be alone with him, but I took comfort in knowing Jules and Franco would ride with us.

Blake's motorbike rumbled to life, and I waved to Louisa as she grinned and wrapped her arms around Blake. They sped off and now I was alone with Sam. I turned around uncertainly, and Sam stared me down with blazing eyes, his jaw set. It was unnerving, but I couldn't tell if he was angry with me, or just as scared of being alone with me as I was with him.

"Are Jules and Franco already in the car?" I asked once I noticed they were nowhere to be seen.

"No," Sam replied as he stalked away. I couldn't help but feel an impending sense of dread. What was I doing? I was supposed to be home in an hour and now I was on my way to some guy's house—to do what?

"Are you coming, or not?"

Sam was already half way down the street and I had to jog after him. I expected to be met with that piercing gaze when I caught up with him, but instead I found amusement in his expression.

"What's funny?" I asked, my voice low, daring him to voice his opinions.

"Nothing, Ava," he said, smiling as he lifted a key and pointed it in front of him. The thud of a lock moving penetrated the darkness, and I saw the orange sidelights of Sam's car blinking. I'd seen his car once before outside the college gates, but I hadn't taken much notice of it then. This time, I almost gaped at it. It was a sleek, black coupe and it looked brand new. All I could think was that he either had rich parents, or a job that paid extremely well. Either way, it was an impressive car, and even though it was evening, I could see my own reflection in the paintwork of the passenger door.

"Nice car," I muttered.

"Thanks." He smirked and climbed in.

The inside of the car was all polished black surfaces, and the sting of leather and spearmint filled my nose as I reached for the seatbelt. Sam turned the key in the ignition, put the car into gear and the engine roared to life. He revved the engine a couple of times, seeming to enjoy himself. I smiled.

"Are you going to stare at me the whole time?" he said, his eyebrow raised. My cheeks flushed with heat, and I quickly faced the window without replying, but his voice interrupted my wave of panicked embarrassment.

"Actually, keep staring," he said. I immediately whipped my head round to face him. Maybe Louisa had been on the money. "I quite like it," he grinned. I'd never seen Sam grin like that before and something inside me leapt. I chewed the inside of my lip to stop from grinning back. I wasn't going to let him win me over that quickly just because we were alone now.

"I don't get you," I mumbled.

"What's there to get?"

"Really?" I said incredulously, watching as Sam continued to stare ahead, impassively. "You've made it pretty clear that you hate me and don't want anything to do with me, but then you say things like that…" I said, gauging his reaction. We'd just come to a set of red traffic lights, so he turned towards me.

"I don't believe I ever said that I hate you," he said,

his expression serious. Now that he was facing me, I could feel the same elastic pull between us like I had in the cinema. I wondered if he felt it too.

"Fine. Then why do you keep asking me to leave you alone?" I asked, my heart battering the inside of my chest. It was partly to do with the fact I hated any kind of confrontation, but also because I dreaded his answer. He remained silent for a moment, his jaw set in thought. Then his eyes locked with mine.

"Because you have a better chance of leaving me alone than I do of leaving you alone."

Suddenly, it was as if all the breath had been knocked out of me. Only the green light glinting in our peripheral vision made him tear his gaze away and concentrate on the road again. I faced forward in my seat, but the atmosphere in the car had changed. It was electric. When I thought about Sam's words, I knew he was wrong. I was already in too deep. I had no chance of leaving him alone.

The suburban road was quiet as we pulled up outside a small detached house with a curving cobbled driveway. Blake's motorcycle was parked up, and I could just make out silhouetted movements through the blinds at the window. I swallowed and heard Sam shift in his seat behind me.

"I can take you home," he said, "if you don't want to go in."

"No, it's fine," I said, but I had to try hard to block out the voice in my head telling me this was a bad idea.

Sam nodded and climbed out of the car. I should've followed, but something was stopping me. This was really unlike me. I didn't go to strangers' houses, or hang out with older guys. I knew it and Sam knew it and Louisa probably knew it too. I wasn't a free-spirit like Louisa. I was the type of person who did exactly what her parents asked of her and normally, I'd be home, curled up on the sofa watching a film. I was here now though, and despite the feeling that I didn't belong, at least I knew Sam didn't hate me. Louisa was right. It seemed that he liked me, but something was stopping him from acting on it. It made me wonder if perhaps I made him as uneasy as he made me.

As I walked up the driveway, Franco appeared at the door, letting us in without a word. I stepped into the small entrance with Sam and immediately heard the low thud of music and voices from a room down the hall. My hands felt clammy, but it was too late to change my mind as Sam was already following Franco through the door to the right.

When I peered around the corner, I found a small front room with dark leather sofas and a widescreen TV, but that was it. The room was so sparse, in fact, it gave off a cold, uninhabited feel. I frowned and I wondered if it was possible for me to feel any more uncomfortable.

"Blake's just moved in," Louisa said. She was sitting on the sofa to my right with her legs underneath her and Blake next to her. I nodded interestedly and felt a little better with Louisa there.

Perching beside her, my eyes drifted to Blake. He was hunched over, fiddling with a small, round silver box, but before I could say anything, Louisa whispered eagerly. “So?”

“What?”

“Sam,” she hissed. “What happened in the car?”

“Nothing,” I whispered back, ignoring the bloom of butterflies in my stomach and glancing over to the other side of the room. Sam was slumped at the end of the other sofa, which seemed to be as far away from me as he could possibly get without leaving the room.

Louisa narrowed her eyes at me. “Nothing?” I shifted uncomfortably. “You’re lying,” she hissed, “Come on. Spill.”

I wanted so badly to spill every detail to Louisa, but I was aware of Blake only a few feet away from me. I glanced up to look in Sam’s direction again and my heart leapt in my throat as he was staring straight at me—black eyes on hazel. I instantly felt drawn into his gaze as I had in the car, but I tore my eyes away and looked back at Louisa.

“Really. Nothing happened,” I said, crossing my arms over my chest despite the warmth in the tiny house. Leaning back on the armrest, I could still sense the pull of Sam’s gaze and it was with great restraint that I kept my eyes downcast. Louisa didn’t push me any further and the room was filled with the gentle thud of music. Only when I heard Blake’s voice did I look up.

“Lou, babe, can you pass me that lighter?” Blake was holding out his hand towards the arm of the chair where a small orange lighter sat. Louisa picked it up and gave it to him.

“Are you sure you’re okay being here?”

My stomach flipped wildly, and I found that I was beginning to enjoy the sensation, but it turned sour as I thought of Dad. He'd be worried and rightly so. I was being stupid. I hardly knew these people, Louisa included. Maybe I should go, but then how did I leave without offending anyone?

"Yeah," I smiled half-heartedly at Louisa, and let my attention float over to that corner again. Sam was lost in thought and had a faraway expression on his face as if he was in the moment of reliving a painful memory. I wondered what it could be. There was still so much I didn't know about him. I hadn't known him all that long either. It made me recall the night we met and how he'd questioned me about my mum. How had I forgotten the fact that he knew about my amnesia? I suddenly felt stupid.

The clicking of a lighter echoed in the near empty room. Blake was holding a long glass contraption and holding a flame near the end of it. I frowned in confusion, but as it lit and the tube filled with smoke, I realised what it must be. He put his mouth over the top and breathed in, and I watched the smoke disappear into his mouth. I shifted awkwardly in my seat as he sat back on the sofa with his eyes closed and slowly blew the smoke out of his mouth. My mum had been particularly overprotective, and I'd never actually seen one in real life, only in films.

Leaning down to Louisa, I whispered in her ear. "Is that what I think it is?"

She giggled quietly, nodding. "Don't worry, you don't have to do it."

I watched as Blake passed the glass contraption to

Jules who took his own lighter from his pocket and lit the end, filling the tube with smoke again. He breathed in the smoke, but as his eyes closed, he held his breath for longer than Blake, before blowing the smoke into the room again. The two continued this ritual with each new song that played. I was just relieved that it hadn't been offered to me.

Smoke continued to fill the room, and I began to feel light headed and a little sick. I couldn't understand how anybody enjoyed feeling like this. The sickly sweet smell of weed filled my nose and I thought I might throw up. Louisa was happily tapping away on her phone, however, so I leant down and whispered in her ear.

"I'm just going outside for a bit."

She nodded and I got up off the sofa and opened the door. Slipping into the hallway, I took a huge gulp of air and headed out the front of the house.

It was dark outside, but the night air felt refreshing in my lungs. I sat down on the front step and breathed in deep breaths until the cold hurt my lungs and I had goose bumps on my arms. Slipping my phone from my back pocket, I started typing a message.

Hi Dad. I'm just at Lou's. I hope you don't mind. Be back soon. X

I hadn't lived with my dad long enough to know what his reaction would be, but I decided it was best to tell him I was at Louisa's. It felt good to have some freedom and not feel like everybody was watching me, waiting for me to change back into the Ava they knew before. I wasn't sure *that* Ava would ever return because right now, I couldn't even imagine ever feeling like that person again.

It seemed like she was gone for good. I wondered what I'd be doing if none of it had ever happened. Would I still have the same friends? Would I still spend every Saturday watching box-sets on TV? Would I still spend every Tuesday after school at Shakes Milkshake Bar? A grim laugh whispered from my lips. A lot had changed. I had changed.

As I sat and stared out into the night, my reverie was interrupted by a low cough, making me snap my head around. Sam was standing in the doorway, smirking down at me. My pulse elevated and I leant to one side so he could get past, but he sank down onto the step next to me, his arm brushing against my own.

"I wondered when you'd make a run for it," he said in a quiet voice, eyeing me with amusement.

I narrowed my eyes at him. "I didn't realise you had a drug problem," I said in the same tone.

"Did you see me smoke any?" he said, his breath coming out in white puffs of air. I didn't answer. "That stuff doesn't do anything for me," he said and continued to look at me, making me wonder if he was lying. I couldn't work this guy out. What was his interest in me? Something was off about him. He was so up and down with his emotions.

"So why are you really out here?" he said. I shrugged noncommittally as he opened his mouth for what was bound to be another smart remark. "You don't talk a lot. I can see it all in your eyes though. You think you hide it well, but you're an open book."

"Thanks," I said with sarcasm.

"Sorry," he said, laughing to himself, "but it's true. At

least… I can see it anyway. I don't think the others have a clue who you are or how you really feel."

"Fine," I said, feeling more than a little overanalysed, but still confident enough to challenge him. "What do you see?" I said, forcing myself to shuffle to face him.

A small smile lifted on his face and he studied my face, his eyes fixing on my own as he considered what to say. "You pretend like everything's fine… but really you're in pain from the loss of your mum, and you don't know how to handle your grief."

I gazed at him for a moment, then lifted my brows. "That's what you see? Wow, I had no idea you were clairvoyant," I said, moving to stand.

He gave me a small nod. "Sit down. I'm not finished." I huffed and cocked my head to one side in impatience, but I sat down, intrigued.

His face became serious, his gaze intent on my own as if he could see right inside me. A long moment stretched out between us before he finally spoke, and this time when he opened his mouth, it was almost as if I already knew how right he was going to be.

"You act like everything's fine because your mum always taught you to be strong, but you feel like you're letting her down because you're not as strong as you think you should be…"

"Seriously?" I muttered, ignoring the fact that every word he'd said so far was correct.

"You wake up in the night because you have terrible nightmares and for a moment you think everything is just how you thought it was and that she's still alive, but then reality crashes down and you realise she's gone and you're never going to see her again."

I held my breath and waited for him to continue.

"You're not close with your dad and you feel alone. You think nobody understands your grief because you think what you feel isn't grief…"

I opened my mouth to speak—

"But it is," he finished. "That feeling inside you that's too big to feel is real. You just haven't grasped how to wield it yet." Sam stopped talking and stared at me transfixed and all I could do was close my mouth again.

I swallowed at the lump in my throat and stared back. Who was Sam? He understood. He actually got how I felt; his words perfectly encapsulated it. There was only one way he could truly understand. He must have been through this darkness too.

The revelation brought relief and pain sweeping over me and I fought to keep a hold on my emotions. I needed to think of something else, but as I rifled through my brain, all I could come back to was Sam and everything that he'd said—including his admission in the car. I had to ask him about it.

"What you said in the car..." I began.

"I meant it," he said.

I hadn't expected him to answer so quickly. "Then I don't understand. Why do you need to stay away from me?" I said and watched Sam's reaction. His eyes averted my own, and I wondered if there was a small flicker of regret that entered them. He remained still and quiet.

"Why do you want to stay away from me?" I whispered.

"I don't…"

I stared at Sam for a moment, but realising how heavy the mood was becoming, I tried to lighten the atmosphere. "Am I that repulsive?" I asked. He smiled and I knew it had worked.

"You're disgusting," he said and I waited for him to say more. I watched as his gaze slipped straight through me; he was lost in thought. When he finally came to and answered, I listened intently, but his mask was back on. "It's more about self-preservation," he said, getting to his feet and looking down at me. "Do you want to go home?"

I wanted to know more, but he'd made it quite clear that he wasn't going to share anymore tonight. The Sam that was willing to talk had gone. I shrugged. "I guess I should," I said. "I'll have to give my dad a call..." I opened my phone and started flicking through to my contacts list.

"Come on," he said. "I'll give you a lift."

I looked up at him from under my eyelashes. "But I thought I needed to stay away from you," I said with a smirk. I knew I was challenging him. "For whatever reason that is..."

Something flashed in his eyes as if he had remembered something. "A good enough reason," he said, shoving his hands in his pockets, keeping his face emotionless.

The journey in the car with Sam was silent, and I watched as the beams of the car headlights curved over hedges and road signs in the dark. I knew it had been a mistake going to Blake's house, but if I hadn't, I wouldn't have found out that Sam didn't hate me. In fact, far from it—he understood me and he liked me. And quite disturbingly, I was sure I felt the same way. It was a strange thought, as Sam had often been rude or obnoxious to me and there were still things he wasn't telling me, not to mention the fact that he seemed certain being near each other was a bad idea. Perhaps he thought being around each other would only make our problems worse, but I saw it the opposite way. All I could do was hope that he might change his mind because I couldn't deny the pull I had towards him.

Feeling my phone buzz in my pocket, I realised I hadn't let Louisa know I was leaving. I opened her message and typed back a reply, but as I did so, I caught Sam watching me out of the corner of his eye. "What?"

"Nothing," he said, returning his eyes to the road without so much as an embarrassed flush at getting caught out. His Adam's apple grazed the inside of his tattooed throat as he gave a small cough, creating the illusion of dancing, black flames on his neck. They were beautiful, curving tendrils rising from the collar of his t-shirt and seemed to become one with his dark hair, which had coiled around the back of his ears. He really was beautiful. It was in that moment, as my pulse throbbed painfully at the base of my jaw, that I knew I needed to ask some questions before I fell for him any further. I just hoped he was willing to answer.

"Can I ask you a question?" I said, swallowing.

"Sure," he said, his voice deep and steady, making me even more nervous.

"When I met you—in the barn—you said, '*Have you remembered how she died yet?*'" He kept his eyes on the road, careful as ever, not to give anything away.

"That's not a question, Ava."

"Fine," I huffed. "Why did you say it?"

The quiet purr of the engine filled the silence and I waited as he thought about his answer. I must have been waiting longer than I'd thought because the car slowed and I saw we'd reached Willow Farm. Sam turned the engine off and everything fell silent in the car. His black eyes shone in the darkness.

"You were screaming that you couldn't remember how she died..." he said. I narrowed my eyes at him, trying to remember that night. It was all such a blur of emotion, but I was sure I hadn't said that. "You were pretty distraught," he muttered. An emotion I didn't understand glimmered in his eyes.

"No," I said, "...there's something you're not telling me." I felt the familiar pulse inside my veins and a sensation like rising water rose in my chest as I stared into black pooling eyes.

"Ava, you were upset that night. You were outside in the freezing cold, and you were tired—"

"No," I said, hearing my own voice shake as my body began to tremor. "It makes me sick to think that I can't remember what happened to my mum, but—I know what happened in the barn. I know I didn't say those things," I said, my breathing hitching. Tears were pooling in my eyes as I grappled with the door handle and climbed out the car without another word.

Slamming the door behind me, my feet crunched on the gravel as I hurried up the front path, and even as I heard Sam's car door open and his voice call out, I couldn't look around.

“Ava, I never meant—Ava! I’m sorry—”

“Leave me alone!” I screamed. “I don’t ever want to see you again!” I cried, yanking the farmhouse door open.

As I pushed the door closed behind me, I slid down onto the floor and let myself be claimed by sorrow. Huge heaving sobs erupted from the deep darkness inside me, encircling me and holding me captor. Tears streaked unbidden down my chin onto my jumper, and I knew I wouldn’t see the rest of the weekend. I was in that dark place again.

CHAPTER *Six*

Sam didn't appear with Blake and the others the following week. As I walked with Louisa out of college, Franco and Jules eyed me suspiciously, and I began to feel guilty for the way I'd spoken to Sam. He'd had a point. I *had* been upset that night and I'd not been myself—not that I knew myself anymore. I was sure I hadn't said anything about my amnesia that night, but the more I thought about it, the more I wondered if I had said something. There were things I didn't know about Sam, but how could he possibly have known that I had no memory of how my mum died? I hadn't even told Dad. On top of that, Sam had tried to apologise after he realised he'd upset me, and I'd thrown it back in his face and said I didn't want to see him again. Well, that was a lie, I thought. He obviously had his own issues, but I wondered if I'd walked away from the only person that truly understood what I was going through.

As I hitched my bag onto my shoulder and wandered across the grassy common towards the library, Louisa glanced at me anxiously for what felt like the hundredth time today.

"Come on, Ava. You're not fooling anyone. Something's happened between you and Sam. Blake hasn't seen him all week and you've been as miserable as sin." She stopped just short of the gates out of college and looked at me seriously.

I shook my head. "Noth—"

"—And don't even say nothing," she said, interrupting me.

I stared at her for a moment, and her expression told me she wasn't going to let up. How was I going to explain to Louisa everything that had happened without telling her I couldn't remember how my mum died?

"We had a fight," I said simply, shrugging.

"A fight?"

"Yes, it's where two people—"

"—Don't be an arse. I know what a fight is, Ava Blume. Give me *details*," she said, crossing her arms in front of her.

"About my mum.... I got upset and shouted at him," I said.

"Why did you fight about your mum?" said Louisa, looping her arm through mine. "Come on, Blume...walk and talk. I'm cold."

It was almost the weekend so there were only a handful of students still milling about in the late afternoon gloom outside the library and computer rooms.

"Remember I told you I'd already met Sam and that he hated me?" I said.

"Yes," said Louisa, "only he *clearly* doesn't hate you."

"Well, yeah, you're right. He doesn't hate me, but..."

I took a deep breath. Maybe I should just tell her. It might be good to tell someone. Miss Peter's words rang in my mind. *Let it in, Ava.* I stopped just short of the library entrance and looked at Louisa nervously. "Please don't think I'm mad. I'm really not," I said, swallowing hard, feeling the emotions rush upwards inside me.

"Lewis Carroll said all the best people *are* mad," said Louisa, smiling patiently.

"I'm serious, Lou," I said. "And I haven't told anyone. Not even my dad," I said, giving her an imploring look.

"Okay," she said, sympathy shining in her eyes as my own bubbled with tears.

"I can't remember," I said through the lump in my throat. "How my mum died, I mean. I can't remember."

I watched as Louisa took in what I'd said. "What, nothing?"

I shook my head and wiped the stray tears off my cheeks. "No, not a thing."

"But I thought you said it was a car crash?"

"I did," I said, wiping at my nose. "I only know that because I spent weeks in hospital being told how lucky I was to survive it. I don't actually remember any of it though, and now I keep having these nightmares about her with all this blood and—"

"Ava, I think you need to tell your dad," she said, putting a consoling hand on my shoulder.

I shook my head violently. "No, I can't," I said.

"Why not?"

"Because he said I should go and talk to someone. You know…a therapist, but last time I did, it just made it worse *because* I couldn't remember anything. I just shut down and couldn't talk."

"Right," she said, coming around to face me. "But you know I'm here, right? And I might not be able to understand completely, but I *do* understand." There was an edge to her voice that made me look up through my tears.

"What do you mean?" I said.

"My dad passed away a few years ago," she said quietly, her confident demeanour changing dramatically as she picked at her nails. "It was a long illness so it was a relief when he went. It meant he wasn't suffering any more, but it was still horrible."

"Oh," I sniffed, feeling horribly self-involved. "I'm sorry, Lou. I didn't know—"

"No, not many people do," she said, tucking her hands in her pockets. "I wanted to keep it private," she said, looking back at me. "So, I do understand…and I understand grief. It's individual and lonely and you can't see the light at the end of the tunnel, but trust me—it does get better." I smiled at her and dug in my pocket for a tissue, which I used to wipe underneath my lashes.

"Don't worry, you haven't smudged your mascara." She grinned, her usual confidence returning. "And don't think you've distracted me from the matter at hand either..."

I stared at her blankly.

"Boys!"

I laughed groggily and shrugged. "I was just really rude. He gave me a lift home from Blake's and I got upset and said I never wanted to see him again."

Louisa raised her eyebrows at me in amusement. "I bet that brought him down a peg or two," she said, grinning, as we walked towards the library. "Don't worry, I'm sure he'll get over it."

"Even so, it's not like me to act like that, and it still doesn't explain why Blake hasn't seen him."

"Maybe Blake was mean to him too," Louisa said, delight painted all over her face.

"It's not funny," I said, nudging her in the arm. "I don't like upsetting people."

"Well just apologise when you see him, then," she said, as if it were the simplest solution in the world.

The weekend had finally arrived and I sat on the sofa in my dressing gown watching TV, absently munching on a piece of toast smothered in strawberry jam. It had been a quiet morning and I was in a good mood. I'd slept well for once and it felt good to be taking time out after a busy week at college.

Light filtered through the window into the tiny lounge, and when I heard the back door open, I almost jumped. Getting to my feet, I wandered into the kitchen where I found my dad bent over on the doormat, pulling off muddy boots. He looked up as I came in.

"Morning, love," he said, setting his boots down and trudging over to the sink to wash his hands. "Any chance of a brew?"

"Sure," I said, getting the kettle and following him.

"I know you've got school work," he said, glancing

at me, "but if you fancy giving your old dad a hand with mucking out the barns, I'd be grateful, love." He pulled out a chair at the kitchen table and slumped down into it with a sigh. He looked exhausted, and I wondered if Sam had avoided coming to work just so he didn't have to see me.

"Okay," I said, reaching for two mugs. I'd felt a lot better after talking to Louisa the other day, but now a fresh wave of guilt washed over me. I still hadn't apologised to Sam. I hadn't seen him to do so. As if sensing what, or rather who, I was thinking about, my dad brought him up, spiking my interest.

"Sam's let me down, so I've been a hand short all week. Come down with the flu, sounds like."

I doubted this. Sam didn't seem the type to come down with flu, but maybe I was overreacting. Maybe he really was ill and his absence had nothing to do with my outburst.

"Have you heard from him?" my dad asked.

"Why would I have heard from him?" I said a little too quickly. Turning away, I busied myself with pouring water into the little blue teapot.

"No matter, Aves," he said, shrugging. "I just know Lou's a friend of his, so I thought you might have heard." Oh—Lou.

"No… sorry," I muttered, swallowing as the guilt that was rooting itself in my veins pulsed painfully. If Sam really was ill, then I felt even worse for not apologising to someone who was sick. I just wondered exactly how sick he was. The morning in the barn came rushing back to me, when he'd appeared as if he was in pain before practically jogging out into the yard.

"Maybe I should go and see him. Where does he live?" I said as casually as I could, but knowing I'd blown it when my dad raised his eyebrows at me.

"I thought you two weren't friends?"

"I never said that," I muttered, grabbing the box of biscuits and placing them on the table. "I just meant that I didn't have his number so that's why I haven't heard from him." I inwardly cringed at my absurd lying, and my dad's expression told me that he believed about five percent of what I was saying. He was obviously feeling kind as he didn't question me any further however.

"He's over near the water mill," he said. "There's a couple of farm houses round the back of the woods. His aunt lives in the one at the end of the lane, nearest to the fields."

"His aunt?"

"He lives with her," Dad said, popping the lid of the biscuit tin and peering inside. "I think his parents died a long time ago from what he's said."

I debated if it was possible for me to feel any worse. Maybe my life wasn't so bad after all. But living with an aunt? I hadn't pictured that. For some reason, I didn't think of Sam as living with parents or some kind of guardian. He seemed like an adult.

Late that afternoon, I climbed off the bus into what seemed like the middle of nowhere. I hadn't seen a house for miles, and when the bus stopped, I'd considered asking the bus driver if this was actually a stop. There didn't seem to be anything other than huge trees on either side of me, and I had to walk part way along the road before I came across a tiny farm track leading down the side of the forest boundary.

The track was only just big enough for a car to drive down and I couldn't quite imagine Sam's elegant black coupe making its way along this road. It was filled with pot holes and littered with enormous chunks of brittle wood that had fallen off the overhanging trees. A rush of wind blew leaves around my feet, whipping my coat open, and I shivered as I travelled down the quiet lane. The autumn breeze was beginning to turn icy and when I glanced up at the sky to see grey clouds descending, I wished I'd put on a more weatherproof coat.

As the lane rounded a corner, I eventually found myself on the other side of the forest with only green fields stretching out ahead of me. I began to wonder for the second time, if I'd got off the bus at the right stop, then I glimpsed a block of stonework through the sparse hedgerow. I was nearly there.

When I finally came to the end of the lane, two small stone and slate roofed houses came into view. Tall trees rose up in the adjoining fields and towered over the houses, making them look tiny.

I stepped onto the gravel driveway and several sheep bleated at me from the embankment as I neared the house. The farm house at the end was long and despite looking too shallow to hold an upstairs, had two sets of windows, one on top of the other. I immediately felt myself scanning each one for Sam, as I took in the rest of the house.

Ivy grew up one side of the building and thorny, brown tendrils hung from the middle of the structure. I imagined the cottage would be covered in roses in summer, but this time of year, it looked withered and dry. In truth, if Sam's car hadn't been parked up, I would have thought the house was empty, uncared for and unlived in.

Raising my hand, I knocked on the wooden door and waited. My hands were so cold that I couldn't feel the ends of my fingers, so I stuffed them in my coat pockets and shuffled on the spot to keep warm, but still nobody came. Maybe the house was empty after all. I stood back from the door and looked along the side of the house for signs of life.

"Hello?" I called, listening hard for a response. I wondered if I'd made a mistake and come to the wrong house, but just as I started to walk away, I heard the door open with a click. I turned back around to a woman with wild, blonde curls and bright green eyes that looked at me expectantly. She couldn't have been more than fifty.

"Oh. I don't know if I have the right house. I was looking for Sam," I said, feeling shy. "I'm sorry if—"

"Sam's here," she said, smiling kindly. "Although, you should know that he's not well." He really is sick, I thought, feeling something inside me constrict uncomfortably. "I'm sure your father told you," continued the woman kindly. Of course, she must know Dad. She must have been the one to let him know Sam wasn't well.

"Yes, he did," I said. "I just thought maybe I could come and see him." I looked down and chewed on my bottom lip, but continued when she said nothing.

"Actually, I was kind of rude to him last week and I've come to apologise."

The woman smiled at me and nodded. Her eyes seemed to glow with some kind of emotion that I couldn't understand. "Of course, Ava. Come on in," she said, opening the door wide for me to come inside.

I stepped into the farmhouse, but instead of feeling warmer, the cold hit me. The floors were a deep dark stone, as were the walls, which seemed to be curved in at places, and I couldn't see a radiator anywhere. No wonder Sam was ill, I thought. Even with the chilly air, however, there was a delicious smell of freshly baked bread wafting into the hallway, and I breathed it in deeply.

"Freshly baked," the woman said, eyeing me with interest. "Why don't you take him some? He hasn't eaten for a few days." I nodded, feeling a little worse all the while, as she walked into the kitchen, her long floral gown floating behind her. I looked after her with interest. She looked nothing like Sam and seemed a lot more personable. I wondered how long he'd lived with her and how long ago he'd lost his parents. She had her work cut out with him, I thought, but who was I to talk?

She reappeared only a few moments later with a tray laden with warm bread and melted butter, which she handed to me carefully. It looked delicious and I felt my own mouth water. My mum used to butter my crumpets like this, so that the butter dripped off the sides. My face must have twitched with the memory as I found Sam's aunt peering at me with curiosity.

"Where—?"

"Upstairs, first door on the left," she said.

I gave her my best fake smile and made my way carefully up the stairs with the tray. I felt stupid. Maybe I shouldn't be here. I'd told Sam I never wanted to see him again and he'd steered clear of me since—or maybe he'd been ill this whole time. The thought was unsavoury, but I pushed it away as I balanced the tray on top of one arm and pushed a small wooden door ajar with the other.

"Sam?" There was no response and I cringed internally. "Sam?" I tried again, pushing the door open and creeping into the room.

It was small and dark with only a glimmer of afternoon light filtering through the curtains, allowing me to glimpse Sam's belongings. To the right, there was a small, unused antique desk and chair, which sat opposite a thick bookcase laden with books with fading leather spines. There was also a pine bedside table overflowing with clutter including sunglasses and car keys. Directly under the window, there was a large iron-framed double bed, on which Sam was sprawled.

His eyes were closed as he slept, and his scruffy black hair flopped onto his forehead. He looked peaceful, apart from the fact that his legs were twisted in the sheets, but what drew my full attention was his bare, muscular chest. I stared.

I'd guessed he had tattoos, but I hadn't guessed the volume with which his body was covered. His torso and arms seemed to be almost entirely embroidered with black markings. I swallowed nervously and crept forward to try and get a closer look. There were all types of design: faces, landscapes, writing, symbols. My eyes travelled down his arm which hung off the side of the bed; there was another large tattoo which looked like an intricate design of an hourglass. Marked in deep black and curving around the muscles on the inside of his arm, it was particularly striking and stood out from all the other tattoos. I felt compelled to reach out and touch it.

I leant closer to get a better look when Sam moaned in his sleep. Mid step, I froze and watched as Sam twisted in bed causing the sheets to slip further down. I found myself staring at the small trail of hair running down from his navel and the heat rose in my face. I definitely shouldn't be here. Placing the tray on the floor, I turned and tiptoed towards the door. Then the floorboard creaked beneath me. I sucked in my breath and waited, air burning in my lungs. I hoped that I might be able to escape without Sam ever knowing I'd come, but then I heard the rustle of a sheet.

"Leaving so soon?" he asked, his voice rough like sandpaper.

I spun around and looked at him impishly. His complexion was grey and his eyes seemed dull with fatigue. He clearly wasn't well, but he still gave me his best self-important smile. "Will you chuck me that t-shirt please?" he said, indicating a long sleeved grey t-shirt hanging off the bed post.

I reached over and handed it to him. He sat up in bed with a small wince and strained the muscles in his chest to pull it over his head. I blushed when I realised he was watching me. He grinned at me darkly and directed his attention to the tray on the floor. "Is that for me?"

"Oh. Yeah." I picked it up and placed it carefully on

the side of his bed. Standing awkwardly, I waited as he took a bite of the warm bread and butter. He undeniably looked sick. His face had a sheen of sweat and dark patches under his eyes. I started to wonder if this was more than flu. There was something about the way he held himself that told me this wasn't the first time he'd been this sick.

"You can sit down, you know. I know you don't like me, but I don't bite."

I felt horrible. "About that," I started, "I was rude to you the other day. I'm not great at talking about my mum—or thinking about my mum. I'm sorry." I fiddled with my fingernails and pushed the thought of my mum away, deep down to that shadowy place inside me. "And I wouldn't be here if I didn't like you," I finished, feeling a little better. I awaited his response, expecting something cocky that would make me regret apologising.

"Apology accepted. Now, sit."

I glanced at him in bewilderment. He chewed on a crust of bread and took me in. "It might surprise you to know that you being upset with me wasn't my top priority to fix."

I looked down, embarrassed, feeling the heat rise in my face again. I'd made a fuss and he didn't seem bothered, but I made myself mumble, "But I *was* a priority to fix?"

Despite the pallor of his face, Sam smirked. He took another bite of bread, and I looked out of the window as he ate. The trees were swaying in the wind, but there was a small glimmer of sunshine shining through their branches.

"I'm glad I pissed you off. You bringing me breakfast in bed has been an unexpectedly pleasant experience."

I laughed. "More like lunch, really," I offered with a shy smile, turning my attention back to Sam. He looked over at the silver clock on his bedside table and raised an eyebrow.

"Looks like you need the rest anyway," I muttered, noticing beads of sweat developing on his forehead. He must have a fever.

"I'm alright." He shrugged, and I saw that his lips were dry. He looked really uncomfortable, and it seemed as though he was putting a great deal of effort into remaining composed in front of me. He leant across to put the plate back on the tray and flopped back in bed, defeated. "Would you mind getting me a glass of water?" I knew it was his way of getting rid of me. His chest heaved and he put a hand to his head as he breathed steadily. He looked like he was going to vomit any second. I mumbled an answer and went downstairs.

The house was empty, so I searched the kitchen cupboards, taking my time so as to give him time to recover. When I found a pint glass to fill with water, I heard him cry out in pain and almost dropped the glass. What had happened? I made to go back upstairs, but was stopped by a calm, knowing voice.

"Leave him, Ava." Sam's aunt was standing in the back doorway. "He won't thank you for pitying him. He needs time is all." Her face was thoughtful, but she quickly painted on her smile. "To get better, I mean. Come outside with me and help me weed the garden, will you?" I was uncertain and gazed back into the house.

"Are you sure I shouldn't go and check—" I began, but she walked out into the back garden leaving me alone to listen to him scream in deep, agonizing pain again. My heart constricted, but hesitantly, I followed her outside. I barely noticed my surroundings as I followed after her. What was wrong with him? It wasn't the flu—maybe his appendix? In which case, he should be rushed to hospital—but no. There was something more to this. Sam was obviously ill, but he seemed unperturbed by it, as if he'd suffered from this countless times before.

"Mrs—" I stopped. I didn't know his aunt's name.

"Seline," she offered, handing me a small gardening fork and bending down at the edge of the bedding.

"Seline… shouldn't he go to hospital? He sounds like he's in pain," I said as calmly as I could, even though inside, I was panicking. Seline seemed to be more concerned with her weeding. She simply shook her head and gestured me to come and sit next to her, which only confirmed what I thought. This was normal for him. I stood stock still on the spot, confused. I wasn't sure how many minutes passed before I finally forced myself to kneel down and start weeding, but my mind was elsewhere, and I accidentally weeded one of the tulips. Seline stopped and studied my face.

"I can see why he likes you, Ava," she said, a smile creeping into her eyes. I raised my eyebrows. "Oh, come on. You're not going to tell me you didn't realise; a smart girl like yourself?"

I did know. Of course, I did, but it was still a shock coming from his aunt. "He's mostly obnoxious," I said honestly, making her chuckle. "And rude—and confusing. And he's probably a little old for me..." I felt my face go red.

Seline laughed again and I smiled in response, feeling a ray of happiness develop inside me. It was gone in a second, however, when I heard another scream issue from deep within the farmhouse. This time we both looked up to the top windows. Seline obviously cared for Sam and hadn't seemed even slightly offended that I'd said he was obnoxious. There was something about her reaction that told me this was something she loved about him. The problem was that with every passing moment, I could feel myself being drawn in deeper, and I knew I was beginning to see in him what she saw. If he really was ill, I wasn't sure if I could stick around. Something twisted sickeningly deep inside me and tears pooled in my eyes.

"Shh, dear, you've got enough on your plate without worrying about my Sam as well," Seline said, placing a cool hand on my shoulder. I wiped the tears from my eyes, feeling embarrassed. "He'll be just fine in a couple of days. He just needs bed rest and home cooked food." She smiled heartily in an attempt to reassure me, but I knew there was nothing that could make me feel better about hearing those screams.

CHAPTER Seven

I didn't see Sam for another week after I left Seline's that weekend, and all I could do was think about the deep, guttural cries of pain I'd heard. He was definitely ill, and Seline had seemed disturbingly calm about her nephew's health. It made me wonder exactly how long he'd suffered from this illness, whatever it was. There was something they weren't telling me, but that didn't make me any less desperate to know if he'd improved. I'd debated so many times over the week whether to phone Seline or even drop by, but I got the distinct impression that I would just be told he'd be fine.

I stared out of the classroom window during English, lost in thought. I'd gone over the details of that day so many times in an attempt to find something I'd missed. I knew I shouldn't care. I'd only known Sam for a short amount of time, but I felt drawn to him. I remembered Seline saying something about Sam just needing time, but how much time? How long did it take him to recover from something like this? Or maybe she hadn't meant that at all. Maybe she'd meant time away from me.

Maybe she knew just how close to the edge he walked, like me. Whatever it was, it seemed like something ongoing that he'd had to fight for a long time. I wondered if he'd continue fighting or if there would come a time…

"…and that's due on Monday," came Mr Jenson's voice. "With no extensions," he clarified, looking directly at Zac, who simply raised his eyebrows.

Shaken from my reverie, I grabbed my bag and made for the door, but Zac soon caught up.

"Hey. Ava, wait up." Although I liked Zac, I cringed internally. I just felt like being alone today to get lost in my thoughts.

"Hi." I hugged my coat to me, having not bothered to put it on in my hurry to leave.

"Whoa, what's got your goat?" he said, standing back and looking at me in mock horror.

"Sorry. Nothing," I mumbled. "I'm just annoyed about all the work I guess." Zac eyed me suspiciously, but he didn't say any more, which I was thankful for. He'd recently found out about my mum and he was being exactly the same as usual, and that's what I liked most about Zac. Over the past few months, I'd really hated people tiptoeing around me as if I might break down any second. With Zac, I could just forget about it all and be normal.

"Well, what's the deal this weekend?" he said, hitching his bag further onto his shoulder and staring me down.

"Not much," I said, knowing full well I'd spend my entire weekend attempting to coax my attention onto homework, but failing miserably and focusing solely on Sam instead.

"Well, have you ever been to a rave?"

I stopped in mid stride and turned to face him. "No…" I said hesitantly.

"Well there's one on Blizzard Street in town. You want in?" He waited expectantly as I thought it through. I'd never been to a rave, and I was aware that most of them were illegal. It didn't exactly sound like my scene, but not wanting to let Zac down, I gave him a lifeline.

"Maybe…" I said, hearing my own voice hitch, knowing full well I didn't plan on going, but not able to tell Zac to his face.

"Cool," he grinned, surprising me by grabbing my forearm, pulling up my sleeve and scrawling on me with biro. "Here's my number."

"Zac! What—" I huffed.

"Sorry, gotta go. That's my bus!" He laughed and grabbed me into a bear hug before shoving the pen in my direction. I took it automatically and watched him jog down the path. "See you Saturday!" he called, rounding the corner and leaving me feeling out of sorts.

Shaking my head in confusion, I slid the pen into my knot of hair before making my way down the same path. Zac's bus was pulling away from the curb, and I wondered how long my own would be. When I looked down at my watch, my eye caught the biro scrawled on my arm and I realised what Zac had done. He'd made sure I would message him first. Cheap move, I thought, but I felt myself smile.

Having stopped in my tracks, I debated whether or not I should go and find some books at the library for my essay. My bus was going to be another fifteen minutes, but truthfully, I knew I wasn't in the mood. I made my way to the bus stop instead, choosing to just wait it out in the cold. Anything was better than sitting in the library mulling over how little work I'd done. My mind was elsewhere and nothing and no one could sway that, or could they?

Standing at the bus stop, dressed head to foot in black and wearing dark sunglasses, despite the distinct lack of sun, was Sam. He leant on the side of the bus shelter with his hands in his pockets, looking distinctly out of place amongst the chattering students beside him. When he saw me, a lazy smile crept up his face. My heart leapt as I walked towards him.

"Hey," I choked out, scanning what I could see of his face for signs of illness.

His smile deepened and he lowered his sunglasses to look at me; they revealed grotesquely black eyes, causing my stomach to contract. I took a step back and felt my pulse miss a beat as I stared into them. Something wasn't right about his eyes. As the smile disappeared from his face, I felt a stab of guilt for reacting as I had. It didn't go unnoticed either as he quickly returned the glasses to cover his eyes.

"Sorry," I muttered.

"You didn't come back," was all he said.

I was confused at first, but then it dawned on me what he meant. I'd left Seline's without saying goodbye, but only once the pain had seemingly subsided and Seline had reassured me that he'd fallen asleep. I felt my face redden and I fixed my eyes on his throat. It was easier to look at his swirling tattoos than at his glasses. It felt like I was in front of one of those two-way mirrors you got in police stations. "You wanted me to come back?"

His smirk returned. "I mean you never brought me that glass of water," he teased, standing up straight. He was almost a foot taller than me and I found myself looking up at him as I spoke.

"What was wrong with you?" I asked, walking beside him as he gestured to follow him. I took a moment to really look at him as we walked. His complexion had returned to a pale pinkish colour, and despite what I'd seen under the glasses, he looked well again, if not better than before.

He stopped and although I couldn't see his eyes, I could tell his gaze was cutting into mine. "Flu… or some kind of virus." He shrugged, turning to walk again, but I caught at his elbow and stopped him.

"*Flu*?" I said incredulously. "I don't believe you."

"And I don't believe *you*," he said swiping my hand from his elbow and grasping hold of my wrist. He pulled it closer to his face and lifted his sunglasses again; this time I knew to avoid his gaze. "Whose phone number is this?"

I stopped breathing as his breath brushed across the inside of my arm. I felt like I'd been caught doing something I shouldn't and I pulled my arm away. Besides, why was he so concerned who I was dating? If that's what it was. Was it a date? Did I want to date Zac? Was I even going to go? Did it matter? Sam might like me, but he didn't want to act on it; he'd made that much clear.

"None of your business," I said, pulling my sleeve down.

"He's not good enough for you," said Sam.

"You don't even know whose number it is," I fired back, feeling amused, enjoying the thrill of Sam's jealousy. At least, I thought that's what it was until his gaze darkened. A cold breeze whipped past us and I shivered. Almost as if he sensed this small weakness in me, he took a step forward, towering over me. I could do nothing but stare. His face was serious as he cocked his head to one side. In the corner of my eyes, I saw his hand twitch upwards and I wondered if he was going to touch my waist, but instead, he reached for my arm.

His hand was warm as it curled around my wrist and I was surprised by how I relaxed at his gentle touch. Warmth spread through me and I no longer felt the chill from the breeze blowing around us. It was as if he'd cast a bubble of calm around us, shutting everything else out. Then I heard his voice as if from a distance.

"Well, all I know is that it's not mine," he said as he slid his other hand around the back of my neck and into my hair. My breathing stopped as I felt his warm fingers trail into my hair and up my scalp, sending shivers down my spine. My lips parted as I felt his hand stop, but with a small tug in my hair, he revealed a pen. I stared unseeing as he held it aloft, his attention still fixed on my now reddening face.

Seeing my reaction, he chuckled, pulled the lid off with his teeth, and proceeded to lean over my arm. My pulse was all over the place with embarrassment and I was sure he could feel it as his thumb rested on my exposed wrist. As he began to write, he moved a fraction closer to me, filling my senses with his aroma and I breathed in deeply. He smelt of a peppery kind of aftershave with a strange undertone of ash, and as the hair on his forehead fluttered in the winter breeze, I itched to reach out and touch it.

He finished by signing my arm with a large, intricate S and looked at me. I glimpsed the black behind his glasses, but this time I didn't fear them, I just felt drawn to them. I stared at my own intrigued face in the reflection of his sunglasses and all I wanted was to reach forward and remove them. I was only vaguely aware of his hand sliding away from my wrist.

"You're staring…" he muttered.

I nodded slowly and continued to watch him. I wasn't sure what had gotten into me, but as he continued to keep a steady gaze on me, I felt braver than normal. "Why the sunglasses?" I asked in the hope of a real answer.

"Kind of a personal question," he teased, his lips quirking up at one side.

"You know what I mean," I said, feeling the sting of my nails cutting into my palms as my usual equilibrium of self-doubt and panic returned, two-fold. "You're not telling me something," I said as I shivered in the cold.

"You're right," he said, sliding his hands into his

pockets and standing up straight.

I inhaled and the cold air shuddered through me. I wondered if he was going to tell me, but as I watched his jaw set, I knew it was a false hope. "You're not going to tell me, though, are you?" I said, relieved and disappointed all at the same time.

He shook his head with a wry smile on his face. "No, Ava. I'm not going to tell you." I wondered what that smile meant.

"Thanks for dinner, love," my dad said, placing his plate on the coffee table and leaning back on the sofa. I watched as he propped up his head with a cushion and closed his eyes.

"No problem," I muttered, putting my own plate down and grabbing the TV remote to turn down the volume. I'd discovered in the few weeks I'd lived with Dad that he was a terrible cook, so I'd taken to preparing most of our meals. My skills weren't much better, but at least they gave us more options than jacket potato or beans on toast. I didn't mind though. It was kind of nice to look after someone else for a change. Sighing in tired defeat, I slumped back against the cushions.

The log fire was crackling as it kicked out heat beside me and as I curled into my chair, I began to feel sleepy. Closing my eyes, I rested my head on the wing of the chair, but my mind instantly began to wander to Sam and what he'd said. He'd as much as told me he had something to hide, and I was torn between ignoring it or trying to find out more. I'd considered the idea of him suffering from a chronic illness to having a drug addiction, but as I reflected on the options, I knew that I wasn't even close. I couldn't explain why. It was if a sense I never knew I had had kicked in, and as I thought through different scenarios, I always encountered a niggling feeling that something wasn't usual. Somehow, I always came back to the notion that Sam was most definitely *unusual*. I just couldn't put my finger on the how or why.

Sitting up and grabbing my phone from the table, I scrolled through my contacts, pausing on the two new numbers I'd acquired. I'd entered them both into my phone as soon as I'd got home so I could have a shower to wash them off and avoid any unwanted questions from my dad. But now what was I supposed to do? Sighing to myself, I chucked my phone down into the side of the chair. I wasn't involved with either Zac or Sam, but somehow it felt wrong to message both of them. Maybe the easy way out was to not message either of them. When had my life become so complicated?

It was dark outside now, and all I could hear was the distant bleating of sheep in the barns. It was eerie how quiet it was out here in the country at this time in the evening. I thought about my old bedroom and how even in the middle of the night, I could see the orange glow of the street lamps and hear the buzz of distant traffic. Climbing to my feet, I went to the window and pulled the curtains shut, but just as I turned around, I saw the light fade on my phone.

Grabbing it from the inside of the chair, I hovered over the unlock button as I breathed in deeply. I stared as the screen lit up, but my heart slowed dramatically. It was just Louisa.

Louisa. *Hey Ava, did we have biology homework? I may have been messaging Blake at this point in the lesson… xxx*

I stared at Lou's message and tried hard not to feel too disappointed. I knew neither Sam nor Zac had my number, so I wasn't sure why I'd felt a rush. I was just being stupid.

Hi Lou, it was to investigate the effects of smoking on the body. Xxx

I watched as Louisa typed back.

Louisa. *Ew… Maybe I can use Blake as my human guinea pig! Xxx*

Smiling, I closed my phone and chucked it down the side of the chair, but Louisa obviously wanted to talk more about Blake as the screen lit up again. Sighing to myself, I picked up my phone and unlocked it—I felt the blood drain from my face. There was a message from Sam. With trembling fingers, I pressed on the message tag.

Sam. *Ava, are you home?*

I stared at Sam's message and suddenly felt wide awake. My heart accelerated to an unnerving speed. I sat up in the chair and glanced nervously over to my dad. His head was lolling to one side as he snoozed. I typed back.

Hi. How did you get my number?

His reply was almost instant.

Sam. *Are you home?*

Frowning at the sense of urgency that seemed to emanate from his message, I typed back. *Why?*

I'm heading to your place.

I felt my mouth drop open in shock. He was so demanding sometimes, it threw me off counter and I struggled for words to reply.

My dad's asleep and I'm busy doing homework. What about tomorrow? I typed clumsily. I waited as he typed back a message.

Sam. *No. I'm coming now.*

Narrowing my eyes at his message, I fiercely typed a message back. *What's so important that it can't wait until tomorrow?!*

I waited, but no reply came. Sighing, I threw my phone back down and tried to mentally prepare myself for something big. Maybe he'd decided to tell me the big secret, I thought.

What seemed like mere moments later, there was a knock on the door, making my heart jump inside my chest. I breathed deeply, attempting to calm myself, but as I opened the door, I knew there was no point. Sam stood in the doorway with a strange expression on his face.

"Hey," he said with a frown as he stepped into the tiny porch. He was inches away from me, but there was something off about him. His usual cocky demeanour was vacant and had been replaced by a closed and distant nature.

“Hi,” I muttered. Something felt wrong.

His eyes were back to a more normal shade of black as he stared at me and he breathed unevenly; I couldn’t tell if he was about to yell at me or kiss me. Then he turned away from me and looked into the house.

“Is there somewhere we can talk—alone?” he said.

“Uh…sure,” I said, looking carefully at his face for any clues. “The kitchen, I guess.”

He nodded and marched off into the kitchen, leaving me feeling confused. Something had obviously happened, but who knew with Sam? I thought back to the night at the cinema when I’d accidentally touched his hand and he’d practically run off. He seemed to scare easily, but as of yet, I couldn’t tell why. He wasn’t exactly a nervous person, and he seemed to take great pleasure in making me feel as uncomfortable as humanly possible.

I pushed the front door to and followed him into the kitchen. Sam leant on the counter with a deep frown on his face, but his eyes flicked to my arm, and a whisper of the Sam I knew appeared on his face.

“You rubbed off my number…” he said, his expression softening.

I felt the heat rise in my face as I nodded.

“Did the other guy get erased too?” he said.

I looked down at my arm, but as I looked up again, he was standing close enough for me to touch. I loosened a breath.

“Ava?” he said in a gravelly voice I hadn’t heard before.

“Mm-hm?” I replied as coolly as I could, looking up

at him. My breath was taken away as he lifted his hand and tucked a strand of hair behind my ear. My blush deepened and I glanced at his neck, briefly concentrating on the ends of calligraphic writing swirling into his shirt.

"I don't think I should be your friend…" he said.

I met his eyes and could see pain in them as a dull ache filled my own chest. I shook my head in confusion. "Why?" I asked.

"Because I—"

"Are you ill? Is that it?" The words came from my mouth before I could stop them.

"No, I'm fine," he said, caught off guard. "I told you—it was just—"

"Flu. Right." I stared him down and could see the inner turmoil on his face. I could tell he hated the way I was looking at him.

"Ava, I just have a lot going on and I think it's better that I don't involve you." He looked me up and down. "You have enough to deal with right now too."

"Sure…" I replied, my voice dripping with sarcasm. This again. "Poor breakable me," I said, hearing the bitterness in my voice.

"That's not what I mean," he replied, his tone just as raw. He fixed me with a blazing stare so that I couldn't look away from him. "There are things you don't want to know—shouldn't know." His hands were trembling and I knew I'd touched a nerve, but I didn't care. I was fed up of people thinking I was weak, least of all Sam.

For a long moment, we stared each other down. I couldn't figure it out. What had made him change his mind so suddenly? It had only been a few hours earlier that he'd been acting like a jealous boyfriend and now he didn't even want to be my friend. Worse than that, he thought I couldn't cope with being his friend—or was it more than that? His breathing was laboured and his jaw was clenched with unspoken words.

"I'm just trying to do the right thing," he stated.

"And what's that?" I said, wondering how far I could push him. I knew I was being cruel now, but I wanted him to admit there was something more to it. "You think the poor little girl whose mum died can't handle a bit more grief?"

"What?" He pulled a disgusted face and looked genuinely baffled. "No. I just told you that's not it."

"Then tell me what it really is," I said.

"No." His expression became guarded.

I inched closer to him so that our toes touched. "Tell me," I whispered, imploringly.

"No," he whispered back. His chest rose and fell a little quicker, and I knew I was making him nervous.

"Why?"

Why wouldn't he just tell me what was really going on? I doubted that anything could be as terrible as he was making it out to be. Since my mum had died, he'd been the only person to make me feel truly alive; not Dad, not a therapist, not even Louisa or Zac—only him. He knew what I felt. He understood that gaping hole inside me and somehow, he was able to make me feel a little better about it. He was in the darkness *with* me. What was the point in us standing alone if we were both in this forest of shadows together anyway? Surely, he could feel that pull between us; like for like. I needed to make him see that. I needed to make him understand.

Hesitantly, I raised my hand and placed it on his forearm, feeling the soft cotton of his t-shirt under my fingers. His eyes widened, but he didn't move. Instead, he stared down at me with more ferocity than before.

"Believe me, Ava—I'm doing you a favour."

"What are you talking about?" I said.

"You won't want to be around me when you know—"

"Know what?" I said, hearing the frustration in my own voice. "Because whatever it is, maybe I wouldn't care. Maybe I *don't* care." I let my hand slip back down to my side as I took a step back from him.

"You'll care," he said, running a hand through his hair. "You're human, Ava. You will *care*—that's what humans do."

"Human?" There it was; the clue I'd been waiting for.

"It's a figure of speech, Ava," snapped Sam.

"No, it's not…" I said, my eyes unseeing as I began to piece together everything I'd seen: Sam moving quick enough in the barn to catch me, Sam's outrageous amount of tattoos, if that's what they were, Sam's mystery illness, Sam's eyes as black as the shadows inside me. I knew he wouldn't say another word if I questioned him about it, so I tested the water.

"Well, maybe I'm not like other humans," I said, but when I said it, I thought of the horrendous guilt I'd felt for not feeling anything more than numb for my mum's death. I'd tried to push this thought deep inside me, but maybe if I shared this secret with Sam…

"You're right. You're not like other people," he said, his expression cold as he stared me down. Swallowing against the bitter taste in my mouth, I looked down at my hands. He already knew. He'd known about my amnesia too, and although he'd said I inadvertently told him, I still couldn't remember saying anything about it that night in the barn. The sting of him admitting he knew how little I felt still hurt though. He agreed with me. I was different. I was cold and heartless. I swallowed hard at the lump in my throat.

"Fine," I said, my voice not much louder than a whisper. I felt sick with guilt, and knowing Sam thought less of me made it a thousand times worse. "I won't come near you again." A long moment passed, but I couldn't look up at him and I couldn't move. I just waited. He'd leave soon enough.

"Ava, I'm sorry," he whispered, moving a step closer to me.

I looked up into his face and knew he truly felt bad for what he said, but he *had* said it. I was beyond ashamed, and if he'd said it to hurt me, to get me to back off, then it had worked.

"It's fine. Just go," I said.

He hesitated, his black eyes wide with guilt. He knew he'd said something that couldn't be taken back, but as I stood my ground, he turned on the spot and walked from the room without another word. I don't know what I'd expected him to do, but now that he was leaving, I felt like a huge chasm was being levered apart between my ribs and I fought back the tears. Thinking as logically as I could about my feelings, I decided I had two options. I could either break down and cry—or deal with it. I chose to deal with it. Before the building emotion could take hold of me, I marched into the front room and flung myself into the chair, grasping my phone and typing a message to Zac.

Hey, it's Ava. We still on for tomorrow night?

I watched as Zac typed a message back.

Zac. *Hey, babe, Sure. Meet me in town, outside Andersons Music. X*

I stared at the text and waited for my breathing to slow to a more normal rate. Maybe this was what was supposed to happen all along. Maybe this was right, but why did it feel so wrong? Something in the course of my life had just changed and I felt it. I felt that elastic pull between Sam and I begin to stretch to an agonizing length, where it quivered. I braced myself for the snap that would break us apart for good.

CHAPTER Eight

I wasn't sure how I'd got through the morning, but I was glad to finally have a distraction from the raw emotion inside me. As I got off the night bus, I dug my hands in my pockets and rounded the corner onto a busy street. There were people climbing in and out of taxis, queuing for club entry, or chatting outside in smoking areas, smoke dancing around their chilly faces. Most of them were smiling or laughing with friends, and I wondered if I'd ever feel like that again. Loosing Mum had already left me feeling alone in this world, but it felt like a hole had been punched in my chest when Sam walked out yesterday. Had he thought about me at all today? Shaking my head, I knew he hadn't. Of course, he hadn't. He was stronger than that. He'd made a decision. He didn't want me around anymore. He wanted me out of his life—*safe*, I thought with a grimace. Swallowing down the feeling of agonizing loneliness, I told myself to get a grip. I needed to get on with life and forget I'd ever met Sam. Tonight, I just needed to let myself go and find other ways of feeling alive.

Looking either way down the street, my shoes

scuffed the pavement as I crossed the road and weaved behind a large set of pillars lining the front of a department store. All the buildings were intricate and grand, made of enormous blocks of yellow stone, and as I headed towards the high street, my shadow stretched out onto the walls; a reflection of how I felt inside.

When I reached Jackson street where Anderson's Music store was located, I immediately spotted Zac hunched in the shadow of a large stone pillar. He was wearing loose fitted jeans, trainers and an oversized sweater with the hood pulled up. Feeling relieved, I walked over to him. Although I craved the independence and freedom that came with growing up, I still didn't feel like wandering the streets on my own at night, but I got the distinct impression that Zac was used to it.

"Hey, you," he grinned, embracing me lazily so that my face brushed the soft material of his hoody. As he stood back again to look at me, I could see that his eyes were a reddish colour, and I recognised the look from when I'd been to Blake's.

"Are you stoned?" I asked, raising an eyebrow. He looked back at me sheepishly through a haze of cannabis and I found myself wondering what it was like. I knew I was an idiot for even considering it, but as I thought of Sam and felt the wound inside my chest opening up, I decided I didn't care. Zac was leaning on the pillar beside me, his eyes half closed as he gazed at me.

"What's it like?" I asked innocently. "Being… you know…."

He stood up. "You want to try?"

I hesitated, knowing full well I was being stupid, but

feeling a buzz of excitement inside at the same time. Maybe this was the way out of the numbness that grief brought and the agonizing pain and anger left from Sam's departure. I hadn't realised it was possible for one person to feel so many conflicting emotions at once. Maybe I just needed to take a few risks. Looking back at Zac, I nodded.

Smiling and reaching into his back pocket, Zac produced a lighter, which he held to the end of the joint, making it glow orange in the night air. As I watched, my heart started beating like a hummingbird in my chest. Was I really going to do this? I knew getting stoned probably wasn't the answer, but I needed something to dampen what I was feeling—anything.

I watched as Zac put his lips to the joint, his chest expanding. After a moment, he slowly he let the smoke drift from his mouth. The sweetened smell hit my nose and the smoke engulfed me. I was suddenly reminded of being at Blake's and how Sam had looked over at me—a private look that had conveyed a thousand thoughts. The memory was like a knife in my chest, and I reached out with determination as Zac handed me the joint.

Zac's blue eyes gazed at me, serious. "Ava, you don't have to—" he started.

"No, I do," I said, "I mean—I want to." I had to.

"Okay…" Zac said, watching me carefully. "Here," he said. "Just breathe it in, then hold it."

Tentatively, I put my lips to the end and breathed in, filling my chest and feeling my throat burn. My lungs felt hot as I held my breath, but as soon as Zac gave a small nod, I let the smoke billow back out from my lips. Smoke wafted in front of me in the cool air and I handed the roll up back to Zac, feeling the overwhelming need to cough. It was an uncomfortable sensation, but I was willing to try anything to feel something other than what I was feeling now. I'd tried to deal with this alone for too long, and when I'd met Sam I hadn't felt so alone. Now, his rejection had pushed me ever so slightly closer to that unending precipice. I teetered on the edge. I needed to steady myself, if only for a few minutes. Looking back into Zac's curious eyes, I took the joint and put it to my lips again.

After a while, the drugs began affecting all of the muscles in my body and the tension started to slip away. The feeling of loss and excruciating nothingness faded to leave me feeling sleepy and warm, despite the fact I was sitting on cold, hard stone. I'd almost forgotten about those deep, black, curious eyes. Almost. Instead of burning the inside of my eyelids, they just seemed to waft lazily in and out of my mind.

I jumped as Zac nudged my arm.

"Sorry," he mumbled, turning to me with a grin.

"S'alright," I smiled back.

He looked at me for a moment, then leant into my shoulder so I could feel his warm breath on my face. All I could smell was the sweet stench of cannabis. "You okay?"

I felt a little queasy, but I nodded and gave him a small smile. Zac really was quite good looking, I thought, as his bright blue eyes shone underneath his mess of dirty blonde hair. Brushing a strand from his face and pulling his hoody over his head, he stood up and casually took my hands from my knees to pull me to my feet.

"Come on," he said, letting one hand drop to his side and leaving his other hand curled around mine. His hand was softer than Sam's. I thought vaguely of how Sam had curled his hand around my wrist that day at the bus stop. Heat had radiated from his touch; actual heat. The word *human* echoed in my mind, but I couldn't quite grasp onto the thought. I was definitely and blissfully high, and as Zac and I crossed the road towards the end of town, I began to enjoy the feeling of his hand on mine. I was sure I could see the hint of a smile on his lips too.

After what must have been at least twenty minutes of walking, we came to a tumble-down back street. It was lined with parked cars, one of which was missing a wheel, and black bin bags were stacked clumsily alongside low-walled front gardens. Yellow eyes glared at me from under a white van and a white cat leapt out in front of and disappeared down another side street. That's when Zac finally came to a stop.

"We're here," he said, sliding his hand out from mine at a set of metal gates, which appeared to have been busted open. The lock had been knocked out leaving a rectangular hole and the frame was bent in as if someone had used a crowbar on it. Zac seemed unperturbed by this and ducked through the opening without hesitation. Glancing briefly over my shoulder, I ducked through the gate too.

On the other side, I found myself in a small concrete clearing with cracked tarmac and several, large industrial dustbins, which reeked of rotting food. I turned my nose up at the vinegary smell wafting through the air and jogged to catch up with Zac who was walking down the side of a long unused red-brick building. The building blocked most of the light from the street as most of the windows were boarded up, and I wondered if we were headed in the right direction. Everything was so dark, but then we rounded the corner.

A huge warehouse stood in front of us, dotted with grimy square windows, several of which were shattered, but the bottom level buzzed with life. Groups of teenagers and young adults hovered outside, waiting to get in, but it wasn't like the clubs in town. There was nobody manning the door or the amount of people going in. It just seemed to be first come, first served.

I felt Zac slip his hand into mine again. "You sure you're alright? You're quiet."

"Yeah, fine," I lied. I still felt a little dizzy and out of sorts, but for these few moments I could enjoy muted emotions. It was like floating outside of myself: aware and yet completely disconnected.

The beat of music filled the air and as we moved closer, the crowds became steadily thicker. A mix of people were filtering in the same direction as us, and as someone stumbled into me, I looked around to find an older girl, wearing a cropped t-shirt with a nose ring and coloured tattoos, smiling back at me in apology. I smiled nervously, but felt Zac's grip tighten on my hand as he pulled me through the doors.

The music was even more intense as we stepped inside the warehouse, which was already full to the brim with hot, clammy bodies. Zac pulled me in front of him as he took off his hoody, revealing a loose white tank top.

He definitely belonged here. I, on the other hand, was wearing jeans with converse, but at least I had worn a small black camisole; something I was glad of in the heat. Unzipping my jacket, I stuffed it in the same corner that Zac had thrown his.

"You ready?" he shouted.

"Yeah," I said, raising my own voice, but it was barely audible.

Zac guided me through the crowds, deeper into the buzz of the party, and right into the midst of the rave where smoke filled the air and strobe lights of all colours flicked through the room like lasers. The sting of sweat filled my nose as raised arms and hot bodies crammed in at me from every angle, but I was too excited to care.

Eventually Zac stopped and turned to me, grinning. Reaching up, he ruffled his hair in the heat of the room and leant forwards, bringing me closer to him, placing his hands on my hips. I could feel the warmth of his hands through my top, and I felt myself blush. As a blonde-haired girl caught my eye, I found myself moving towards Zac and resting my hands on his upper arms. In the corner of my eye, I watched her slink back into the mass of bodies.

Zac smiled down at me, pulling me against him as we began to move to the steady thud of the music. He seemed to be in his element, and as he leant his head back and closed his eyes, I felt myself relax too.

The atmosphere in the room was vibrant and I watched the beams of colour change incessantly from red, green, blue, indigo and back to red. It was hypnotic and I found myself held captive by the colour filled smoke. It was only as I was pushed closer to Zac that I was shaken out of my hypnosis and thrown back into the present.

Over Zac's shoulder, I could see more and more people gathering to look at something. Standing on tip-toes, I craned my neck over the crowds. There, in a small clearing, was a girl swinging a glowing hoop around her arm. It was mesmerizing to watch and as she stretched up high, the hoop swung gracefully down her body to spin around her upper rip cage. Both women and men had stopped to watch her as her entire body twisted and flowed to the rhythm of the music, all the while keeping the hoop aloft. I couldn't take my eyes off her until I felt Zac's lips brush my ear.

"Balloons," he said, eyes directed behind me. I turned to see someone dressed in black making an exchange of money with a guy wearing a sweat drenched t-shirt. He took a black balloon from the vendor and put it to his mouth. I watched curiously.

"It's laughing gas," I heard Zac say.

I faced him questioningly. "Laughing gas?"

He nodded. "Yeah," he said, laughing. I watched the guy breathe in the last of the gas from the now tiny balloon. Lights flashed across his face as he swayed and bounced back off into the party. This place is insane, I thought, shaking my head and sweeping my hair over one shoulder to cool down. Closing my eyes, I leant my head back and listened to the sound of the synth and drums echoing into the room. The dizzy feeling had seemingly subsided for now and I actually felt good. I felt almost normal; free from all of the intense emotions that had crippled my every waking moment over the past months. I felt seventeen. I felt human again. *Human. Humans care. You'll care.* I frowned to myself. It was almost as if he was implying that—

"Ava."

My eyes flicked open to look at Zac. "Yeah?"

"You want?" he said, holding up a small white bottle with a mischievous grin.

I looked at him suspiciously as he turned the cap and held it out to me. I took it from him and put it to my nose. It was hot and the smell caught in my throat, but before I thought any more about it, I put it to my lips and took a sip. It burned as it slipped down my throat, and I pressed my hand to my lips as I swallowed. It was strong and tasted like pure alcohol. Zac laughed at my expression.

Nudging him in the ribs, I handed it back. He took two swigs from the bottle, pulling the same face as me, wiped his mouth and laughed again. I shook my head and turned around, but as I did so, he caught me around the middle and pulled me towards him, making me jump.

"Zac," I muttered, but he couldn't hear my voice over the music. We weren't dancing anymore and as he searched my face with bright blue eyes, my heart was beating hard in my chest, but not with anticipation. He leant forward and brushed my nose with his, making my lips part in response, and then he was kissing me. I felt myself kiss him back hesitantly, but I wasn't thinking of Zac. This was wrong—a sudden cry from the other side of the room simultaneously broke us apart.

Across the crowds, people were moving away from the door as police in yellow and black uniforms entered, flanked by more police wearing helmets and holding large rectangular shields. I frowned in confusion at the riot police, lined up like toy soldiers. Then people began to shout and something hit one of the shields hard, making my anxiety spike.

"Come on," Zac said in my ear, taking my hand and leading me towards the back of the warehouse, but we weren't the only ones trying to make a quick exit. People from all angles started to push and pull us. I felt Zac's grip tighten around my hand, but it was a second too late as a huge muscular body barged into us, breaking us apart. I looked up and saw a broad-shouldered guy staring down a younger man who had a bloody face.

"Come on then!" The bulkier man shouted towards the other guy, who was stumbling backwards. The bigger guy threw a punch, but he missed his target and flew into the ring of spectators that had formed. Everybody was trying to stay out of the way, I could see the hoop girl moving away from the scene, but as I readied myself to dodge any flying punches, I didn't see the bottle coming at me until the last moment.

I raised my hands to cover my face, but it came with such force that I immediately felt a sharp pain through my wrist and forearm before being shoved into the crowds. Stumbling on my own feet, I fell to the floor amongst a sea of legs. The floor was cold and damp and I got to my feet as quickly as possible to make my way over to the edge of the room where I leant against a cold metal post.

I searched the crowds of people, trying my best to see Zac, but couldn't spot him anywhere. All around me was chaos. People were panicking as more fights broke out; shouts and screams echoed through the emptying warehouse, but all I could think was that I needed to stay upright. I was beginning to feel dizzy and when I looked down, I saw that my arm was glistening red where a huge gash had opened on my wrist. As if seeing it for the first time made it real, it throbbed painfully and a wave of nausea washed over me. My head began to spin and my vision blackened into a tunnel. Just as my legs turned to jelly and gave way, I felt Zac's arms around me, scooping me up.

CHAPTER *Nine*

Blood rushed in my ears, deafening me as I stared down at her, her golden-brown hair disarrayed on the pillow around her face and her hands clasped neatly together on her rib cage. She could have been asleep, but the pallor of her face said otherwise. She looked like my mum, but there was none of the energy or passion that was once there. She was a stranger.

Sadness gripped at my guts as I reached out and took her cold, white hand in mine. It felt light, too light. “Mum?” I whispered. Her eyes fluttered open and my heart leapt at the prospect of looking into those eyes that made me feel loved and safe; those eyes that looked just like mine. Although, instead of that hazel gaze that warmed my very soul, I found myself looking into hollow black pupils. My heart turned to ice, I flew backwards and found myself sitting bolt upright in a sterile bed.

“Mum?” I said, glancing around my surroundings. It felt like she was still there—but she wasn’t. I was alone, sitting on a bed made up with crisp white sheets, in a cubicle cordoned off by rough, blue curtains. I felt the sting of disinfectant burn the inside of my nose, and a cry escaped from my mouth as the night before came flooding back and I realised where I was. Looking wildly about, my heart rate elevated.

I ripped back the cold white linen from my knees, revealing a hospital gown, and my feet hit the chilly floor as I swung my legs from the bed. My head swam as I stood up, and I stumbled forwards, grappling at the curtains. I was hardly aware of my shock as they flashed apart, revealing a short, round nurse with stern blue eyes.

"Oh, no, you don't," she said, her hands outstretched. "Back in bed, young lady."

Her stern exterior blocked my exit. "I can't," I whimpered, feeling sickness bubbling in the pit of my stomach. The smell of this place set me on edge and I had to get out before my body shut down completely. I could already feel my heart beat threatening to shatter my ribs, but as I side stepped the nurse and made a desperate play for freedom, I stumbled into someone else.

"Ava?"

My dad's face was full of concern as he grasped my upper arms. "Hey… Hey, Ava. Calm down," he said. Tears pooled in my eyes and my heart pounded painfully in my chest. I didn't want to be in here. People died in hospitals. *She* had died in hospital. *I* had almost died.

"Come on, Ava, honey." The nurse's voice was patient and kind, but I couldn't stop. My throat was constricting, I couldn't breathe, but nobody was listening. I was like a caged bird, unable to stretch my wings in order to escape. I wasn't about to give up.

Pushing hard against my dad's grip, I ran towards the door to the ward, reaching it with a thud and pulling hard on the handle. It shuddered under my protests, but as I yanked hard on it for the third time, I found myself undeniably held captive. That's when my determination slipped.

"Dad. Please," I pleaded, turning to him. I could feel the burn in my lungs as I continued to breathe around the lump now lodged in my throat.

"Ava…" His voice was soft as he edged towards me, with a pained look on his face. "You can't leave just yet, love—"

"N-no," I stammered, feeling my legs wobble. I slid down the door into a heap on the floor and sobbed hard, the pain stinging my throat. It was all too much—the dream, the smell, the hospital, being trapped—nobody seemed to understand.

"I can't breathe," I whispered, between rasping breaths.

The nurse knelt down in front of me so she was eye level with me. "Ava, honey, look at me."

I looked into her concerned eyes.

"Just take deep breaths in through your mouth and out through your nose, okay? Nice and steady…"

But I couldn't. Even when I tried to imitate the nurses breathing pattern, I couldn't rid myself of the sensation of a belt tightening around my chest. Maybe this is how it would end; I'd just stop breathing.

"Ava." The nurse's voice was stern this time. "Ava—look at me."

I looked into her expectant face, but as her eyes flicked down my body, I followed her gaze and I saw it. My right arm and wrist were bandaged and I could see red blotches of blood seeping through the material. I automatically felt my stomach convulse violently, and I bent double and retched, bringing up what I'd consumed the night before.

Huge pains ran through my stomach and I had to gather myself onto all fours as I heaved, empting the remaining contents of my stomach onto the floor. My whole body seemed determined to cleanse itself and I couldn't stop it.

When the retching finally stopped, I wiped my mouth with my good arm, sat back on the floor and took a deep breath. I still felt like I needed to get more air into my lungs. Silent tears ran down my cheeks, leaving a burning sensation behind. Is this what it had come to? Months of grieving and I was still at rock bottom. Looking down at myself, I began to feel ashamed of what I'd let myself become. Was I this person now? No wonder Sam had declared he no longer wanted to be friends with me. I was a mess. He'd known all along. I couldn't even cope with my problems, let alone his too. At least one of us was sensible enough to walk away rather than cause a whole new world of hurt and destruction.

"Ava, love," my dad whispered, kneeling in front of me and gently placing his hands on my shoulders. I looked at him, and had never felt so low—so afraid. “You need to let the nurse help you. Then we can leave the hospital, okay? But they can’t let you go until they’ve done some more checks on you.”

I nodded reluctantly and my body gave a wild shake. Seeing my bloodied, bandaged arm had been a shock. Dad knew I didn’t like blood, but I realised my moments of anxiety were multiplying. I hadn’t voiced what was really going on inside my head and it had reached the point where my body was regularly trying to declare its unease. I just hoped he didn’t decide to send me to a therapist. That would be the last nail in the coffin, I thought bitterly.

“Come on,” he said, pulling me to my feet and directing me back towards my bed. I went without protest this time. The sooner this was done, the sooner I could leave.

The sheets were cool as I climbed onto the mattress, careful not to put any weight on my damaged arm. As I sat back on the pillows, Dad pulled the covers up to my waist and eyed me with an edge of disquiet.

“You okay?” he mumbled.

My body was trembling involuntarily and I looked at my knotted hands. “I’m sorry, Dad,” I whispered on the brink of tears. “I was stupid last night.”

He sighed heavily and leant forwards, brushing my hair back from my forehead. “I thought I’d lost you,” he said.

I swallowed uneasily as I tried to recall how I’d

miraculously gotten to the hospital, but I couldn't remember. All I could remember was when Zac found me. I'd been so relieved that I'd felt like crying right before I passed out.

"I don't suppose you're going to tell me who you were with, are you?"

I fidgeted with the sheets. Did I really want to get Zac in trouble? It was my own fault. I'd decided to go to the rave. Zac never forced it on me. I didn't have to go, or smoke a joint, or drink alcohol underage—but I did, and at the time, I hadn't cared. Last night I hadn't thought about anything other than the need to get rid of the pain that felt like someone slowly twisting a knife in my gut.

"Ava?"

I glanced to my dad's blue flecked eyes. "Sorry," I muttered.

The curtain pulled back. "Right, Ava. We're going to have to change that dressing for you," said the nurse, bustling over to my bedside. "It was all cleaned out last night whilst you were out for the count."

I cringed internally as I thought about what kind of state I must have been in. Maybe that's why Zac had left too. I really needed to sort my life out, and I wondered if it was possible to feel worse in any way.

"You had some stitches put in, but it all looks like it will heal," said the nurse, stretching my arm out with her blue gloved hands. She placed a small cardboard tub underneath my wrist and began to peel back the sodden bandage.

I looked away. Blood always made me feel sick.

"Are you going to be okay?" The nurse stopped what she was doing.

"Mm-hmm. I just don't like blood," I said, trying to swallow with a dry throat.

"Okay. Well…" she said, reaching to the shelf on my bedside table and producing another cardboard bowl exactly like the kidney shaped one already under my arm. "If you're going to hurl, do it in here," she said, with a small smile.

I nodded and held it. I could feel her peeling the bandage back from my arm, then a sharp twinge traveled through my hand, making me inhale sharply.

"You're alright, love," Dad said, putting a hand on my shoulder.

"She severed an artery so there was a lot of blood, but she'll still able to move her fingers." I could feel pressure on the inside of my arm as the nurse spoke. "No tendons were damaged. Look. Wiggle your fingers, honey." I cautiously moved my fingers up and down on my right hand without looking. "You're a very lucky girl, Ava," the nurse chimed.

"She might be lucky, but when I find out who took her to that rave…" I looked up at my dad, shocked. "Was it Louisa?"

"No!" I countered.

"Was it a boy?"

I blanched at this and simply shook my head, making him raise his eyebrows.

"Okay, so we know it's a boy then…" he said, his jaw clenching. Oh crap. "Was it Sam?"

Sam. The knife twisted in my gut. "No," I whispered, feeling my mood drop a few more degrees. Was it truly over between us…before it had even begun?

"You're doing really well, Ava," came the nurse's encouraging voice again as she dabbed at my damaged arm, making me grit my teeth. I breathed through my mouth and brushed my hair away from my warm face. The sound of my phone vibrating was a welcome distraction.

Before I could protest, Dad picked it up. I observed cautiously as he raised an eyebrow and placed it on the bed in front of me.

Louisa. *Ava! I'm at the hospital. What the hell happened? Which ward are you in? Lou. xx*

I breathed a sigh of relief as I read the message, but before I could type back, my phone was hooked out of my grasp and put back on my bedside table. "I'll go and find her and get a coffee on the way," Dad said, moving towards the curtains and drawing them back. "Are you going to be okay?" He looked at my arm.

"She's all done," the nurse piped up, taking the cardboard tub away and leaving me with a fresh bandage. "Well done, Ava."

"Thank you," I mumbled, but when I looked up, Dad was gone. Sighing, I wondered how long I was going to have to deal with him being angry with me.

"Don't worry. He'll come around," whispered the

nurse. "It's a man thing. They like to suffer in silence." She gave me a wry smile before squeezing my shoulder and leaving the cubicle. I looked after her as she left and hoped she was right.

As I glanced over to my phone, I wondered if I should message Zac. He must have gone home. I just hoped I hadn't got him into too much trouble. Before I could even think about constructing a message, a familiar, assertive tone penetrated the silence of the ward, making me smile.

"Ava Blume. Yep. Where?"

The curtains pulled back and Louisa appeared. Her hair was a mad wind-swept mess and a large purple scarf was wound around her neck. "Ava! What the hell?" she said, flinging her arms around my neck.

"Hi, Lou," I mumbled into her shoulder.

"Your dad's just been questioning me about some rave," she said, leaning back to sit on the bed. "You need to fill me in—and fast!"

I knew I could trust Louisa not to say a word to anyone—not even Blake, so I took a deep breath and told her the whole story. I started with Sam and then went on to explain meeting Zac, smoking pot, kissing Zac and finally the fight at the rave, which explained the huge gash on my arm. As my story came to an end, I inhaled deeply and waited for her onslaught, but it never came. Instead, she gazed at me with pursed lips.

"Is this about your mum?" she murmured.

Her question caught me off guard as it wasn't the

reaction I'd expected from her. I opened my mouth to try and put some words together, but when nothing came to mind, I shrugged.

"Ava, I know I don't know exactly what happened with your mum, but I know grief can do strange things to you…" She sat back on the bed and studied my face and I felt like a little sister being reprimanded.

"I guess," I muttered, fiddling with the bandage on my arm. It was the truth. It had been to do with the grief that weighed down on me, but also because of Sam. I hadn't been aware of just how much I'd wanted to forget the feelings of guilt left behind after my mum's death, but I'd blamed my mood mostly on Sam. In truth, it had just been an amalgamation of everything that had happened over the last few months. It was just that Sam walking out was like my one last spark of hope being ripped away. I'd thought doing a few careless things was my answer.

"I just needed to not care for one night," I said. I'd been selfish though and I'd dragged Zac into it all.

"Damn that stupid boy," Louisa said with a sigh.

"It's not his fault," I whispered, feeling ashamed. "Zac didn't force me into going. It was all me."

"No," Louisa retorted. "Not *that* boy." She looked me hard in the eyes with such ferocity that I knew she'd worked it out. How did she do that?

"Oh…" I said, feeling my face redden at the thought of Sam. I really wished my body wouldn't react to the simple mention of him. He'd made his choice and, somehow, I needed to respect that.

"You know," Louisa said, leaning forwards, "he was in a foul mood last night." At that, the knife in my stomach yanked out hard, leaving me breathless and in a moment of selfishness, I hoped it was because of me.

"You saw him?" I asked, feeling that familiar flutter come with a vengeance.

Louisa nodded. "Yeah, at Blake's. Although, it wasn't for long."

"What do you mean?"

"I don't know… I think they were arguing about something, and when I turned up, he left."

I frowned at Louisa in confusion. "What were they arguing about?"

"No idea, but whatever it was, Blake was pissed," said Louisa, leaning over and inspecting my arm. "He was all red and sweaty," she said, trying to lighten the mood. Despite the way I felt, I smiled.

"Was that before or after you left…?"

Louisa narrowed her eyes at me. "*You* have a dirty mind," she said.

This time I laughed out loud, wincing from the pain in my arm.

"Seriously, Ava, be careful!"

"I'm fine. It's just sore," I said, turning my arm over to check for blood.

"Did they say what you damaged?" she asked. "Did you tear any tendons? Do you need physio? Did you sever an artery or anything gruesome?" She sounded excited by the prospect of blood and guts, and I shriveled my nose at her.

"You're sick," I started, "but yes—the nurse said I severed an artery, but I was out of it."

"Wow, you're lucky. You could have bled to death, Ava." She gave me a grim look as she leant over to fish her phone from her bag.

"What?" I swallowed as I felt the blood leave my face. I didn't know that. No wonder Dad was so angry with me.

"You didn't know that?" It was Louisa's turn to go pale.

"No." I shifted, uneasy.

"Well, the main thing is that you're okay." Louisa recovered quickly, placing her hands on top of my free hand. At the sound of someone entering the ward, she turned. "I should go," she said, giving me a hasty squeeze around the shoulders. "I can hear your dad coming, and I want to avoid another interrogation." I smiled as she got up from the bed. "It could be dangerous seeing as you've imparted all of your scandalous secrets with me now!" She winked at me and gathered up her bag and phone as I heard my dad's voice just outside the curtain talking to the nurse.

"Oh, and do you know when you'll be discharged yet? It's the Battle of the Bands Thursday night," she said. "We could go together. Zac's playing with his new band, Fortitude. That's if it's not too…you know—weird with you two."

"Yeah, sure," I nodded, feeling a little nervous at the

thought of talking to Zac about how I really felt. "If I'm allowed out that is…"

"I doubt it," came Dad's voice.

Louisa and I both turned to see him appearing from behind the curtain. He had a coffee in his hand and was scrutinizing Louisa. At that moment, Louisa's phone began to ring. Blake's name flashed on the screen and I wondered what had happened between him and Sam last night.

"I'm just off, Mr Blume," said Louisa, picking up her bag. "I've got a hot date!" She held up her phone and smiled widely at my dad, but he wasn't in the mood.

"Huh. Any idea who tried and failed to date my daughter?" He fired back at her. She widened her eyes at me, as if to say *good luck!*

"Bye, Lou," I muttered as she left the cubicle.

"That one's lively," Dad grumbled, slumping in the armchair next to my bed. I wanted to apologise, but I knew it wouldn't make any difference, so I sat in silence. As he sipped at a maroon paper cup, I let my mind wander over what Louisa had said. She'd said Sam had been in a horrible mood, but was that to do with me or another matter entirely, and why had he left as soon as Louisa had arrived? Sighing to myself, I wondered if I'd ever find out, or if I'd be kept in the dark for eternity. I shook my head. I already knew that I couldn't just slink back into the shadows. He'd unlocked something inside me and now I had to find out more.

CHAPTER *Ten*

We were on our way home from the hospital and as we trundled along the winding, country road, I gazed out the window at the mist. It was low to the ground today and made the trees in the fields look as if they were hovering. The weather had been terrible the whole day and it was still cold and damp outside, causing the tyres to spray mud along the hedgerows as we travelled along. It was cosy inside the cab of the car, though. The radiator was on high and the radio produced a low hum of chatter, but I hadn't listened to a word of what was being said. My mind was still going over what had happened the night before and how lucky I'd been. But worse than that was the constant replay of the few words that Sam had shared. *There are things you don't know...shouldn't know.* What was so terrible? I knew it must be bad, but I just couldn't put my finger on it. He'd tried to drive me away, but he'd only made me more intrigued. Now, I had to know.

As the four-wheel drive slowed and turned onto the uneven track leading to Willow Farm, my shoulder knocked into the car door, making me tense. I was cradling my right arm in my lap and dreaded seeing red liquid seeping from underneath it, although the nurse had reassured me that it should be fine. I had stitches and would need to go back for a check-up, but other than that, I was all fixed.

When we rumbled to a stop in front of Willow Cottage, Dad climbed out, shutting his door behind him with a metallic clunk and left me listening to the whispered buzz of the car radiator coming to a stop. Silence erupted around me and I felt goosebumps course up my arms. My dad had been unnervingly quiet ever since he'd stepped foot in the hospital, and I wondered how long it would last and at what point he might lose it and get angry. I at least knew him well enough to know it was just beneath the surface. He was someone who bottled all his feelings up until the last minute, then he'd explode like a cannon. Like father like daughter, I thought with a grim smirk on my face. I reached gingerly for the door handle, but it was pulled from my reach.

"Here," Dad said, taking me under my good elbow as I slid awkwardly down onto the gravel driveway. I shivered in the hard winter air. "The door's unlocked," he said. "I'm just going to get some wood for the burner."

I watched him walk away towards the barn and resigned myself to the fact that the next few days off wouldn't be as relaxing as I might have first hoped. He was mad at me—really mad, and I wasn't accustomed to living with him enough to know the effects this might have on day to day life.

Sighing to myself as I made my way around to the

front door, I hoped I would at least be able to catch up on my overdue assignments. I'd been so wrapped up in everything happening with Sam lately that my college work had suffered, but now that he was officially no longer a friend—I froze. Zac was slumped on the doorstep with his head in his hands and as he looked up at me, relief spread over his face.

"Zac… What are you doing here?"

"Oh, my god, Ava," he mumbled, getting to his feet. "I'm so sorry." He searched my eyes. "Are you okay? What happened? I couldn't find you…"

"It's okay. I'm fine," I said, giving him a small smile. "I've just got back from the hospital. All fixed now." I held up my arm and a shadow passed over Zac's face as he saw the bandages covering my wound. "It's not as bad as it looks," I said, shrugging and trying not to remember the feeling of sickness as I'd seen the blood running down my arm.

Looking up at Zac, I could see that he was pale with tiredness. He looked worse than me. "I don't know what happened last night, Ava. It just went crazy in there."

"Don't worry about it," I muttered, shivering in the cold. "I was stupid last night. I probably deserved everything I got." Zac shuffled on the spot. I could tell he felt bad, but I didn't want him to get into more trouble. "Look, you should probably go. My dad's really angry," I said, glancing over my shoulder. "He'll be here soon, and I don't want you to get the blame for what happened. It was my fault."

"Yeah, I thought he'd be angry," Zac nodded, "but I

should show my face. You know…apologise."

"Yeah, I really don't know if that's a good idea," I began, but Zac's face paled further and I heard the crunch of gravel; I knew it was too late.

"Hi, Mr Blume—"

"Don't tell me…" said my dad, stopping in his tracks, his hand gripping a bucket of firewood. "You're the one responsible for injuring my daughter?" His eyes were wide with fury and I felt my stomach flutter uneasily.

"I am. I'm so sorry, Mr Blume. I never meant—"

"For her to get hurt?" He put the bucket down, his blue eyes glazed with anger. "What the hell do you think you were doing?"

Zac swallowed and a puff of white came from his mouth as he exhaled. "I don't—"

"My daughter had never touched a drop of alcohol or a single drug until you came along."

That wasn't entirely true. I recalled downing alchopops with school friends when I was fourteen. It had been a dare and I'd foolishly tried to fit in, which had resulted in feeling horribly ill the next day.

"Dad, it's not his fault. I'm seventeen. I'm practically an adult and it was my decision."

"Then you're not an adult, Ava," he stated, fixing me with a glare I'd never encountered before. "Adults don't make stupid decisions." I dropped my eyes to the ground as Dad glared at me, making me feel like a child. "I can't believe how stupid both of you have been. You could have *died,* Ava."

At that, my eyes flicked back up to him in shock and

hot tears burned my eyes. Breathing shakily, I blinked them away and felt the bitter wind sting my cheeks as I did so.

"Pete," came another level voice. Dad moved aside and Sam came into view. "Is everything alright?" My stomach twisted involuntarily. My face heated with embarrassment, but I couldn't look away. His dark hair was ruffled from the wind and he was wearing a long-sleeved t-shirt, old jeans and boots caked in mud. His eyes travelled over me, up to my face and down to settle on my arm. His jaw clenched.

Breaking my gaze from Sam, I pulled my coat around me to cover my arm. I didn't need to be reminded how stupid I'd been by Sam as well, and from the look on his face, I knew that's what he was thinking.

"I think you should leave, Zac," said Sam, not taking his eyes off me. I wanted to tell him it wasn't his place to say that, but I knew it was better if Zac left.

"Sorry," I whispered, turning towards Zac. "I'll call you later."

"Sure," he mumbled, looking beaten. He hesitated a moment before turning and slouching down the paved path and out the gate. As the gate fell shut behind him, I immediately felt all eyes on me again.

"Inside, Ava," snapped my dad, picking up the firewood from the doorstep and disappearing inside. I watched him go and became all too aware that I was alone with Sam. Keen to avoid being rejected again, I decided to avoid his gaze and not say a word. If he wanted to talk, it was up to him. Letting my hair drop around my face, I made my way to the front door, feeling an ache in my chest with every step.

"Ava…"

I turned slowly to face him, trying to keep my face expressionless in an attempt to appear untroubled by yesterday's conversation.

"Your arm…" he said, stepping towards me.

"Stop," I said, immediately losing my cool and stepping back. I knew if I let him touch me, I'd lose all my strength. I'd thought a great deal about everything that had happened with Sam, and I'd come to the conclusion that if he wanted to be friends, he'd have to trust me enough to tell me what was going on. How I was going to let him know this without actually saying it was another matter. As I opened my mouth, I found that not even one word was available.

"I was just going to ask if you were okay," he mumbled, a look of hurt crossing his face.

"I'm fine," I said, watching as he stuffed his hands into his pockets. "I just think it's better…" I mumbled.

"Right. The no-friends thing," Sam said, pursing his lips. "You're right." He looked directly into my eyes. "I told you you'd be better at this than me."

I stared at him, surprised that he'd brought up the conversation we'd had in the quiet of his car. The memory only made me think of how he'd said he couldn't stay away from me, and I found myself asking him one more time. "Why are you doing this?"

"Because I have to," he said, standing up straight and searching my face impassively.

“You have to? Who says?”

“I do.” He fixed me with a glare, but there was no anger there—just pain. It was then that I believed the decision he’d made had not been easy for him. I just wished I was stronger to help him carry the burden of whatever haunted him.

All I could say was a simple, “Okay.” In that moment, the nurse’s words floated back into my mind. *He’ll come around. It’s a man thing. They like to suffer in silence.* I just hoped that when he did come around, I was strong enough to handle whatever truth came my way.

That night I dreamt of the operating theatre doors that I longed to open. This time there were no nurses or doctors or that stinging sensation of disinfectant though. There was no rushing and no blood—just doors looming ahead of me. They remained closed, my hand outstretched in front of me, always just out of reach. I knew something behind them held the answers I needed, and it seemed like each dream brought me closer, but this dream felt wrong. Something was keeping me from discovering the truth, and I wondered if I’d ever remember what had happened to my mum.

The following morning, I awoke with a stinging sensation in my arm and the heaviness of grief in the recesses of my chest, pinning me to the bed like a dead weight. As I stared at the ceiling, I wondered what the point of it all was. I’d felt like this for month upon month now and my emotions were wearing thin. Despite not being able to remember what happened the night my mum died, my insides still roiled at the thought of that fateful night. On top of the constant frustration and agony, I felt like every tiny thing reminded me of her, and in amongst all this confusion, there was Sam. It made me want nothing more than to curl up in Mum's arms, breathe in her perfume and listen to her tell me everything would be fine—that everything would make sense in the end.

A tear slid down my cheek as I pictured her rosy cheeks and wicked grin, usually when she'd been teasing me. My chest felt empty. I didn't want to feel like this anymore and I wasn't sure I had the energy to keep pretending I was okay. And with Sam avoiding me too—the one person who'd seemed to have the power to ease these feelings—I felt more alone that ever. It was as if I was standing in a crowded room screaming at the top of my lungs, but nobody could hear me.

Sighing in frustration, I knew the only thing I could do was carry on as normal, despite feeling far from it. Pulling on my cardigan and a pair of slippers, I stomped downstairs to breakfast, ready to face another day of acting as if everything was fine. All I could do was hope that someday this would all stop and the light would finally return to me.

The house was eerily quiet and the kitchen empty. I padded over to fill the kettle, looking out the window as I did so. It was a relief to find that my dad was already out working. At least I didn't have to tiptoe around him to avoid being questioned further about the rave. He'd been so quiet last night that I was glad to finally be able to say goodnight. Even though when I'd got to bed, I'd found myself slipping into a fit of silent tears. I'd even ignored Zac's calls despite feeling horrible for ignoring them.

As I flicked the kettle on, I wondered if he'd been in trouble with his parents. From what he'd said before, it sounded like they were overbearing at times. Maybe he wasn't the only one that had wanted to forget.

Wiping a tear from my eye as I yawned heavily into my arm, I slumped down at the kitchen table to wait for the kettle to boil. I was still so tired, feeling like I was constantly running on empty. I closed my eyes and attempted to let the silence of the empty cottage clear my mind, and it was working for a moment until my dad came bursting through the back door. I sat up with a start and stifled another yawn.

"You're up. Come with me, young lady."

"What—now?" I started.

"Yes, now," he said, chucking me a pair of wellies. "Put these on."

"But I've only got my pyjamas on—"

"Doesn't matter. Come on." He stared at me pointedly as I reached uneasily for the wellies and stuffed my bare feet into them. What job could he possibly want me to do at this time in the morning with an injured arm? I suppose I deserved it, I thought, as I moved through the back door.

The cold nipped at me as I followed my dad around the outside of the house towards the barns and I began to regret not having showered and dressed before coming downstairs. I should have known my dad would have me working on the farm, but as we climbed the stone steps to the driveway, he stopped. Climbing the last few to stand beside him, I realised he was looking at a small purple car.

"I've actually had it for a while, but I've been trying to fix it up for you."

I turned to him incredulously. "What?"

He wore a wistful expression. "It's been a tough year. God knows…" he mumbled. "But you're going to be eighteen soon and you need your space."

"But you—"

"I'm still angry with you," he said. I nodded, feeling dizzy with confusion and fear and excitement all wrapped into one. "But I understand that you need your freedom and I think this will help." He pulled a pair of keys from his pocket and handed them to me. "Maybe I've been a little over protective what with everything that's happened, Aves. I just want you to know it's because I care."

"Dad…" I said, taking the keys. "You didn't have to." He was giving me a car. I'd never had my own car, and after my mum, I'd not had much interest in saving for one.

"I know," he said. "But I wanted to and I think it will do you good. I know your mum would agree."

Mum. I swallowed down the lump in my throat and looked back at the tiny car. I couldn't believe it. Dad was giving me a car after everything I'd put him through lately. It was a brave move on his part, and I could see him watching me with caution. "Thanks…." I muttered. "I know I don't deserve it..."

Huffing to himself, he put an arm around my shoulders. "We all make mistakes, Aves, even adults. I was wrong last night. By the graces, I know I've made my fair share, and I know I can be overbearing. Your mum used to tell me as much. I just hope you've learnt your lesson. If you don't want me breathing down your neck every second of the day, then you need to take care of yourself too. You're old enough now."

I fiddled with the keys, unsure of what to say. This morning I'd been wondering how much longer I was going to have to endure the silent treatment, and now it seemed it had come to a surprisingly abrupt end.

"Call it an early eighteenth birthday gift," he said.

"Thanks, Dad," I mumbled.

Climbing inside the tiny car, the smell of mechanics' oil and rubber wafted through the interior, but I didn't care. I finally had my own car which meant *freedom!* I put the key in the ignition and started the engine. It coughed and spluttered a little, but as it rumbled to life, I smiled through the open door at my dad. He seemed in a good mood, and I remembered what Louisa had said about Battle of the Bands on Thursday night. Maybe now was the time to ask, before he changed his mind on the whole freedom thing.

"So, is it ready to drive?" He nodded and I thought about how to ask about going to the concert without mentioning Zac. "Because there's a concert at college on

Thursday night that Louisa wanted me to go to. It's a music thing and she has no way of getting there…" I looked at him as he considered what I was saying. My mood dropped as I saw him stuff his hands in his pockets and frown down at the floor.

"Never mind," I said. "It's just a music competition. I'll tell Lou I can't—"

"You can go," he said.

I looked at him, surprised.

"But I want you back by ten."

I nodded frantically. I'd agree to eight if it meant I could just have a little guilt-free freedom. Suddenly, life was looking a fraction brighter. Although before basking in the light, I needed to wade through the shadows. I needed to face Zac and tell him I'd made a mistake.

CHAPTER *Eleven*

"So, your dad kept it a secret?" Louisa asked, running her hand along the dashboard. I watched as she craned around to look in the back of the car and then turn back and open the sunshield at the front. She adjusted the tiny mirror and wiped something from the corner of her mouth.

"Uh-huh. I had no idea," I said.

"So apparently trying to kill yourself works a treat. Maybe I should try it with my mum."

I glanced over at Louisa through narrowed eyes. "I did not try to kill myself."

"Then what were you trying to do?"

"I was trying to have fun for once," I huffed. "It just went wrong."

"Alright, cool it, drama queen. You're not the only one with a dead parent." She laughed under her breath and gave me a sideways glance. Shaking my head in distaste, I pulled into the college carpark. It was almost pitch black, even though it was still early evening, but I managed to find a space near the back of the carpark underneath some huge oaks whose roots had broken through the tarmac.

"So, have you spoken to Zac?" Louisa asked, gathering her things from the foot-well. During our conversation in the hospital, I'd told Louisa about kissing Zac and owned up to how I really felt. She hadn't been surprised.

"We messaged a few times." I shrugged. "Nothing serious. He just keeps apologising. I haven't brought up… you know."

We climbed out of the car into the night air and walked to the sports hall where the bands would be playing. Other students were queuing up outside the double doors to buy tickets, but, thankfully, Louisa had had the hindsight to buy them the week before, so we casually made our way past them towards the doors.

The heat hit us as we came into the entrance hall, and I could hear the thud of music ahead, even though the concert wasn't due to start yet. They must be getting in a few last-minute practises before the competition, I thought. I slid my coat gingerly over my injured arm and proceeded to pass it to the cloakroom staff in exchange for a pink ticket, which I stuffed in my back pocket.

Louisa had sloped off and was waving through the glass windows at someone. She'd taken her coat off too, but looked quite the opposite of me—grown up. She was wearing black skinny-jeans, ankle boots and a red camisole. No wonder Blake found it acceptable to date her. She looked like an adult, whereas I barely looked my age in my jeans and converse. Feeling self-conscious, I swept my hair round to one side in an attempt to look a little more feminine next to Louisa. I was glad I'd at least gone to the effort of putting in some earrings.

"Who are you waving to?" I said, moving beside her.

"Zac," she said, pointing into the dark room. "He's over by the stage."

I squinted into hazy, smoke filled room and could just make out Zac. He was standing with a small group of other boys from our year group in college and was indicating for us to come in.

"Come on," Louisa said, pushing the doors open.

As we approached, I could see that the stage was littered with wires which trailed off to various amps and microphones. At the back, there was a drum kit and in the middle of the stage, there was a boy with long blonde hair leaning over a bass guitar. His fringe kept flopping over his face so that he had to keep blowing it away as he plugged in various wires to the base of his instrument.

"You made it," Zac grinned, giving us both a bear hug. "I wasn't sure you'd be allowed out. Especially seeing as I'm such a bad influence," he said, leaning over to me with a dry smile.

"Yeah, I didn't exactly mention you'd be here," I said, returning his smile. I was glad he was happy. He'd spent most of the week messaging me and apologising, but, it seemed, he'd finally got the message that it was just as much my fault as his.

"How's the arm?" he asked, leaning in to talk over the sound of a bassist testing the amps.

"Much better thanks. Just a bit sore…"

Zac glanced over at Louisa who had busied herself with talking with one of the other band members. I knew she didn't know him. She was giving me a chance to talk to Zac. I was both thankful and a little annoyed that I couldn't just pretend everything was fine.

"Good. Look, Ava. I'm really sorry—"

"Stop apologising. My arm's fine, Zac," I said, but as he shuffled on the spot, I had the uneasy feeling that I knew what was coming. "Oh. You're sorry about…"

"No, not sorry," he said. "I'm not sorry about that. Only that I think it was misplaced. I kind of got the impression that you and that guy at your house…?" He waited expectantly as I opened and closed my mouth thoughtfully. What was I supposed to say to that? But before I could conjure an answer, Zac went on. "Louisa might have mentioned him a few times too. I kind of guessed she might be trying to tell me something…"

I was sure I was blushing. "I'm really sorry, Zac," I said, feeling ashamed. I'd not been fair to Zac and he'd been a really good friend to me. "I don't know what's going on with me at the moment," I muttered, embarrassed.

"Look, it's fine," he said graciously. "As long as you're going to stick around and watch me play. Maybe you'll see me in a whole new light and that other guy will seem like a pussy in comparison to the rock god that I am." Zac grinned at me and I knew I was forgiven. He was a better friend than I deserved.

Zac nudged me in the shoulder. "Cool. Well, I'm glad you both came, but I'd better go and set up. I'll see you later." He smiled at Louisa before moving over to his band members and disappearing behind the stage.

The main doors to the hall opened and the crowd from outside dispersed into the open space, filling the room. The lights dimmed and the coloured stage lights lit up, throwing the place into an atmospheric bustle. I felt a lot lighter, and Louisa grinned at me knowingly.

"Drink?" she said, leaning over to me.

I nodded and we made our way to a small hatch over the other side of the hall. There was already a small queue, and as we joined the end, a deep voice made me jump.

"Hello, Louisa… Ava."

We both turned our heads to find Mr Jenson standing behind us. He was wearing jeans and a t-shirt, which made him look strangely out of place at college. He was normally dressed in suit trousers and a shirt.

"And who might you be here to support?"

"Fortitude," Louisa replied with a smile. "Zac's band."

He nodded politely. "Of course. He's a very talented bass and guitar player, Mr Brands informs me. Although, there are a number of very talented musicians tonight."

"Which teachers are judging?" asked Louisa.

"Well Mr Brands, of course, Mrs Richards and myself." He smiled at us. Louisa was unfazed by casual conversation with a teacher, but I wasn't sure of the protocols for this kind of situation, so I glanced down at my shoes, only half listening to their conversation.

"Anyway, it looks like I'm being summoned already. I'd better go. Enjoy your evening." He excused himself and marched off in the direction of the stage where Mrs Richards was waving him over.

"You're quiet," said Louisa, watching me hand over my money to the girl behind the counter. "Did you sort everything with Zac?"

"Yeah," I said, giving her a small smile and wedging a drink can under my good arm. "It's just weird talking to teachers."

Louisa laughed. "You're such a nerd," she said, handing over her own money for a drink. "He was just being friendly. Besides, he's only a few years older than us."

"More than a few," I said, following Louisa out of the queue. We walked over towards the stage where Mr Jenson was standing in the centre with a microphone, and as he brushed his hair back, Louisa turned to me with an impish grin.

"Well maybe so," she said, "but he is kind of hot."

"Ugh, really? A teacher?" She almost spat her drink out, making me laugh.

"First up, we have a heavy metal band. Please welcome to the stage *Venom*." Mr Jenson stepped off the stage and three guys from our year slouched onto stage, all dressed in oversized black hoodies and jeans. Two of them had long hair and I recognised one as the guy that had been playing bass earlier. The third had short ruffled brown hair and he stepped up to the microphone. Louisa and I exchanged looks, unsure what to expect from this band, but as they began to play, it was quite impressive, and I found myself wishing I could play an instrument like them.

After several more songs, the next band came on stage, which was a rock group called *Wasters*. That was then followed by an alternative, mellower band called *Florescence*, which Louisa enjoyed dancing to, and another, which was similar to the first, called *Demons and Knives*. Finally, Zac's band was introduced.

"Next up is a fantastic new entry into the Battle of the Bands this year. I hope you all enjoy their music. Introducing... *Fortitude*." Mr Jenson stepped off the stage just as Zac appeared holding an electric guitar in one hand. Two other boys I didn't recognise followed him on stage. One of them moved to plug his bass into the amp and another taller guy with a sweep of brown hair stepped up to the microphone. The last guy seemed to have appeared from the back of the stage and was concealed behind the drum kit.

"Hi everyone," called the one with scruffy brown hair holding the mic. "Are you ready to rock?"

Everybody cheered and turning to Zac and the drummer, he nodded to them. Zac grinned as he looked down at his guitar.

"This is a song called *See Me Through to the End*."

The drummer started with a steady beat and as it built, Zac started playing some mellow chords that hung in the air like fireflies. The atmosphere in the room had changed completely as everybody watched and listened. The music built and the bass joined in to give the music richer, deeper tones.

I closed my eyes and listened carefully to the echoes of *Fortitude*. Considering the metal undertones to the music, it was surprisingly cathartic, and the tension inside me began to lift. The hall filled with the sounds of Zac's guitar riffs and symbols crashing, and as I opened my eyes, I could see that Louisa was just as impressed as me.

"I have to admit," she said, leaning over, "Zac has just become far more attractive." I laughed and she grinned mischievously. As I looked over at Zac, I knew what she meant, but it didn't compare to the feelings Sam evoked in me. Zac was very talented though, and I wondered if his parents knew how well he played.

He smiled to himself and adjusted something on his guitar, waiting for his band members to be ready for the next song. Just as they were preparing themselves, something near the fire exit caught my attention. Mr Jenson was standing in the doorway looking agitated as he spoke to someone just outside in the hallway.

"What's going on over there?" I said, nudging Louisa.

"Probably some kids who haven't got tickets," said Louisa, shrugging and glancing over. As she opened her mouth to speak again, she paused; Blake had appeared. The blare of the guitar had started, and although we could see that he was arguing with Mr Jenson, we couldn't hear what was being said. "What the…?"

I watched as Mr Jenson practically pushed Blake outside, and before I knew it, Louisa was pulling me through the crowds of people towards the door.

"Lou, wait," I breathed, as we reached the exit. "Be careful. You don't know what it's about…"

She glared at me. "Well, not yet, anyway," she said, pushing the door ajar and peeking out. The coast was clear as she slipped through the exit into the hallway. I followed close behind, and as the music became a distant thud, I became vaguely aware of a ringing in my ears.

"Where'd they go?" I whispered as Louisa began to creep down the empty hallway.

"This way," said Louisa, nodding towards the end of the corridor. There was an exit that opened onto the field at the back of the building, so they must have gone outside, but before we even reached the corner, we heard raised voices outside.

"I don't give a damn, Jenson. He's risking it for all of us." It was Blake's voice. Louisa and I exchanged darkened glances.

"I appreciate that, but this is neither the time nor the place, gentlemen," came Jenson's cool, calm voice. A beat passed before he spoke again. "I suggest you all go home."

"I'm not leaving," came another voice, making my blood run cold. Louisa flicked her eyes around to meet mine and in that instant, we knew who it was. "Look, Ava doesn't suspect a thing. Why would she?" I felt my pulse race.

"Then why are you here?" said Blake.

"You know why I'm here."

"Do I?" spat Blake. "Because I don't know if I can trust you anymore. You were supposed to—"

"I know what I was supposed to do!" yelled Sam, making Louisa look round to me anxiously. There was a long moment of silence, and I wondered whether they had gone, until Sam spoke again. "I know what I was supposed to do. That's why I'm here."

"Sam," said Mr Jenson's voice, which held an edge to it that I'd never heard before. "That's all very well, but I'm just not sure it's a good idea. It's a little crowded tonight."

Louisa gave me a curious look, but I could only swallow nervously. I had no idea what they were talking about, but the fact Sam's reason for being here involved me only made me want to see him more. I knew it made no sense considering the conversation I was overhearing, but my feelings were beyond my control.

"Go home, Sam," said Mr Jenson.

"No," breathed Sam. "I can't go home. You know I need it."

"And who's fault is that?" said Blake. I could imagine the look on Sam's face as Blake spoke to him, but what was this? Was it something to do with drugs after all? It seemed like a reasonable explanation, but what connection would that have with me?

"Please…"

"Fine." This time Mr Jenson's voice was final. "But you're to claim what you need and leave." I listened hard as silence followed. "Got it?"

"I think we should go back," Louisa hissed urgently; I could see the anxiety in her eyes. I nodded and together we made our way back without a word.

Back in the hall, I was surprised to find myself feeling genuinely relieved that we hadn't been caught eavesdropping. There was, obviously, something going on that neither I nor Louisa knew about, and it seemed like the others were angry with Sam for what must have been the smallest indiscretion. After all, I was still completely and utterly in the dark when it came to Sam. It seemed silly, therefore, to feel the buzz of excitement in my chest at the thought of seeing him. Mr Jenson had said he'd allow Sam in for whatever he needed, but what did he need so desperately that involved me, and why did they know about it too?

CHAPTER *Twelve*

When we saw Mr Jenson enter the hall completely unaffected, I wondered what else had been said between him, Blake and Sam. He seemed oddly calm as he walked onto the stage to introduce the new band. I couldn't come up with any connection between him, Blake and Sam. It just seemed like such an odd mix of people, and I was beginning to realise Sam's secrets might not just be his own.

"So? Enjoy the music?" Zac asked, bringing me back to the present. As I turned to Zac, I could have sworn Mr Jenson's blue gaze briefly locked with mine. My heart hammered in my chest. Did he know that Louisa and I had just been eavesdropping on his conversation? Was he still looking at me? I didn't have the nerve to turn back to check. Instead, I immersed myself in conversation, trying hard to ignore the tremble in my hands.

"Yeah, it was great. Everybody really loved it," I said, watching as my words made him grin, whilst half aware of a figure leaving the stand and disappearing backstage.

"Lou?"

"It was brilliant," she said. "I reckon you'll pull tonight." She grinned, making him laugh.

"Ava," came a cool, hard voice. My heart leapt into the mouth. Turning away from Zac and Louisa, I came face to face with Sam. His gaze sliced right through me and I was entranced. Before I could say anything, his eyes flicked over to the stage and I didn't need to follow his gaze to know who he was looking for. The tension in his shoulders told me he didn't want to be seen with me—or couldn't be seen with me.

"I need to borrow your…friend," said Sam, his gaze on Zac, ignoring Louisa completely.

Zac frowned as he looked back at Sam. "Sure," he answered uncertainly.

Sam led me through the crowds and away from the concert. My pulse was thumping in my ears as Sam marched through the main entrance, which was now deserted, and into the open air. I shivered, and I could see he was edgy, his shoulders hunched and his eyes darting around our surroundings.

"What the hell are you doing, Ava?" He spoke with such raw anger and I was taken aback by his tone. He'd never spoken to me like that before. "You're worth more than this—than him," he said, baring his teeth.

"What?" I said, incredulously. Had he really pulled me out here just to yell at me? "This has nothing to do—"

"No, don't you dare say it has nothing to do with me. It has everything to do with me," he argued, his black eyes flaring, even in the darkness; but I wasn't focusing on that. All I felt was frustration and anger. What was his damn problem?

"God! You are so confusing, Sam!" I couldn't keep up with this constant status changing. Did he want to know me or not? And what the hell was he mixed up in? Shaking my head in frustration, I pivoted on my heel to go back inside. Enough was enough, one of us had to break this vicious cycle. One of us had to end this friendship that was so quickly becoming volatile. I wasn't going to put up with this—

"Do you like him?"

I froze. Sam's voice was so quiet and confused that it knocked the wind out of me. How could he change his mood so quickly? An uneasy minute passed, before either of us spoke. I didn't turn around.

"Ava, I don't have time for this… do you like him?" Sam's voice was soft, yet this time I caught the tension in it as he awaited my answer.

I turned back towards him, unsure of which version of Sam I would be met with, but I no longer saw anger. He stood alone on the empty expanse of the carpark, anxiety stretched taught in him as he searched my face for an answer.

"Does it matter?" I said quietly. He said nothing, letting his eyes drop to the floor. I knew I wasn't going to get an explanation for his behaviour. Whatever he was going through, whatever he felt for me, he still couldn't tell me anything, so what was the point? I sighed in defeat.

Turning back towards the doors, I made to go in, but Sam's hand caught my elbow and curled around my arm. His touch was so soft that all the anger I'd felt before, evaporated. I looked over my shoulder at him and he tugged me backwards against his chest, and in that moment, it was like nothing else and nobody else mattered. It was just him and me, and this time I looked right into his eyes—those endless black eyes that seemed to promise the world. It was with sadness however, that he lifted my arm and pulled down my hoody sleeve revealing my bandage.

"Does this matter?" he whispered into my ear, his breath sending shivers down my neck.

"That wasn't Zac's fault. It was mine," I breathed, feeling his chest tense against me as he turned me around to face him.

I looked up into his face and I could see confusion as he gazed at me—and something else. Was that fear I could see?

"I was really angry with you," he said with unnerving calm. He gritted his teeth and closed his eyes, baring his teeth as he dragged air deep into his lungs. "No—I *am* angry with you." He opened his eyes and glared at me.

"Well, that makes two of us," I said with as much venom as I could muster, even though I felt quite calm inside. Breaking our contact and pulling my sleeve down, I looked him in the eyes as he continued to bare his teeth. It was like staring down a vicious dog, but I held my own, acting on instinct. Then ever so slowly, Sam's breathing calmed and his eyes dimmed to a more human consistency.

"Why were you angry with me?" He sounded so earnest, and I couldn't believe I'd actually have to explain. In fact, no, I wasn't going to explain that; I was angry because he'd blown off even being friends with me. He'd have to work it out for himself. Why should I give up all my secrets when he kept so many from me? Resigning myself to the fact that I wouldn't be getting away from him anytime soon, I pursed my lips and held my tongue.

"Why were you angry with me, Ava?" His voice held an edge and it made me recall what I'd overheard: *Ava doesn't suspect a thing.* What wasn't he telling me? Two could play at that game.

"What do you want from me, Sam?" I asked, surprised by how strong my voice sounded. "You say you don't want to be friends, yet here you are—"

"It seems your actual *friends* aren't much use," he muttered, glancing at me darkly. "And after the other night, you still feel the need to be around him…" His gaze became luminous in the dark and it hit me. I couldn't believe I'd been so stupid. Sam was jealous. That's what had changed his mind. He was actually jealous of Zac. My heart fluttered in my chest.

"You don't like Zac?" I asked, innocently. His eyes were bright as he watched me, but he said nothing. I tried again. "Why don't you like Zac?" Still no response. Frustrated, I took a step towards Sam so that I could have reached out my fingertips to brush his clothing. "What do you want?" I implored.

I watched his resolve slip. "You know what I want," he answered straight away, the tension evident in every muscle in his body.

"No, I don't," I said, quite simply, blinking at him. I'd thought I did, until he told me he didn't want to be friends—or couldn't be friends. Now, I was more confused than ever, thrown by his ever-changing mind. He stared at me for a long while, face neutral and no teeth bared—unblinking and calm.

"You," he said quietly.

"But—"

"I want you, okay?" He sounded almost annoyed, but I wasn't sure if it was with me or himself. He closed the gap between us so that I could feel the heat of his chest against mine, and as I met his gaze, my pulse started thudding in my ears. I held my breath as he reached up and ran a thumb down my cheek.

"I was so angry," he breathed, shakily. I could tell he was fighting the anger inside him that had so freely flowed before. Even his eyes were overflowing with that deep, dark emotion, causing me to feel a sense of dread. He moved his hand to my arm and gently caressed my wrist. "If only I'd got to you earlier…"

I frowned. Then his words sank in.

"You were there?" I said, feeling shocked. "*You* took me to hospital? Did you *follow* me?" I couldn't believe what I was hearing.

"I've told you, I can't stay away from you," Sam muttered as if it was obvious.

"So, what—" I stammered, "you thought it was perfectly acceptable to stalk me?" Sam at least had the decency to look awkward. He stuffed his hands in his pockets and looked up at me from furrowed brows, but I saw hurt there. What was he so wound up about? If anyone should be annoyed, it should be me. "How long were you following me?" I asked.

Sam grit his teeth and his frown deepened, but he still

fought to keep that anger checked.

"How long?" I repeated, but when he continued to say nothing, I wondered if he'd seen me smoking or drinking or—

"Oh," I whispered. If I'd thought Sam was upset by all the stupid, reckless things I'd done that night, he was most certainly upset about my last mistake of the night. "You saw Zac—"

"Please don't remind me," Sam snapped.

"But I didn't—I didn't want—"

"I know," he said, his voice softening a fraction.

I blinked away the rising emotion in my chest. Sam had seen Zac kiss me. I felt exposed and foolish. I just wanted the ground to open up and swallow me. Sam had been there all along. I'd been trying to forget all my feelings for him and he'd been watching me the whole time. I wondered if he'd stayed in the hospital with me. Knowing Sam, he'd probably been there the whole time—even during the spewing incident. I cringed internally, then remembered the conversation I'd had with Louisa.

Sam cocked his head to one side and searched my face, but I was thinking about what Louisa had said, trying to make sense of everything. "When I was in hospital, Louisa came to see me," I said. "She said you were at Blake's and you were arguing."

Sam crossed his arms over his chest and kept his face carefully still. I could tell that he hadn't expected me to know this. His eyes were fractionally wider and he swallowed. Although I felt a pang of guilt at making him feel this way, I couldn't help but feel hopeful. Had I just found a chink in Sam's hard exterior?

"It was because you followed me, wasn't it? That's why you argued with Blake. He thinks you should stay away from me too." I watched Sam intently, but when relief crashed over his face, I knew I was wrong.

"No," he said simply. "It was nothing." He tucked his hands in his pockets and was careful not to show anything more on his face.

"Sure," I said, with a sigh.

"It was—"

"No, it's fine, Sam. I know you're not supposed to tell me. I get it." When I looked up at him, his eyed were narrowed in my direction. I needed to backtrack. I didn't want to give away that Louisa and I had overheard his conversation with Mr Jenson and the others. I had to keep that one for when I really needed it. "I mean, I know there are things you can't tell me."

"Who says?" he uttered, leaning towards me.

"Just my intuition, I guess," I muttered, hoping that my nonchalance would convince him. As he moved towards me however, I knew I wasn't fooling him.

"Well, for now," he whispered, leaning even closer to me and brushing my hair over my shoulder, "just keep your intuition to yourself—for your own safety." His eyes were serious and his proximity was unnerving. I felt the need to be back in the hall with Louisa and Zac.

"Sure," I murmured, swallowing. "I should go back to the hall. I think Zac has one more set before the concert ends." Sam's eyes flickered as I mentioned my friends, but this time he didn't say anything. Instead, he stood back and let me go. I walked away, but when I reached the door, I was suddenly overcome with doubt. As unpredictable and complicated as Sam was, I needed to know I was going to see him again.

"Sam?"

"Yeah?" he said, sliding his hands into his pockets.

"Are we friends now, or…?" I trailed off, unsure of what I should say, but he simply smiled.

"Sure," he said, his tone resigned. "Friends." A dark shadow flashed across his face telling me that this wouldn't be an easy ride.

On entering the lobby, I was breathless and warm, despite having been outside in the late November air, so I made a short detour to the toilets. After spending that amount of time with someone equally unnerving as he was stunning, I felt the need to recover my equilibrium.

In the girl's bathroom, I splashed cold water on my face and waited until my heart rate had slowed to a normal pace, bracing my hands on the sink. That turn of events had not been expected tonight, and I'd been unprepared. After all the heartache of the past week, Sam had decided that we could be friends after all. His indecisiveness was sending me in a spin, but I was already becoming accustomed to having that dizzying feeling back in my life. I just hoped it was for good this time.

As I looked in the mirror, I realised I'd lost more weight and I mentally scolded myself. My cheek bones were more prominent than normal and I looked tired. I was letting my feelings get the better of me. I really needed to start looking after myself, I thought, as I took a paper towel to dab at my wet cheeks. I was feeling a lot less flushed and ready to face the crowds again.

There was another band playing on stage as I entered the busy hall. It was heavy music and the singer just sounded like he was screaming. It wasn't music I could relate to at all and my face scrunched up in distaste. Clearly, the majority of the audience felt the same way as half of the crowd had drifted over to the drinks stall and the teachers were struggling to serve everybody. At least that would make it easier for me to find Zac and Louisa, but glancing around the hall, I couldn't see them anywhere.

A deafening scream echoed around the hall, stopping everyone in their tracks. Even the music came to an abrupt halt and my heart pounded uneasily in my chest. Nervously, I headed towards the staging area, where a low hum of chatter had started to emanate. As I approached, I dreaded whatever had caused such a desperate, guttural scream. But as my mind went over all sorts of horrible scenarios, I noticed Mr Jenson over by the double doors again—only this time he was with Sam. I stopped. Mr Jenson's face was serious as he spoke briefly before holding the door open for Sam. Sam slinked out without a backwards glance and a sense of unease settled in me like someone had planted an icy cold hand over my heart.

I felt sick. Closing my eyes and taking a deep breath, I exhaled slowly, attempting to disperse the anxiety building inside me. Who *was* Sam? It was becoming apparent that he could be bad news. Maybe I was being paranoid, but I had no time to dwell on this as Mr Jenson's voice boomed over the microphone asking students to make their way out of the hall. Before I could move, Louisa's arms were around my neck.

"Ava!" she sobbed.

Pushing her away gently, I looked at her tear streaked face and her eyes immediately widened in fear.

"Ava—It's Zac—" The icy hand squeezed my insides, catching my breath.

"What about Zac?" I asked shakily.

She looked at me—lost. She wasn't telling me something. Pushing her away from me and forcing myself through the dregs of the crowd, what I saw made my heart stop. Zac's body laid sprawled on the floor as Mr Brands pumped desperately on his chest. I could tell by the way Zac's mouth was ajar that he wasn't conscious.

"Zac," I choked, moving towards him, but I felt cool hands on my shoulders, stopping me.

"Ava, he needs space," came a female's voice. Mrs Richards. But I couldn't look away. "Ava." This time her voice was firm, but I couldn't move. I was frozen—forced to watch on helplessly. I sank to the floor and as Louisa sat down next to me, the whirr of sirens closed in.

Florescent yellow and green jackets blurred in front of me as the paramedics took over from Mr Brands. Their movements seemed so calm and collected however, and I wanted to scream at them to move faster. They pulled Zac's t-shirt up revealing his bare flat torso, and I watched as they began pumping his chest with such force, that his stomach protruded with each compression. It was hard to watch, but I couldn't tear my eyes away as the second paramedic stuck white pads onto Zac's upper chest.

How was this happening to my friend? Zac was such a kind, genuine soul, and I couldn't quite understand what had gone wrong. He looked like my friend who had spoken to me only moments before, but his face was sickeningly grey.

His entire body jumped as the machine administered shock after shock, but when the paramedics exchanged a brief glance, a chill spread through me. It was as if I was in a dream as I watched the medics lift Zac's chin and place his face into an oxygen mask. Yet, I knew it was useless. Unable to breath, all the colours in the room started to blur into one and then the blackness closed in as I hit the floor.

CHAPTER *Thirteen*

I was aware of the dead weight of my body on the mattress as I lay in the early morning light. It was chilly outside the duvet and my arms had goosebumps, but I couldn't find the life inside me to move them. I was lost. My soul had given in and left me alone in this abyss of numbing agony. It was all so unreal that my mind failed to comprehend what had happened. Had I really lost my friend? Only a week ago I'd snuck out of this very room to hang out with him and now, as I lay staring blankly out onto the expanse of my room, I kept seeing his unresponsive body lying on the floor of the college hall. His soul had left his body and all in a moment, Zac's life had ended—much like my mum's had. He no longer existed in this world.

The endless darkness pushed in at me from above, like an enormous bird of prey, opening its huge talons over my soul. The feeling was disturbingly familiar and I couldn't believe I was back here again so soon. I wondered if Zac might somehow exist in another dimension which my mum had gone to, or if he was simply another soul floating adrift the river of existence.

Was he waiting to take host of another body and another life? Or maybe that was it and he was gone forever, leaving only memories in the minds of those that knew him.

A gentle knock at my door stirred my mind and I focused on the inanimate object I had aimlessly been staring at—the desk chair. It was strange, I thought, that sometimes you could become so lost in your own thoughts that you ceased to be able to see, despite your eyes being wide open.

"Ava, love? You awake?" My dad's voice was quieter and gentler than usual, but I couldn't find the will to speak. If I stayed quiet, he'd think I was still asleep and I could drift off into my sea of thoughts again. I waited silently. Sure enough, the creak of the floorboard indicated his departure.

It wasn't until the second knock came at the door that I realised I'd drifted off into a light sleep. My body had finally given into exhaustion and let me fall asleep, if only for a short while. As I glanced at my phone, I saw that a few hours had passed, and I felt a tinge of relief at having successfully made it through two hours of the day.

"Ava?" The door opened a fraction and I felt dread yawn open before me. I didn't want to talk—not yet. His head appeared around the door, his eyes filled with concern. "I've brought you some tea and toast, love," he said, nudging the door open with his shoulder and stepping into my room. Placing the tray down on the floor next to my bed, he looked at me.

"I know it's hard, love, but try and eat something." He gave me a sympathetic smile which I didn't return before walking out of my room again, closing the door behind him with a small click. At least my dad understood me, probably more than my mum ever had. Mum would have been coaxing me out of bed to go for some retail therapy rather than leaving me to wallow, but somehow, he knew to leave me alone. I couldn't face anyone or anything today. My mind was full of Zac, and I began to wonder if he'd still be alive if I'd never met Sam.

Glancing over the side of the bed at the tray of toast, I hadn't even the energy to turn my nose up at the food. I simply was not inclined to eat. Pulling the duvet over my head, I listened to my steady breathing until my phone buzzed on my bedside table, making me jump. Irritated, I pushed the duvet off my head and reached out for my phone. As I grasped it and brought it to my face, I felt a small pang of disappointment, mixed with guilt, that it wasn't Sam. It was Louisa.

Feeling suddenly hot, I flung the duvet off my legs, swung around and sat up. It was the most I had moved since last night and my head spun, sending tiny blue white smears in front of my vision. I blinked and rubbed at my eyes, wincing as my arm throbbed.

Looking down at my bandaged arm, I remembered how Sam had pulled my sleeve up. *Does this matter?* he'd said, holding me against his chest and then finally admitting his feelings for me. But his use of the words '*I want you*' seemed strange now. Was this in the romantic sense or was it another cryptic phrase I had to make sense of? As the spots cleared from my vision, I glanced down at my phone to look at Louisa's message.

Louisa. *Hey babes, I hope you're ok. Well not ok, but you know what I mean. xxx*

I stared at Lou's message for a while longer, then chucked it onto the bed without another glance. I didn't have a response for that. Getting up, I crossed to the window. Maybe some fresh air would inject some life into me and allow me, at least, the cathartic release of tears. Gathering the curtains away from the glass, I opened the latch and pushed the window open, breathing in the chilly morning air. My lungs cooled, and I felt the goosebumps travel down my arms, but I felt no more alive than I had a moment ago. I was still numb and empty. It was like I had forgotten how to cry and had no recollection of how I had done it before.

But as I stared out into the fields, something caught my eye and I blinked, my heart missing a beat. Sam was standing on the edge of the field, looking up at my window. Our eyes locked and he stood deadly still with a dark expression that made me go instantly cold.

A shock of fear ran through me, and I ducked inside the window, closing the latch and letting the curtains fall shut. My heart was beating hard against my rib cage as if trying to escape, and the floor felt precarious beneath my feet. It was then that I felt the usual looming of eternal darkness—but was it everything that had happened with Zac or was it fear I felt?

The weekend passed in a cloud of toxic emotions, and I found myself almost glad to go back to college on

Monday, if nothing more than to force myself to face reality. I'd already dodged the huge display of flowers at the front gate but there was only so much longer I could stick my head in the sand. Soon enough, I'd have to face facts. It was when I reached class and saw the gaping empty seat next to me, that it finally hit me hard, like an arrow in the chest. Zac wouldn't be there. He never would be. The universe had simply continued without him as if the loss of him was miniscule in the grand scheme of things. Perhaps it was—but it didn't feel like it. It seemed oddly melancholy in that tiny space, as if some dreadful ghost would remain there in his stead.

"Ava?" Mr Jenson's inquiring voice halted my thoughts and I flicked my eyes up. "Are you okay?" His voice was quiet and caught me off guard. The memory of his stern, authoritative voice from the other night had altered my opinion of him, and now here he was, altering it all over again.

"Yes," I smiled with some effort. Everything inside me was screaming for me not to press my mouth into a curved line, but I managed it despite the all-consuming feelings of constraint inside my chest. The smile felt empty though, and reminded me of how I'd been after my mum's death. I'd been so broken and fearful. The thought was disturbing and I wiped it from my mind as quickly as I could, but it was too late. All those sleepless nights came rushing back to me: the screaming, the stench of disinfectant in my nostrils, the blood running down my face that turned out to be tears. I raised a hand to my face and was shocked to find that there were tears now.

"Ava..." This time, the voice was Louisa's. Her eyes

were wide with concern as she reached forward to take my arm.

"Girls, perhaps I should call Ava's—"

"She'll be fine," was all Louisa said to Mr Jenson, giving him a glance of cool suspicion, which didn't go unnoticed. As she grasped my hand and led me out of the classroom towards the girls' bathroom, I began to compose myself, already feeling foolish for crying at the sight of Zac's empty chair. I needed to get a grip. I couldn't go back to how I was before, and I needed to be more aware than ever right now, what with Mr Jenson keeping a close eye on me.

As I glanced at Louisa, I knew she would have been going over all the same things that had happened this weekend involving Sam, Blake and Mr Jenson. I suppose I should have been glad that at least I wasn't in this alone. Especially if, if it came to light, they knew something about Zac's death.

The girls' bathroom mirrors were smeared with lipstick and finger prints, and as I looked at my reflection, it brought back memories of the other night when I'd been internally scolding myself for not eating properly. But now, it seemed I looked worse, if that was possible. My eyes stared back at me blankly, without life or meaning, and my cheeks looked pinched in at the sides. I looked more exhausted and drawn than ever.

"When was the last time you ate something?" Louisa asked, concern etched on her face.

I shrugged absently and noted my appetite stir inside and then mellow out again. I turned towards Louisa. "There's something weird going on, Lou," I said.

"Yeah, it's called grief. That's why you haven't eaten or slept or—"

"No," I interrupted her. "Not that. I saw how you looked at Mr Jenson. You think he has something to do with Zac too, don't you?" She pursed her lips and lowered her gaze. Nodding silently, she drew in a shaky breath and leant against the sinks. "Yeah. Blake's involved too. I don't know what it is though."

"What makes you think Blake is mixed up in it?" At this Louisa raised an eyebrow at me as if to question my sanity. "I mean, I know we heard him the other night, but what else have you seen to make you wonder?"

Louisa thought for a moment before shaking her head slightly. "I don't know exactly. It's just that there's this dynamic in the group—like there's some kind of male testosterone war going on, but… it's different. Before, everyone listened to Sam, but lately, Blake seems to be—" Louisa sighed in frustration. "I don't know. Maybe I'm imagining it all. It's just weird. They do everything and go everywhere together, but it's more than just a group of friends hanging out…" Louisa trailed off; her eyes seemed to see straight through the cubicle door in front of her. "I remember this one night when I arrived at Blake's, they were all really high on something. I don't know what it was, but it was unnatural. Blake's eyes were completely black." I listened intently as I recalled Sam's eyes. "And those marks. They all have those marks like it's some kind of cult," she said, meeting my gaze. "There's this one mark and I know it sounds stupid—"

"An hourglass?" I whispered.

"Yeah. You've noticed it too?"

I felt sickness in the pit of my stomach. What was Sam involved in, and how was I going to stay clear of him? Did I have the strength to stay away? “Sam has marks all over his body,” I muttered. Louisa arched an eyebrow at this, but I continued regardless. “But that hourglass tattoo on his forearm. It seemed to stand out from the other marks. I hadn’t thought much of it until now.”

“Blake has the same. Franco and Jules do too.”

A thought flicked into my mind. “You don’t think Mr Jenson has one too, do you?”

Louisa’s complexion paled before she pursed her lips defiantly. “I don’t know, but I’m sure as hell not going to wait around to find out.” Without another word, Louisa grabbed her bag and headed for the door with me in close pursuit.

“Wait! Lou, what are you going to do?” I hissed, grabbing her by the arm. “You can’t just march on up to him and say *‘Hey Mr Jenson, I think there’s something fishy about you. Show me your arm.’*”

Louisa looked indignant. “What do you take me for, Ava Blume? I have far more panache that that!” She grinned widely, showing off her pearly white teeth, hitched down her top a little and marched down the corridor. I knew there was no point in chasing after her. Once Louisa had a plan in her head, there was no diverting it and maybe she would get lucky. In the meantime, I decided to make my way to the college computer suite to do some snooping of my own. Even if I found nothing, it would distract my mind from thoughts of Zac for a few minutes. Those shadows were looming precariously close today.

To my relief, the tiny room was almost dead, so I found myself a quiet spot on the far wall. I chucked my bag under the computer desk, opened up a browser and paused for a moment, my hands poised over the keys. I quickly typed *cults in the local area.* A number of pages popped up including a news article on a satanic cult who had mutilated a pony in Dartmoor, but nothing spiked my interest. I tried again. *Local cults with hourglass tattoo.* I knew I was being crude, but I didn't want to leave any stone unturned. Again, there was nothing.

"Damn," I whispered before simply putting in *hourglass symbol.* A few pages popped up amongst computerised images of hourglasses, none of which looked like the tattoos I'd seen. I clicked on a link that said, "Hourglass Symbol and its meaning." The page opened and I scrolled through the information.

The hourglass has been used as a time keeping device for years and even today is used to symbolise time passing. The symbol is up for personal interpretation but in the past, some have said that the two triangles represent the dichotomy of existence and the cycles of life. However, others believe it to represent nature: one part symbolising the sky and the other, the earth.

I clicked back and tried another link.

The hourglass is seen as the emblem of life and the eternal passage of time. The sand slipping away reminds us that life is limited and we should make the most of the time we have on earth. It also symbolises the eternal loop between life and death.

My heart was in my throat as I clicked another link.

The hourglass is a symbol of time and death. The irreversible sand indicates the fatal aspect of time slipping away with nothing to do and no power to stop it.

Time and death. Could they really have something to do with Zac's death? Clicking on the search bar again, I decided to try one last search. I quickly typed *hourglass and life and death cults,* but there were just the same pages. Sam's cult must have been so underground that there was nothing on the group. I sighed in frustration as I cleared my search and leant down to grab my bag from under the table.

"Find everything you were looking for?" came a male's voice which I recognised. I ducked back above the table and turned around in my chair. Mr Jenson stood directly behind me and as guilt washed over me, I had the irrational fear that I hadn't wiped the browser page behind me. Just as I had the thought, his gaze flicked behind me and back again, but held nothing in it.

"Yes, thank you, Sir," I smiled, trying hard to relax my posture. He leant on the table behind him, bracing his hands on the side, and I noticed that his sleeves were pulled up. They were bare. I felt a sense of relief at the same time as a small stab of disappointment. I'd felt like Louisa and I were onto something, and now, neither of us had come up with anything.

"Are you sure you're okay, Ava?" His voice was quiet and his eyes, although searching mine, seemed genuine. I began to relax. Louisa and I had run away with ourselves. Maybe Mr Jenson was innocent. He seemed to be just another teacher concerned for his student. I nodded.

"I know what it's like to uproot, and it's tough going. You've had it tougher than most. I just wanted to check in to make sure you're okay."

"Yeah. I'm fine," I said, pulling my bag over my shoulder as I stood up.

"Well if you need to talk to anyone, there's me or plenty of other teachers that can help or lend a listening ear. I just wanted you to know." With that, he smiled, tucked his hands in his pockets, and turned to walk away just as Louisa appeared. She eyed Mr Jenson as she walked past him without a word and went straight to me. Flinging herself into a chair next to me, she huffed in indignation.

"Well, that was a wild goose chase and he was here with you all along."

"His shirt sleeves were rolled up. There were no marks," I said plainly, and Louisa's shoulders dropped in disappointment.

"And I'm guessing you haven't been researching for that essay by the look on your face…"

"Nope," I said, relaxing back into the chair now that Mr Jenson was gone. "Nothing on cults. I just looked up hourglass symbolism. Essentially, it represents life and death and the slipping away of time," I said.

"But what does that have to do with the tattoos they

all have?"

"I don't know..." I said, "Unless, they're in some kind of cult that's to do with life and death. I don't know..."

Louisa frowned. "You don't really think they've killed anybody, do you?" Louisa's face had paled some, despite her usual steely resolve.

I shifted in my seat nervously. "I don't know," I said quietly, "but it's odd that they were all acting weird when..." Louisa and I had the same expression of loss on our faces. *Zac*. I was aware that my own complexion had probably lost its colour as I thought about Zac's lifeless body, but I needed to stay focused. Finding out what was going on with Sam would be my distraction from Zac. Maybe that was the way to deal with grief. Plus, if Sam was mixed up in some kind of life and death cult, what did that mean for me? I was beginning to think I was more involved than I wanted to be.

CHAPTER *Fourteen*

Had I fallen for a monster? The last few days had been agony—avoiding the one person that sparked life into me when that's what I needed the most. Not that I had heard from Sam, but my guess was that he was giving me space after what had happened, sensing that that's exactly what I needed. Or was it a guilty conscience? My mind was a muddle. Some part of me still wanted to believe Sam would never hurt me, but the image of him slipping inconspicuously from the sports hall had haunted my every thought since that night. The idea that he might belong to a life and death cult only fueled my doubts, but the fact was, I trusted him with no logical reason as to why. It just seemed right. But whether I was right or wrong, I knew at some point, I needed to face the truth of who—or even what—he was. I needed to ask that inevitable question, whether Sam liked it or not, but for now, I needed to try to say goodbye to my friend.

Yet, as I stood outside in the cool afternoon air, dressed entirely in black amongst a crowd of mourners, I couldn't ignore the pang of guilt rattling through me. I still couldn't shake Sam from my head. Something just didn't add up. I looked down at Zac's dressed coffin, and I couldn't help but think that death seemed to follow me lately. I knew—I just knew— Sam's presence had something to do with it.

I glanced around the gravesite at all the people Zac had known and felt a terrible responsibility for his passing. His mum and dad stood at the end of the grave, looking at the box that held their son and I could practically see the nothingness hanging over them, as if someone had ripped away part of their being. His mum dabbed at her eyes with a handkerchief as the vicar's voice floated across the scene. His father simply stared into oblivion.

"For as much as it had pleased Almighty God to take out of this world the soul of Zacharias Goodwin…"

The coffin began to lower into the grave. All the brief moments I'd shared seemed to flash in front of me like a film trailer. I'd only known Zac for a short time, but a deeply traumatic time when even the briefest of friends mattered more than ever. He'd been a bright light in my darkness, and it felt wrong to be saying goodbye so soon. Zac shouldn't have died this way.

"…we therefore commit his body to the ground, earth to earth, ashes to ashes, dust to dust, looking for that blessed hope when the Lord himself shall descend from heaven…" I'd stopped listening. I'd become aware of eyes on my back and I looked behind me. Sam was leaning casually against a tree, fixing me with a level gaze, and it struck me how relaxed he looked amongst the tombstones.

My eyebrows knotted together, unsure of why he was here, but I didn't feel scared. I felt an odd sense of peace settling inside me instead, leaving me even more perplexed.

"...shall we ever be with the Lord, wherefore comfort ye one another with these words."

I jumped when a sob erupted into the air like a bullet. It was Zac's mum as she threw a handful of earth onto her son's coffin. Louisa was dabbing at her nose with a tissue, her face streaked with tears. There were other people from college standing either deadly still with hands in pockets, or shuffling awkwardly on the grass. Most had silent tears rolling down their faces or brimming at their eyes. I, on the other hand, must have looked out of place as I stood with my hands clasped in front of me and not a tear in sight. It was as if my emotions had run empty and I had no more to give.

Eventually, the funeral came to an end and the mourners started to disperse across the stone scattered, grassy expanse, leaving me alone with Louisa, whom I said my goodbyes to. She headed off towards her car, and I turned to where Sam stood, taking my car keys from my bag. He immediately stood up straight and waited for me to approach. Taking a deep breath, I made my way over.

"Hi," I muttered, as I walked up to him.

"Hi," he said, searching my face. "You okay?"

I nodded, but felt the need to be acquitted of my lack of emotion. "Do you think I'm heartless for not crying?" I asked him. He looked surprised for a moment, and I half wondered why I was asking Sam, but his reaction quickly changed to thoughtfulness.

"No," he said simply. "There's no right way to grieve. It's…" he paused, thinking of the right words, "it's ever-changing. Look." He pulled down the neck of his t-shirt to reveal an intricate marking over the right side of his chest. It looked like Latin. "It means grief is ever-changing, like the flow of water." I glanced up at him, waiting for him to explain. "Sometimes it's rough and sometimes it's calm—and sometimes there's a drought leaving you with nothing." He let his shirt fall back, and I could tell that he was talking from experience. There was a great sadness in his eyes and I knew he was telling me he understood how I felt too. He couldn't be the bad guy.

It seemed strange to have such a morbid tattoo, but then maybe it wasn't supposed to be morbid. Maybe the words represented hope. The life cycle of water carried on no matter what. Settling on this conclusion, I allowed myself to take comfort in his words, even if his experiences were questionable. I took a deep breath. Now was the time to get some answers, I thought, even if I didn't like what I heard.

"Sam, why are you here?" I whispered, feeling my heart beat increase. "I mean, what do you want from me—really?" His shoulders dropped, but as he continued to search my face, it was if he could sense my fear and his demeanor stiffened. He slipped his hands in his pockets, and I recalled something I read once about if somebody puts their hands in their pockets, then they're either nervous or have something to hide. In this instance,

I knew it was the latter.

"I thought we'd had this conversation," he said, his eyes shining iridescent black in the dim winter afternoon.

"We did, but I don't think I got the whole truth," I said. His gaze flickered with exasperation, sending my heart fluttering like a rogue butterfly.

"What do you mean?" This time his teeth were clenched, and I noted that his skin tone was brighter today, causing the tattoos on his neck to stand out. He inched towards me, but I leant away from him.

"What are you?" The words came out of my lips before I could stop them. I'd said it—*what* instead of *who*. I knew I'd caught him off guard, and he seemed shocked. He pursed his lips in stubbornness and took a step towards me. I backed away.

"Tell me," I pushed. "I want to know."

He seemed to consider this for a moment before answering. "No, you don't," he said calmly, taking yet another step towards me; I stood my ground. So, I was right. He *was* different. My heart was thudding against my chest so hard that it was almost painful and blood rushed in my ears. It was deafening. Then, the words slipped from my lips before I could stop them.

"Zac died, Sam," I said. I didn't know why I was rushing to voice my thoughts. Sam was obviously frustrated with me for questioning him, but I needed the truth, so I continued recklessly. "You were there and then you left—just as he was found. I know you belong to some kind of weird group with Blake and the others. You all have the same tattoos. Louisa's seen them too." Sam was standing right in front of me now, but I wasn't going to run. I was going to face whatever was coming my way. "What happened, Sam? I know you had something to do with it. What did you do to him?"

"Nothing," he whispered.

"I don't believe you."

He glared at me and I could see his eyes clearly now. They were darker like the time I'd seen him with the sunglasses, but this was different. They seemed to swim with a kind of vivid fluidity, and I felt myself being drawn into them. My arms became slack at my sides and all the tension went from my jaw as I felt something akin to warmth wrap around me, holding me close. Then I felt my car keys being plucked from my hand, but I was too incapacitated to care. The warmth flickered as Sam leant in close.

"Ava…" His voice was soft and I felt myself relax even further, my muscles tingling as if some drug was spreading through them. "Trust me." His breath tickled my neck, sending a shiver down my spine. "I'm not going to hurt you." All I could do was nod as I didn't have any breath in my lungs.

"I would never hurt you. I couldn't," he said, his gaze swimming in front of my vision. All the fight had gone out of me and I felt like I could have curled up and gone to sleep; I was that relaxed. Despite the unease he normally produced in me, I believed he wouldn't hurt me.

Sam stepped back slowly and I felt his eyes assessing me. Then, lifting a finger, he brushed it against my cheek and, bringing it in front of my face, I saw that it held one lone tear.

"So not completely heartless, then," he murmured, a sympathetic smile playing about the side of his mouth. "Come on. I want to show you something."

Sam's car glided along the long, winding road, taking us further away from home and deeper into the recesses of countryside. I found myself wondering if I'd done the right thing. What if my judgement had been off and I was wrong about Sam? My head was in a spin, but as I looked out the window onto endless green and mud churned fields, I knew I had to accept that what would be, would be. Sometimes life had to take its course and we just had to believe that we would be dealt the right hand—whatever that might be.

As we rounded a u-bend, the road started to climb a steep incline, which seemed to go on forever, snaking around patches of trees and bracken. Finally, the horizon came back into view, along with blue sky, and we were out of the shadow of trees.

"Where are we going?" I asked, but Sam simply smiled and pulled the car over onto the side of the road.

"Stay in the car," he ordered, climbing out and walking around to the passenger door. I turned to get out but he stopped me. "Ah—what did I say?" he chastised. I flushed at his tone but sat back in my seat.

"Turn the other way," he said, nodding through the car to the driver's seat.

I hesitated, unsure of his motives, but as he held my gaze, I did as he told me. I turned and looked out at the trees on the far side of the road, but something black came down over my eyes. Sam had blindfolded me. I immediately tensed up, hating the dark, but as Sam's capable hands slid onto my shoulders and his breath tickled my neck, I felt a mixture of excitement and fear bubble inside me. This was definitely not what I had expected.

"Are you scared?" he whispered through the blindfold into my ear. I shook my head as confidently as I could, but I could hear Sam chuckling quietly behind me. "Okay then, my fearless lady, come forth." He slid his hands around my wrists to guide me out of the car, but as I stood upright, I felt his hands brush my stomach. My skin tingled.

Sliding around the back of me, he placed his hands on my shoulders and proceeded to guide me forwards. I nervously took one uneasy step at a time across what felt like grass, then something harder, and then grass again, all the while feeling the burn of his grasp on my shoulders. I wondered if he was enjoying the contact as much as I was.

"Where are we going?" I breathed.

"Somewhere that will make even the darkest parts of you feel alive again," he said with anticipation, continuing to guide me to our destination. His words stung with deadly familiarity, making me glad to have the blindfold over my eyes. I didn't want Sam to see how his words had affected me, although he probably knew. At times, he seemed to know me better than anyone ever had, not that I would admit that to him.

"We're nearly there," he said, slowing my pace to a halt. "Okay, beautiful, you're going to have to listen really carefully here." *Beautiful*. His words hung in the air like the aroma of honeysuckle, and I felt my resolve slip a considerable amount.

"Okay," I whispered.

"You need to take one big step up."

I raised my foot and felt my toe hit something hard. Lifting even higher, my foot came down on what felt like a rock, and as I pushed up, Sam's hands slipped from my shoulders to my hips, before he climbed up behind me, himself.

"Just a little further," he said, guiding me forwards. "...and stop."

Breathing unevenly, I became aware of how chilly it was on top of the rock, and as my dress whipped around my legs, I knew I must be up somewhere high. With Sam's arms around me though, I felt perfectly safe. Sam pinched the blindfold away from my face and as I blinked, I felt overwhelmed by the breathtaking view before me.

"Wow," I gasped, staring out onto vibrant green pastures, which stretched out far below us. As I took in the view, I felt as if I was a giant looking down on a tiny toy set. Minute woollen sheep dotted the fields, which surrounded a lake that looked like a wobbly silver-blue blob up here. A matchstick train track ran alongside the water, all the way to the end of the cliff. There were also tiny block houses—only a few, but dense.

"This is where I can breathe," came Sam's voice, bringing me back to reality with a snap. "I come here when I need to remind myself how lucky I am to be alive." I frowned. "Do you like it?" he said, running his hands down my arms.

"It's incredible, Sam," I said, turning carefully to face him. I was very aware of my standing on the edge of a cliff, and my legs were beginning to feel a little like jelly. Sam had been right about waking even the darkest parts inside me. It was strange, I thought, that the prospect of death could make you feel so alive. The fact that Sam knew this too, made me feel even more electrified. I had finally found someone who would dip down into the shadows with me and scoop me up with him, rather than all the others who would simply fling me a rope. Sam *understood* and that was the difference.

"Ava," he began, taking a deep breath. "I didn't hurt Zac."

I stared at him as his black hair whipped in the wind and his eyes shone earnestly into my own. I believed him. My mind whirled with a thousand questions, but it didn't seem right to muddy this place of beauty and destroy the peace it brought Sam. I knew I wasn't the only one fighting an unseen battle every day. Sam didn't want to tell me what he was yet, and I should respect that. There must be a good reason for him holding back the truth, even if it was simply that he didn't think I was ready.

I took a deep breath. "Okay…" I said, "Maybe I'm mad, but I believe you." I felt like a huge weight had been lifted. Giving him a small smile, I watched his eyes gleam.

He smirked and tugged me gently towards him, curling my chilly arms around him. I could feel the heat of his skin underneath the soft cotton of his t-shirt and when I looked up, I knew I must be blushing. He was smiling down at me, amused. Just as quickly, his amusement faded and his eyes widened and flicked down to my lips. My pulse immediately jumped and I bit down on the inside of my lip nervously. He moved towards me, his hair tickling my face as his lips gently caressed the corner of my mouth and the butterflies inside me flipped. Then, as my own lips parted, he kissed me, igniting my insides.

CHAPTER *fifteen*

As I sat on my bed trying to concentrate on the biology essay I'd avoided all weekend, I found myself intermittently glancing at my phone. I hadn't heard from Sam since he'd dropped me home yesterday afternoon, and I'd begun to wonder if he regretted kissing me. Panic rose in me, and I started to go over every detail of what had occurred. Doubt crept into my mind as I started to convince myself that, in fact, I had kissed him, not the other way around. I knew that wasn't true, but why hadn't I heard from him?

The thought that he was with Blake and the others made me wonder if I'd been a fool. I felt out of my depth. Sam still had secrets. Maybe I was just a pawn in some game that I had no concept of and as much as I wanted to believe I was fine, I knew I was more vulnerable now than I had ever been. Then his words hung in the air—*Ava doesn't suspect a thing.* What was he hiding from me? What were they all hiding?

Locking my phone for the hundredth time, I turned to the blank pad of paper in front of me. Doing coursework was impossible when all I had scorched in my mind were Sam's deep agonized eyes, gazing at me, and the memory of his breath on my face as he leant in to kiss me, sending shivers through my entire body.

Throwing myself back on my bed in frustration, I looked over at my clock, but I knew there was little point attempting to do the essay. It was already nearly eleven and I hadn't even written a hundred words. My head was filled with questions that Sam wasn't ready to answer as well as doubts that he was taking advantage, so I decided it was time to take the detective work into my own hands. As much as I wanted to respect Sam's privacy, I felt like I was swimming into deeper waters with the threat of being swept away with the rip tide at any moment. I needed to look after myself. After I heard my dad stomp up the stairs to bed, I silently pushed on some trainers and stuffed my keys into my hoody pocket.

I was relieved to see that the ice hadn't yet settled on my windscreen as I climbed into the car. I was also glad that the engine wasn't more powerful. It started with a quick splutter and I reversed as slowly as I could down the gravel drive, avoiding revving too loudly.

The roads were misty and my anticipation grew as the headlights threw pools of yellow over the undergrowth. Even if I was just overreacting, surely Sam would be happy to see me. Either that or he'd think he'd made a huge mistake and never speak to me again. I cringed at my own insanity.

The tiny farm track came into view, and I rounded the edge of the forest that obscured Sam's house, stopping just before I got to the driveway and pulling up on the side of the road instead. I turned the engine off and glanced over my shoulder. Silence and darkness surrounded me. This seemed like a good spot to park as my car would be hidden from view if either he or Seline looked out the windows. Although my car blocked half of the road, I decided there was no way another car was coming down this road at this time of night.

As I walked along the lane, my anticipation spiked when I saw Sam's car on the drive and lights on in the front room. He and Seline must be in. I considered knocking, but then I thought I'd get Sam's usual cold exterior, and for once, I just needed answers. My feet crunched on the stones as I navigated my way along the gravel driveway, and I hoped that whatever Sam was, he didn't have super hearing. I shook my head at this thought. Since when had this kind of thought process become normal?

As I crouched down next to the shrubbery in front of the window, I listened hard, but all I could hear were muffled groans. I wondered if perhaps I'd overreacted and he was just watching television, so I gazed through a tiny crack in the curtains. I couldn't see much through the tiny sliver, but I could just make out Seline's back and she was kneeling on the floor next to the sofa, her shoulders hunched and her arms taught. What I saw when she got up made my insides go cold, and I had to stifle a gasp.

Sam was laying on the sofa, his eyes completely in the back of his head with only the whites showing. His back arched on the sofa and I could see the beads of sweat covering his entire inked torso. His chest heaved and the muscles in his arms strained as he screamed in pain. I wondered if this is what he'd been going through when I'd come to see him last. My chest ached at the thought.

I turned my eyes away, but I couldn't block his screams from my mind. Crushing my hands to my ears, I lifted my gaze to the window again to see that Seline was dabbing him with a cloth, which she dipped into a bowl of liquid at her side. Each time she dabbed the cloth onto his skin, his body convulsed violently.

My heart hammered frantically in my chest as I stared helplessly as Seline pressed the palm of her hand to his head. He relaxed at her touch, immediately slumping onto the sofa, breathing heavily. It was then that his eyes snapped open again, revealing the same unnerving black pupils I'd seen before. Noticing Seline, he lunged forwards and grasped her shoulders, uttering angrily at her.

She stood up with great effort and stepped out of his grasp, but he caught at her arm before she could turn and leave. It looked hard enough to hurt her, but he instantly recoiled, growling. He cradled his hand as if burnt, like touching her caused him pain. Giving Seline a lingering gaze full of fury, he stormed from the room and I realised he was heading straight for the front door.

My heart leapt into my mouth, and I scrambled to conceal myself around the side of the house, not caring about the noise of my own frantic footsteps crunching and skidding on the gravel. Just as I managed to hide myself, Sam appeared from the house. He was wearing black jeans and an open hoody and his hair was slick with sweat. He climbed into the sleek black car, and as the engine roared to life, I remembered that my car was parked in the way of the road. I stepped forwards, thinking I could make a run for it, but a hand closed over my mouth and around my middle, heaving me backwards with great effort. I turned wide eyed and came face to face with a breathless Seline.

"Stay quiet, girl!" she hissed, and I heard the car tyres spin on gravel and skid away from the house. Her hair was disarrayed and her normally collected disposition was edgy.

"Seline," I mumbled against her hand, which she dropped to her side. "My car—" I began, before her eyes became wide. "It's in the road. He'll know I'm here."

"Run," was all she said. I stared at her, but when she grasped my shoulders and pushed me to the back of the house, I knew she was serious. "Go!" she insisted, "He can't see you here."

But I needed to know. "What's wrong with him?" I urged.

She shook her head, "No. He'll never forgive me, Ava." I saw fear in her eyes. I stared back for a moment, then fumbled up the grass ledge to the back of the garden. Then I heard the dreadful scrape of car tyres reversing on gravel. I didn't look back; Seline's warning was enough. I kept running past the flower beds to the hedgerow right at the back of the plot, but froze there. Sam's voice called out into the darkness with a ferocity I'd never heard before and I never wished to hear again.

"Where is she?" he demanded. I heard Seline stammer something before he shouted again with a deep unbridled anger. "Tell me—*Witch*!" Witch? I stared into the blackness, able see the dark outline of the farmhouse, but terrified to run any further. If Sam really was dangerous, he'd not think twice about hurting his aunt—if that's who she really was. I couldn't leave her, so I crouched down and squeezed into the braches of a nearby fern, my lungs still burning from the cold.

As I listened hard, I could hear Seline trying to reason with Sam, but it didn't seem to be affecting him. I'd always known there was more to Sam than met the eye, but this was beyond anything I could have imagined. I felt goosebumps prickle on my forearms.

"Ava!" he bellowed out angrily. "I know you're out there—I've seen your car!" My eyes widened in trepidation and I gripped part of the fern as I heard him stomp towards me across the grass. Where was Seline? He stopped and I could hear his rasping breath.

"Ava!" The anger in his voice was raw and ground so deep into my bones that I started to tremble. Who was this? It wasn't the Sam I knew. It wasn't the same Sam that had kissed me—or was it?

I stretched up to glance through the branches of fern that I'd hidden in. His body looked taught with anger and desperation all at once, and his eyes held a hunger as they flicked across the hedgerows. I held my breath. He opened his mouth to say something else, and I felt a gush of wind pull at my clothes. It swept up from the floor, directly to the spot where Sam stood. He cried out in fury, clawing at the air blindly, as if the wind was holding him prisoner. His eyes slid into the back of his head and he cried out again, enraged.

It was then that Seline's voice came through the cold night air. She was muttering words in a strange foreign language. Her voice became louder, and as I peered through the long branches, I saw that she was moving towards him with her palms outstretched. She continued to force the words into his being and he visibly began to weaken, falling to his knees with a thud. His eyes returned to normal, no longer blinded with anger, but dread, as he screamed in agony. Seline was hurting him. His chest heaved in desperation and his eyes flicked about wildly as he fell forwards and dug his nails through the grass into the dirt below. His back arched as he barely stayed poised on all fours, then he gasped.

"Seline—please," he whispered with the last breath he had, before slumping to the ground in a heap, unmoving. Seline lowered her hands, eyes fixed on Sam as if she expected him to wake. But after a moment, she relaxed and looked in my direction. I thought I was well hidden in the huge overgrown fern, but something told me Seline didn't need to be able to see me to know where I was.

"It's fine, Ava."

I rose to my feet and trod cautiously out of my hiding place towards Seline. Her wild, blonde hair was flailing in the breeze as she stared down at Sam's body lying face down on the ground. She glanced at me, a warning in her eyes.

"Help me get him inside," she said, lifting his arms in the air. I obediently moved towards Sam and hesitated as I saw the hourglass mark on his forearm. It was a sleeker black today and unnatural to the point of reminding me of the reflective sheen on his car. It looked dangerous as I stared into its depths, and I noticed that Seline had placed her hand just above it so as not to directly touch it. I briefly wondered if that's why Sam always wore long sleeved t-shirts. Maybe it wasn't just to hide it, but to stop others from touching it as well.

"It's fine. He won't hurt you now," offered Seline. The word *now* echoed in my mind. Would he have hurt me? I let the question form in my mind, but didn't allow it any life. I nodded without thinking too much and bent to lift Sam's legs. Together, we heaved him down the grassy bank towards the house.

It was dark inside the kitchen, and as soon as we entered, a pungent tar smell filled my nose, making me cough. Seline seemed unaffected as she bent and lowered Sam onto the tiled floor. I followed suit and we stood back and stared at his limp body. His eyes were closed and the black tattoos that covered his arms and chest gleamed black against his pale skin, making him look deadly, but the curls on his forehead made him look more cherub-like.

"What is he?" I whispered, at the risk of sounding stupid. Then again, I had just seen Seline use magic to bring him down. Seline the witch. She gazed at me with an impressed glint in her eye.

"Finally, you're asking the right questions," she said with a smile. "He said you'd asked him…" I stared back at her, awaiting an answer. "Unfortunately, that answer isn't mine to give."

Feeling disappointed and a little relieved, I nodded and gazed again down at Sam's muscular body lying on the floor. I couldn't help but feel a heady mixture of fear and longing. Tonight was the first time I'd truly felt scared of Sam, and my instinct told me to run for my life. Life was about making mistakes, though, and I knew this was one I wanted to make, however dangerous it got. It could end badly, but I'd never felt more alive. Despite not knowing the truth about Sam, I couldn't walk away from him anymore than he could walk away from me.

CHAPTER *Sixteen*

Adrenaline coursed through my veins and I spent the remainder of the night staring into the darkness, turning over the night's events in my head. I couldn't decide if spying on Sam had been a bad choice or a huge breakthrough. Seline was a witch who could do real magic. I'd seen her use it to bring down Sam. His voice still lingered in my mind. It had been so raw—so animalistic. What was he? I felt like my entire reality had come cascading down around me to reveal a whole parallel world I'd never noticed, right under my nose. What else was real that I'd read about as a child? It was as exciting as it was intimidating. Then I thought of Sam and the way Seline had reduced him to a begging heap of pain. It was horrible watching him suffer, but I didn't want to imagine what could have happened if Seline hadn't been there.

As I stared blindly at the strip of morning sunlight on the ceiling, I found myself wondering if Sam had woken up yet. Seline had assured me he'd be fine, but I doubted anyone could be *fine* after that kind of torture. All the same, I'd come home and tried to take comfort in the knowledge that she knew him far better than I did. She had explained the very least to me; she was trying to help Sam. I'd asked her what kind of help, but she'd simply smiled. I knew that meant I had to wait. Sam needed to be ready to tell me.

Shaking off the residual nervous energy still pent up inside me, I climbed out of bed and got my things ready for college. I needed to get up and get going if I was to make it through today. I just hoped my lessons would be enough to distract me so that the day wouldn't feel like a year. Who was I trying to kid? Nothing would tear my mind from thinking about Sam. I needed to see him, but I knew that was unlikely to happen today. If he had any recollection of last night, he was sure to avoid me so he didn't have to answer any questions. So I made a promise with myself, that if I did see him today, I wouldn't ask him any questions. Seline had assured me that he would tell me when he thought it necessary, and I believed her. Perhaps he'd feel inclined to tell me a little quicker if I feigned disinterest. Reverse psychology: a phenomenon that my mum used to use to great effect on me, that was until I learnt about it at school.

An hour later, I pulled my car through the college gates and parked beside the sports hall, reminding me of the night Zac had died—the night Sam had told me how he felt. A pang of guilt sprung up inside me. What was I supposed to do with that memory? Was it a happy one or a sad one? Pushing the memory from my mind, I gathered up my things and climbed out of the car into the chilly carpark. I had maths first, but it didn't start for another hour. I thought I might as well go to the library and work on that biology essay I'd been avoiding. At least then I could pretend I was doing something productive, even if all I did was mull over every tiny moment I'd had with Sam in the past few months. I knew I should probably try to find Louisa and share with her what I'd found out. She'd want to know. If Blake was the same as Sam, she deserved to know, but selfishly, I wanted to keep this to myself for the moment. If Sam found out I'd been sharing secrets with Louisa, I was sure he wouldn't trust me enough to say more. My gut instinct was not to utter a word more about this.

It was still early as I entered the library and it was deadly quiet, apart from one other student returning books before class. Relieved, I made my way towards the steps and climbed up to the third floor. The third floor was very rarely used and just held a collection of very old anthologies and encyclopedias, so I knew if there was anywhere to hide away, it would be here. I found a quiet spot near the back of the building behind a row of dusty bookshelves with books that clearly hadn't been touched in years. Although tucked away in a dimly lit corner, I could still glimpse the world outside, from my hiding place. A small vertical window stretched from floor to ceiling and looked out over the grassy common. I watched as students and teachers bustled off in different directions oblivious to my eyes on them. I should have been here to do work, but as soon as I slumped down in a chair, I knew that wasn't going to happen. It was the perfect place to think, away from any prying eyes. There was no pressure to put on a mask of calm, which was good as my mind was racing.

I was attempting to process everything. As I pictured Sam and the look in his eyes last night, a thousand feelings stirred inside me. The most dominant was disappointment; disappointment that I probably wouldn't see him for weeks on end now. I'd wondered whether or not I actually wanted to see him, but I still couldn't forget the way he'd kissed me. There had been something so hesitant, almost shy, about the way he'd pulled me close and brushed his lips against mine. It was almost as if he'd expected me to run at any moment.

Picking up my pen, I began to write the title of my essay, but a rough cough sounded behind me and I jumped. I whipped around, and Sam was standing directly behind me, looking at me wearily. An unexpected terror ignited my insides as I stared into the same face that had growled my name into the night, but his eyes were drained and apologetic, and his posture showed his fatigue.

"Sorry. I didn't mean to startle you."

I swallowed nervously. His eyes were black, but not unnaturally black and he looked tired.

"You're working hard, I see," he tried. I stared back at my blank page, embarrassed. "Can I sit?" he said cautiously, pointing to the chair on my other side. I nodded and watched as he slumped next to me. He usually held an air of power, but today, it struck me how grey and ill he looked. I remembered I'd promised myself I wouldn't ask any questions, even though a million of them immediately fluttered to the forefront of my mind. Forcing myself to look away, I began doodling absently in the margin of my paper.

"Seline told me what I did," came Sam's gruff voice.

I glanced back at him briefly before turning back to my doodles. I didn't know what he wanted me to say, but then his warm hand crept up my arm and fixed on my wrist. I turned to him, wide eyed.

"Do I scare you?" he spoke, darkness clouding his vision. I became aware of my breath hitching, and I was torn between pulling my arm away and keeping it in Sam's grip. I shook my head imperceptibly, looking down at my trapped wrist.

"Sorry. You probably want me to get the hell away from you," he said, his hand snaking away from me.

"No," I offered quietly with a small shake of my head. I chewed on my bottom lip awkwardly.

He raised his eyebrows in surprise. "You're right—maybe I don't know you as well as I think I do." I knew we were both thinking of the night we'd met and how far we'd come, but that just presented more questions, so I turned away and gazed out the window, afraid if I opened my mouth to talk, questions would come tumbling out. I could sense Sam staring at me, waiting for me to say something. He gave in and spoke first.

"You don't want to talk about it?" he questioned.

I faced him. "I'm not asking questions today," I said, watching the look of apprehension on Sam's face turn slowly to amusement.

"Are you saying that…I act like a complete raving lunatic and you *don't* have questions?" he asked incredulously. I realised how ridiculous it all sounded and I looked sidelong at him and gave him a wry smile.

"It's not that I don't have questions," I muttered,

checking that we were still alone. "It's just that I've decided to let you off for today. I'm turning over a new leaf; going with the flow."

He made a sound halfway between a laugh and a grunt of relief before slipping further into his chair and plucking a book off a nearby bookcase. He flicked through the pages, pausing to read chapter titles. "Although, I hope you realise that this doesn't change the fact that I have a question for *you*," he said.

I braced myself.

"What were you doing at my house so late last night?" He eyed me darkly, making me blush and avoid his eyes.

He'd caught me off guard and I didn't have an answer. I couldn't very well say I was spying on him because I thought he regretted the kiss and that I thought there was a possibility he might be involved in a murderous cult. My heart rate accelerated and I thought quickly.

"You don't answer any of my questions, so…" I said with what I hoped was a nonchalant shrug.

He laughed bleakly. "So that's how you want to play it…"

"Yep," I said smugly, turning to him with an air of confidence.

He stared back into my eyes, his jaw set, before letting his gaze travel to my lips and back. "Okay…" he began thoughtfully, "What if I answer one of your questions?"

I reminded myself once more of my promise, but this was too good an offer to pass up. Sam reached to massage the back of his neck, letting his sleeve slip down his wrist a little. I could just see the edge of his tattoo. It was still a vibrant black. His complexion was pale though and as he moved his head from side to side, I wondered if he was still in pain from Seline's onslaught.

"Fine. It's a deal," I said, trying not to let my feeling get the better of me. I needed a clear head to think of a good question.

"I thought that might sound like a tempting offer to you," he murmured, his smile sly.

I took a deep breath and levelled his gaze. "Why were you talking to Mr Jenson the other night?"

Sam considered the question for a moment. If he'd been shocked that I knew this, he hid it well.

"I was helping him get people out of the hall," he stated simply, keeping his expression blank.

"No, before I saw you. I heard you talking to him outside. Louisa and I heard everything." The blood drained from Sam's face in realisation. The light-hearted Sam that had been there moments before disappeared in an instant.

"How much did you hear?" There was an edge to his voice.

"I heard a lot about risk taking…" Sam stared back at me, not giving anything away. "And I heard you say, '*Ava doesn't suspect a thing…*'"

Sam was quiet, his eyes fixed on my face, then he took a deep rattling breath. "Yes," he stated simply through gritted teeth, not giving me anymore.

"What aren't you telling me?"

"I can't say." His tone was clipped as he straightened

up in the chair and braced his hands on the desk.

"Why?"

"Because it would put both of us in a lot of danger." Sam's softer demeanour had vanished completely now, replaced by a cold outer shell and in an instant, he was on his feet. "I have to go."

"Did one of them have something to do with Zac?" I asked, getting to my feet too.

"Ava—" he said warningly, glancing down the corridor of books, "you need to be careful what you say."

"Did Blake do it?"

"Ava—" The fear was evident in his face now.

"Did Jules?"

Sam said nothing and continued to stare at me uncertainly. He was hiding something, and I was beginning to feel frustrated. Zac had *died*. "Tell me."

"No," he said brusquely, brushing past me to leave.

"Sam, please. I need to know. What aren't you telling me?" I implored, gripping his arm and pulling him back.

"I can't say," he muttered, staring down at my hand.

"Yes, you can—you just won't!"

He stared at me defiantly and the black in his eyes whirled like storms, but then he closed his eyes. He took a deep breath and when he opened his eyes again, the storm had gone. He looked exhausted.

"Please don't force me to say things I'm bound by law not to tell," he said. He took my hand and lowered it gently to my side. "I need to go. I have to meet the others." With that, he turned and walked away from me.

Seeing him walk away so calmly snapped something inside me. Frustration bubbled up inside me like molten lava and I didn't care who heard anymore. Enough was enough.

"Why are you *protecting* them?" I shouted, just as he turned the corner. My breathing was ragged, and I thought for a moment he'd gone, then footsteps thudded as he marched back towards me, his face full of fury.

"Will you keep your voice down?" he hissed, as he reached me. "I'm not protecting them. I'm *trying* to protect *you*!" I was so confused. Why did I need protecting? As if reading my thoughts, he gazed at me imploringly. "Yes—you, Ava," he stated.

I was unsure of what to say and my voice shook as I spoke. "I don't understand. Why do you need to protect me from them?"

He was angry but as he continued to gaze into my eyes I could see him begin to calm down. "You don't need to understand," he said, keeping his voice quiet and willing me to accept what he said. I knew I should leave it, but so much had happened. I needed to know. I looked into his blazing black eyes with resolve.

"Why is Blake angry with you?"

Sam ran a hand through his hair. "Let it go, Ava."

"I can't," I said, shaking my head. "I'm already missing half the story with my mum's death. I don't want more holes."

"That's different," Sam stated, turning away from me, walking to the wall and plucking another book off the shelf.

"What do you mean? How is it different?"

"I don't know. It just is," he said. He placed the book back on a shelf and faced me. There was something so sad in his expression. "You're never going to let this go, are you?"

"I can't," I said with a shrug. "Too much has happened for me to let it be water under the bridge, Sam. I need the truth, no matter how awful it is."

He looked at me shocked, but I could still see it there: sorrow that stretched beyond anything I'd ever felt before. I wanted him to tell me what was wrong, but I knew that he wouldn't. He seemed determined to go this alone. He reached out and ran his fingers down through the ends of my hair as his eyes flicked down to my lips. I knew in that moment that he wanted to kiss me, but he didn't. An invisible wall had been built between us casting great, terrifying shadows over us both. Only time would tell who would emerge from the dark depths first.

CHAPTER *Seventeen*

After parting in the library, an agonizing three days passed, and I hadn't heard a thing from Sam. Not only had he avoided working on the farm, but he'd ignored all my messages. After one last attempt, I'd given up and resolved to find another way to get through to him. He was finally opening up to me bit by bit, and I wasn't going to give up now. I knew he'd come around eventually. I just needed to give him time.

"Are you going to eat that, or just poke at it all morning?"

"What?"

Louisa was staring at me with a blank expression. After our failed attempt at connecting Mr Jenson to Zac's death, she'd lost all drive and enthusiasm for life, and I knew where her mind dwelled.

"I'm not really hungry," I mumbled, pushing the muffin towards her. She tucked into it without another word.

"You seeing Blake today?" I asked, to lighten the heavy mood between us, more than out of actual interest.

"No," she said through a mouthful of blueberry muffin. "He's ignoring me." At this, my ears pricked up.

"Why?" I asked, trying not to sound too eager.

"Don't know, don't care," she said, but as her throat bobbed, I knew the opposite was true. She cared. She cared as much as I did and if I didn't get to the bottom of this for my own sanity, I at least needed to try for hers.

Grabbing my phone from my pocket, I dialed Sam one more time. It went straight to voicemail, but I was surprised to find that this didn't produce doubt in my mind—only suspicion. A suspicion which deepened Thursday afternoon when I was waiting in my car to turn out of the college gates.

I recognised the roar of the motorcycle first and then I saw him—Blake. I stared as he passed, and when his eyes locked with mine, I saw accusation in them. In that moment, I was sure that Blake was responsible for Sam's disappearance. I knew Sam was loyal to him for some reason, but I was not. I was free to make my own decisions—and I made the decision to get some answers.

It was later that evening that I found myself pulling up on the road where Blake lived, preparing to spy on someone for the second time in a week. As I turned off the engine, I cast myself into darkness and silence. I felt myself tense, but the adrenaline coursing through me kept the demons at bay. This was it. Tonight, I would find out what was going on. I just hoped it would be something I could cope with.

The road was scattered with a few other cars and, squinting out of the windscreen, I just made out Blake's motorcycle on the driveway and Sam's car parked on the curb directly outside. My interest spiked and my eyes strained in the night in a desperate hope of glimpsing him. As minute by minute ticked by on the digital clock of my dashboard however, I felt the crush of disappointment creep up on me. I wasn't going to see him unless I went further.

Unclenching my icy hands from the steering wheel, I took my keys out of the ignition and climbed out of the car, closing the door behind me as quietly as I could. Hesitating, I knew Sam would want to keep me safe and away from Blake, but I was involved whether he liked it or not. Besides, I was stronger than he thought I was. Even I'd come to realise that. I hadn't run for the hills when I'd seen his true colours the other day. It had surprised me as well as him.

The evening air was damp from rain, and I trod carefully, making sure not to disturb any unsuspecting neighbours' dogs. It was a quiet street and seemed like the type of area where curtains would twitch and eyes would always be watching. It made me wonder if anyone had witnessed anything strange since Blake had moved in, but I also hoped I wasn't being watched now. Feeling self-conscious, I pulled up my hood to conceal my face.

As I reached the driveway, I could see that the blinds were closed and the lights were off. If Sam's car hadn't been parked out the front, I would have thought nobody was in. Suspicion had already got the better of me, and I decided to go and check it out further. Wandering to the wood paneled fence, I peered down the side of the house and strained to hear voices. Nothing. Instead of settling my pulsing heartbeat however, this just put me on edge. Why was everything so quiet? What were they doing? I glanced at the time on my phone and knew that there was no way they were all asleep at ten at night.

A gust of wind caught at my hair and I tucked it inside my jacket before I stood high on my tiptoes and reached over the top of the gate for a lock. I smiled as I touched a metal bolt with my fingertips. Sliding it open as quietly as I could, I continued along the paving to thc back garden, where I paused.

It was quiet and small and only had a patch of overgrown grass with an even smaller patio, littered with used cigarette butts. I turned my nose up at them, but then my eyes were drawn to light pouring from the other side of the house.

When I reached the corner, I held my breath. Light flowed out from a kitchen window, lighting the adjacent wall and the whole side of the house. I could hear chatter from inside. I ducked down immediately and glanced up to see a small rectangular window ajar. It looked as if it was the kitchen. Keeping down low underneath the windowsill, my heart pounding, I slunk forwards so that I could hear what was going on inside.

"…nice riff. Listen." I heard music being turned up. It was a metal band and the guitar solo rang through the open window, concealing anything that was being said. Sighing in frustration, I leant against the wall and waited for the song to finish, and thankfully, when it ended, they turned it down again.

"Yeah, okay, I'll give it to you," came Blake's voice, over a quieter metal song, which continued to hum in the background. A loud clatter sounded out from the open window and they all jeered.

"Hey, man..."

"Sorry... It's gone to my head." Jules's voice.

"Yeah," came another voice, which from the lilting Italian accent, I guessed must have been Franco's. "Two beers... that's what it is." Blake laughed lazily, and I immediately thought of what Louisa had said about them all being high on something once.

"Does Jenson know?" said Blake. His voice was serious.

"No," replied Jules.

"How many?"

"I think he lost count," muttered Franco.

"How many, Jules?" asked Blake again.

"Around five..."

"Five? Five in one day? Jules, you're an animal!" Blake said. He sounded jovial as if he had been drinking too. He'd gone from sounding relatively serious to impressed.

"I was bored. This town is dull," replied Jules. I heard Franco and Sam laugh. *Sam*. My chest immediately contracted, but I didn't know whether to feel glad that he was okay or let down that he was with Blake again.

"What? They were calling to me..." said Jules, innocently.

"Sure..."

"Sure, maybe five was excessive. I'm kind of baked."

"You could learn a thing or two from Jules, Sam," drawled Blake. Silence followed, then he spoke again. "Whilst we're on the subject—any luck with the girl?" I tensed.

"No," came Sam's voice. It was a tone I'd become familiar with, which invited no more questions, but where I would back off, Blake pushed on.

"You can't keep her as a pet. You know it's the order—"

"I know," growled Sam. My hands were slippery with sweat as I clenched them.

"Just reminding you, big guy…"

"He did take out the guy at the college. At least we know he hasn't completely lost his touch—" said Jules. My whole body froze, and I bit down on my knuckles to stop a sob from erupting. *Zac*. Sam had killed Zac; and not just that, but it sounded as if Jules had murdered five innocent people. *Murder*. What the hell was this? Sliding down the wall, I slouched against the rough brickwork, defeated.

I felt the cold of the night stab right into my bones. Sam had told me he had nothing to do with it—*and you believed it*, came a snarling voice in my head. Then there was me. They were talking about me. I didn't even want that thought to form in my mind. I closed my eyes tightly and tried to block out the truth. Suddenly, firm hands grasped my arms and pulled me upright. I gasped in fright and found myself staring into those familiar jet black pupils.

"Are you trying to get yourself killed?" growled Sam

in a hushed tone. His eyes were black and angry and his grip was firm. He was leaning towards me, the heat radiating off of him. I could already feel myself weakening at his proximity, but no. This was wrong. It was all wrong. Gathering all my strength, I ripped away from him and stumbled backwards. He looked at me, his eyes wide. Glancing over his shoulder, he spoke quieter, but with just as much force.

"You shouldn't be here. Go home. *Now.*"

"You killed him," I whispered, breathing hard. "And me—you—"

Sam froze and I watched as every tense muscle in his face dropped. "No, Ava. No—I—"

"Are you telling me I heard wrong?"

Something like pain flicked over Sam's face before he reluctantly shook his head in despair. "You don't understand. I didn't kill him, Ava, and I would never hurt you. You have to believe me," he said, taking a step towards me, his hands outstretched.

I took a step back. "I did believe you," I whispered. He opened his mouth to speak, but no words came. He was looking at me as if I'd slapped him. I'd never seen Sam look at me like that before. Before either of us could react, there was the scrape of shoes on the paving stones and Blake, Jules and Franco appeared around the corner. They flanked Sam and each of them had a differing level of animosity in their gaze. A horrible smirk crept onto Blake's face.

Sam hadn't moved a muscle, but as I looked at him, I could see fear in his expression. His lips moved almost imperceptibly, but I could just make out what he was saying. *"Run,"* he mouthed at me, his eyes wide. The look on his face told me all I needed to know and before my brain could register it, my legs began to move.

I ran along the side of the house and out onto the open driveway. The wind ripped past my face, and I heard Blake's bark of laugher, but when I glanced over my shoulder, he was nowhere to be seen. They weren't chasing me, but that didn't stop my hands from shaking violently as I reached my car and scrambled for my keys. I jumped in and prayed the engine would start as I jammed the key into the ignition. Thankfully it blazed to life, as if sensing my fear, and I slammed my foot on the accelerator, driving away as fast as my tiny car would allow.

CHAPTER *Eighteen*

Sam's lips mouthed *run,* over and over again in my mind, like a film clip on repeat. Had I just run away from Blake and Sam? Did Sam really kill Zac? Did he want to kill me? He'd denied it and said that I didn't understand. I was so confused and I couldn't stop my hands from their incessant trembling. When I'd got home, I'd run as quietly as I could up the stairs and thrown myself under my duvet. It was something I used to do as a child if I was afraid of something, but as an adult, I was beginning to realise it wasn't quite as effective.

As I listened to my breathing under the covers, I wondered if I should call Louisa to tell her what had just happened. I knew I couldn't though. What if they found out I'd spoken to her? I didn't want to put her in danger. How would I explain what had just happened in a message anyway? My mind was on overdrive. Whatever Sam's involvement with Blake was, it didn't seem to be a connection that he would break lightly, no matter how much he liked me. Maybe I should just walk away now before it got even more complicated. That's if Sam would let me. I knew he was as drawn to me as I was to him. I cursed under my breath. Maybe this was all part of his plan.

What would my mum say? *Just make sure you don't put your heart on the line.* That's what she would say, but my situation was probably a little more literal than she'd ever imagined. Mum had always been a guarded private person, but I took more after my dad. I wore my heart on the outside for all to see and it was clear that Sam knew this. He knew I was hooked on him like a drug – a highly addictive drug. What had I got myself into?

Sighing to myself, I turned to look at the clock. It was two minutes past midnight and I still hadn't done my biology essay. Well that's not happening, I thought to myself, my inner voice dripping with sarcasm. Since when did I not care about college work?

Turning onto my side, I stared out from under the covers and wondered what I'd been thinking. I'd known something wasn't right yet I went to find out anyway. Blake and Sam's connection wasn't a normal friendship, but I'd never imagined hearing what I heard tonight. Was it some kind of death cult, like Louisa and I had thought, or was there more to it? The word *human* echoed in my mind. Was it just some big joke, or was I really considering all of this? I must be mad.

Yawning, I pulled the covers up to my chin, even though I still had my clothes on. What was the point in changing when they could be coming for me any minute now? I closed my eyes, trying hard to breathe through the impending darkness inside me. No. Sam wouldn't do it, but then… what if he had no choice?

My phone buzzed on my bedside table, making me jump. I looked over, to find Sam's name blinking on the screen. My heart was immediately in my throat as I reached out for my phone.

Let me explain.

No, I replied, before shoving my phone away as if it were Sam's hands on me; his cold, murderous hands.

I'm not asking you, Ava. Hear me out.

God, he was so obnoxious! I wasn't entirely sure how I'd put up with him for so long. I was beginning to think I should have stayed well away from him. Maybe it would have saved Zac. I reluctantly messaged him back.

I'm not asking you either. You LIED to me.

I waited for a response and sure enough, I watched as he began to type, the ellipsis blinking on the screen. My heart was still racing in my chest.

I can't discuss this by message. I need to see you. Please.

I stared at his message. I read it through and through, but all I could see was '*please*'. A small plead. A reasonable request. A sign that he really wasn't the monster that I'd started thinking he was—but no. Shaking my head, I turned my phone off.

Flopping back in bed, I pulled the covers up and turned over, attempting to push everything that had happened from my mind. It was only as I awoke with a jolt however, that I realised exhaustion had pulled me into a fitful sleep.

Sitting up in bed, I looked down at my blank phone. I knew I'd have a message from Sam, but I wasn't going to look. I needed to give myself space from him. The fact was, he'd killed Zac, or at least something to that effect. It still didn't add up. I couldn't quite believe it, but the thought sent waves of terror through me. I wondered if I should tell the police, but then I had no evidence.

Besides, something told me this wasn't something they could help with. I cursed under my breath. How had I managed to get myself involved in this?

A soft knock on the door made me jump. It must be my dad. I didn't feel much like explaining why I was still awake, so I shuffled further under the duvet. "Yeah?" I mumbled, trying my best to sound as if I'd been sleeping for hours already.

The door opened a crack and Dad raised one eyebrow as he stared at me with wistful amusement. "You're as good a liar as your mother was, love." Eyeing me in bed, he pinched his own jumper and wiggled it. I looked down at my hoody and grimaced. He shook his head before coming over and sitting on the side of my bed. Did he know I'd been out tonight? I wondered if I was going to have a lecture about staying safe, but when his face showed concern, I sat up in bed and turned the bedside lamp on. My dad's silence was beginning to worry me.

"What is it?" I asked.

He looked at me resolvedly. "Look, love, I know you get on well with Sam, but…" He took a deep breath and looked across the room as if searching for his next words. "I'm not sure he's right for you, love. At least—not at the moment." He knew I'd gone out and he thought I'd been with Sam. There was no other reason why he'd be talking to me about this at – I looked at the clock – one in the morning!

"He's a good kid, but he's obviously got a few demons of his own to deal with and—"

"If you mean because of Mum—" What was I saying? I'd just found out he'd killed Zac.

"Well, I do actually. He's had a rough start and he's

not very reliable, love. That's why I gave him a job. I wanted to give him a chance. I thought it would ground him. You know, do him good, but… I don't want you getting in too deep. Just think about what Mum would say for me, okay?"

I shrugged impatiently in response. I was already in too deep and despite finding out what I had so far, I needed to know more. I hated Sam for making me feel like this, but maybe I did need to hear him out. Maybe it really was nothing to do with him. Maybe he'd been dragged into this as much as I had. As much as I wanted to ignore it and run away, that niggling feeling in my gut was persistent.

I looked at my dad. "Fine. I'll be careful, but I'm not going to stop seeing him. He's my friend." I watched as the word *friend* sunk in and a little of the concern left his face. Somehow though, the word *friend* felt wrong on my tongue. I wasn't sure if it was because he'd come to mean more to me, or because I didn't want him to mean more to me. I watched as Dad nodded and took a deep breath, seemingly satisfied that I'd listened, but I could tell he still had something on his mind… In fact, why *had* he decided to talk to me now, at this time in the morning? He hadn't questioned me about going out…

"Look," he said, taking a deep weary breath. "That being said, Seline phoned and… Apparently he's upset you." Dad watched me curiously.

I shrugged. How else was I supposed to react?

"I know I'm going to kick myself for saying this," he said, "but Seline said he wants to see you. He's been hurt. It seems he upset a few of his friends too, and they decided to deal with it in their own way, but he's refusing to accept help until he can see you. Seline said he wants to apologise to you. I suppose I can't be angry with him for that…" Dad sighed deeply.

I furrowed my brow suspiciously, and wondered if he really had been hurt. I wasn't sure what to expect from Sam now. He'd already proved to me that he could lie to my face and not feel bad about it. Then again, would Seline lie for him?

"What else did she say?" I asked, looking for clues.

"Nothing much, but I told her I'd let you know." He watched me for a moment, concern etched all over his face. "This doesn't mean you need to go running off because he's demanding to see you though, love. I'm sure he'll be fine. Seline said she can patch him up, and I'm sure he'll have the sense to let her help soon enough. I said we'd be round in the morning."

Morning. I wasn't sure I could wait that long. I wasn't sure I could let Seline deal with him alone either—not after what I'd seen the other night.

Dad coughed. "Are you and Sam…?"

"I should go," I said. All thoughts of avoiding Sam evaporated from my mind in an instant. Something didn't sit right. It seemed odd that Seline had called me. I knew Sam had probably tried phoning me to be faced with a voicemail, but to get Seline to call me… Unless he really was hurt…

"You can go in the morning, love. Seline can take care of him."

"I can't. I mean, I should go now—" I stammered, surprised, as emotion rose inside me. I suddenly felt a wave of guilt wash over me. If I hadn't gone, none of this would have happened.

"We'll go tomorrow, love—" Dad started.

"No, I should go. He's hurt, Dad." I looked at him imploringly.

He sighed deeply. I knew he was having an internal battle. He wanted me to have my freedom, but I knew he was feeling particularly protective of me after what had happened at the rave. "Ava…"

"I have to go," I said, surprised at how strong my voice sounded. "It doesn't matter what you say."

"He's a little old for you, isn't he?" he tried. I knew he was trying to convince me to stay on reasonable terms.

"You were older than mum," I said, blanching slightly at the word *were*.

Dad watched me carefully. "Yes, I was..."

I remembered a conversation I'd had once with Mum. "And Mum told me how you met," I said, watching his reaction.

He took a breath. "Did she now…?"

I wondered how far I could go with this. "She said you met in a homeless shelter," I said, cautiously. I'd never spoken to Dad about this, but I got the distinct impression that I knew more than he wanted me to. "She helped you."

Dad rubbed the back of his neck, then he looked at me, his hand dropping to his side. "I had no idea she'd told you," he said. I gave him a small nod. "What else did she tell you?"

I swallowed. "She always just said that your dad wasn't particularly nice to you and that you were… ill." I looked at him carefully and wondered if he'd clarify what I'd always wondered.

"Ill," he said, a grim smile on his face. There was no

humor there. "Trust your mother to make me sound like the victim." He looked me in the eye. "I was suffering with depression, Ava. It took over my life and I ended up in a bad place. I did some things I'm not proud of," he said simply. "I never intended to end up like that, but I left home and got desperate. That's why I was so angry when you went to that rave," he said, his eyes like ice as he recalled what had happened. "I didn't want you going down the same path that I took." He took a deep breath and a small smile rose on his face. "I was suffering and didn't know where to turn and then… I met your mum."

I smiled and waited for him to continue.

"She was the most beautiful woman I'd ever met and she made me laugh. I always looked forward to seeing her at the shelter." He came to sit next to me on the bed. "I probably would have died on the streets if I hadn't met her."

I wanted to know how Mum had helped him, but I was aware of needing to see Sam, so I held my tongue. I promised myself I'd ask him someday. I looked up at him and found his eyes already on mine. Then he put his hand on my knee and I felt the tension in the room lift.

"Go and see him, Aves," he said, and a small, sad smile rose on his face. I knew what he was saying.

"Thanks," I said and for the first time in a long time, I found myself leaning over and hugging my dad. He squeezed me back, before standing up.

"Just… drive safely," he said, opening the door, "and let me know what's happening, okay? I know Sam's hurt, but I need you to look after yourself too." I nodded before whipping the covers off and collecting my phone and car keys from my bedside table.

"And... you'll be—you know—*careful*? I mean... not just driving...but *careful* careful."

I faced him and saw embarrassment there, and I realised what he was saying. My face reddened. I was *not* having this conversation with him.

"You *really* don't need to worry about that," I said, turning away from him to grab my jacket. Of all the times he could try to have *that* conversation with me, why now? Now was *not* the time for *that*. I picked up my bag and could see my hands shaking with nervous energy. All that was on my mind tonight was answers.

"Come in," Seline said, opening the door. I walked into the farmhouse and followed her into a small snug room with an open fire, the same room I'd looked into a few nights before. There was a TV in the corner, next to the window, and the room had a low ceiling held up by dark wooden beams, scattered with dried flowers. There was also a bookcase crammed with dusty volumes and a blue winged chair with a foot stool on the other side of the room. Against the nearest wall on a small weathered sofa was Sam.

"Sam." His name slipped from my mouth in shock. He was slumped on the tiny sofa, his arm cradling his ribs over a blood-soaked t-shirt. The blood looked like it had mostly come from his face where there was an enormous gash on his cheek and a cut on his bottom lip. One of his eyes was half closed and looked as though it was already bruising. Seline had obviously tried to clean him up a little, but dried blood stained the whole underside of his jaw and neck, and when he opened his mouth gingerly to speak, I felt myself shake with anger.

"Ava—" he croaked, shifting towards me with determination. I crossed to sit next to him and pushed him gently back onto the sofa. "Ava, I—" he stopped and swallowed, etching pain on his face.

"Don't speak. It hurts," I said, dropping my bag to the floor. "You don't need to explain right now."

He looked at me reproachful. "I wouldn't hurt—I wouldn't—" He obviously wanted to explain everything.

"It's okay. *Later*," I coaxed, but he continued to stare at me as if looking away meant I would leave. I nervously raised a hand and brushed his damp hair back from his forehead. He closed his eyes at my touch and leant his head back on the sofa, seemingly satisfied that I wouldn't leave. He was exhausted, and as my fingers swept through his dark curls again, I couldn't cool the thrill that ran through me. He was a complicated mess, but I knew in that moment, that he was my complicated mess. I wondered if my mum had thought the same of my dad when they'd met.

Despite what I'd overheard, I knew I couldn't just walk away from Sam. I'd known it the moment I'd set eyes on him. There was a pull between us then, and there still was now – and I knew he felt it too. *What if he's a murderer?* I shook the thought away. I didn't want to think about that right now. Not when I felt hatred running through my veins as I pictured Blake hurting him. Sam couldn't be the bad guy. It just didn't fit.

As I looked down his broken and battered body, I noticed that his sleeves were pulled up and his hourglass tattoo was completely on show. My pulse raced as I openly stared at it. This was the first time that he hadn't covered it up in front of me, and I knew I could quite easily reach out and touch it. Glancing nervously at his closed eyes, I ran my fingers over his bare hand, feeling his burning skin beneath my cool fingertips. When I reached the inside of his forearm, I ran my finger carefully around the tattoo, making sure not to touch the intricate design.

Sam's breathing quickened.

I looked up into his face and felt my chest heave in air. His eyes held a fear I hadn't seen before and it produced a rush of emotion inside me. His jaw was tense, and he was ready to stop my hand, but I slowly reached up to the sleeve gathered at his elbow and pulled it gently over the mark. He immediately relaxed and stared into my eyes. This time, *I* wanted to kiss *him*.

I swallowed nervously and saw what I thought was a ghost of a smile on Sam's lips. Edging towards him, my hands were shaking as I leant forwards. He lifted his head to meet me, and in that second, I saw his eyes blaze and the gap between us was no more. His hands wound round my back and he was pressing his lips onto mine. His kiss was desperate for all of a second, then he winced. I broke away immediately. I'd forgotten about his lip.

"Sorry," I whispered, feeling the heat in my cheeks, but a slight shake of his head told me he didn't want me to stop. I moved carefully forwards again, and when my lips met his, his kiss was softer. I felt his hands skim along my back, pulling me closer, and my heart raced as I slid my arms around him. Heat radiated from his skin and everything inside me screamed for more, but I had to stop. This couldn't happen. Not now. Not whilst he still had secrets.

"Sam…" I whispered. He was tracing tiny kisses along my jaw, and I had to push him gently in the chest to get him to stop. "Sam, stop…" He broke away and I couldn't help but laugh a little at his disappointed expression. "I just…" What was I supposed to say? That I couldn't kiss him because I didn't trust him? Because I did. I just needed to know the full story. "I think…"

"It's okay," he croaked, nodding and leaning back on the sofa with a small wince.

"And I don't want to hurt you…" I tried, apologetically.

"I can handle it," he managed to whisper, still giving me that all-consuming grin.

"Well, I can't," I retorted. "You need to rest." Up close, I realised just how unwell he looked. As well as the split lip and huge gash underneath his bruised eye, he had a greyish hue to his skin, and I saw that the tattoos protruding up his neck weren't as vibrant as the other day. I frowned.

"What?" he whispered, straining to sit upright on the sofa. His arm tightened around his ribs and he coughed, covering his mouth with his other hand. When he took his hand away, he glanced quickly at his palm before balling his fist up and stuffing it into the sofa. I narrowed my eyes at him and grasped his wrist to try and look in his palm, but he resisted. He was still strong enough to hold his fist closed against my efforts.

"Let me see."

He groaned in frustration and opened his fist revealing blood. I looked into his face and he returned a look that said, *you asked.* He shrugged and took his fist back.

“You should go to hospital,” I said, but the expression on his face told me that was a ridiculous suggestion and deep down, I knew it was, but I didn’t yet know why. There was so much I didn’t know and so much I couldn’t even begin to understand.

“I’ll”—he stopped and swallowed—“be fine.”

“How? How will you be fine?” I asked, feeling frustrated.

“I just will,” he managed to say. Holding his ribs as he took a deep breath, he whispered, “Trust me.” He shifted the cushions next to him and lay back on them.

“I do trust you, but I’m beginning to think you don’t trust me. You say it’s to keep me safe, but I found out some pretty terrifying things tonight and I’m still here.” I stared at him. He was a mess and there was every chance he was bleeding internally. How could he possibly be fine? “You need to start talking if you want me to stick around,” I said.

He fixed those eyes on me and I could have sworn there was a flicker of fear there. “Fine. I’ll – t-t-t… talk,” he said with a grimace, “—about… me.” He seemed to be struggling to speak more than before, but he’d asked me to trust him; to trust that he would be ok. He looked so uncomfortable though and I watched as he shifted on the sofa and doubled over. He pressed a hand to his chest and I wondered if he was going to be sick. Then he took a deep breath, but this time *I* winced. It sounded like he had phlegm in his throat but I knew better. He took a few more breaths, but something wasn’t right and next thing, he coughed deeply and blood spewed on the floor.

“S-Sel…ine,” he croaked, turning a darker shade of

grey.

I was instantly on my feet, and within minutes, Seline was by Sam's side, coaxing him to open his mouth.

"Chew it," she said in a quiet, steady voice. She'd produced a small bundle of herbs which she'd soaked in a dark liquid. I hadn't asked her what it was. She hadn't said a word to me. Now, we both watched as Sam chewed gingerly on the herbs, and when I glanced sideways at Seline, I could see her lips moving almost imperceptibly.

"Spit," she said, holding a small glass dish under his chin. Sam glanced my way, and I gave him a small smile as I came to sit next to him on the sofa.

"Next time," Seline said, "just let me help straight away." She gave Sam a pointed glare, like a mother reprimanding a son, then walked from the room without another word.

"So," he croaked, "What do you want to know?"

"Huh?" I asked, perplexed.

"You wanted to ask me questions."

I looked at him as if he had grown another head. "Yeah," I whispered, "but that was before you nearly died."

He laughed a little, but gasped and held his ribs. "I did not nearly die," he said.

"Then why did you beg me to get Seline?" I said, feeling edgy.

"Because I couldn't speak to you," he said, all of his usual cockiness returning.

I shook my head in disbelief. "See, this is what I struggle with… You just act like everything's fine, but it *really* isn't."

He searched my face. "I know. I'm sorry, but I do

want to make it easier for you."

"Why? What's changed?" I said. As much as I wanted to fire questions at him, I couldn't understand his sudden change of heart.

"You," he said. "I thought I was protecting you, but after tonight… I just want you to trust me…" he said.

"Okay…" I whispered.

"So, what do you want to know?" he said, gently.

He was actually going to talk. I needed to make the most of this. What had changed his mind? Had it been the threat of losing me, or did he think I'd already worked out too much anyway? I looked away from him to clear my head and thought what to ask first. The word *murder* immediately floated to the forefront of my mind. I took a breath and tried to keep my hands from trembling as I spoke.

"Did Jules really murder five people?"

"Next question." Sam's eyes were hard.

"You said you'd talk."

"I said I'd talk about *me*," he said, fixing me with a look that warned not to push him further.

"Fine," I said, grimacing, but my distaste faded quickly as I thought of Zac. I had to quell the rising emotion inside me before I spoke again. I wasn't sure what my reaction would be if Sam said yes to this.

Closing my eyes and taking a deep breath, I asked, "Did *you* kill Zac?" Sadness welled up inside me as I waited for that one word that would surely destroy everything between us. Slowly, I opened my eyes.

"No," he whispered, hurt all too clear in his face. I let a tear slip down my face, but I wiped it away quickly as I thought of my next question.

"Why were you there that night?"

I watched as Sam eyes widened fractionally, before speaking. "I wanted to talk to you," he said. He looked away, but I could see the jealousy in his eyes again, and I knew he was thinking of Zac.

"Why did you follow me to the rave?" Was it just a need to be near me or was it something else?

"I've already told you. I couldn't stay away." He spoke as if this was the most obvious thing, and I leant back on the sofa, still facing him. His face softened as I stifled a yawn. I felt exhausted from everything that had happened and I was getting nowhere with these questions. I thought hard. Then it came to me. I swallowed nervously.

"When I met you, did I really say I couldn't remember how my mum died?" I gave him a look that told him I already knew the answer.

This time Sam looked guilty as hell. "No," he muttered, looking down into his lap. "I'm sorry. I shouldn't have lied to you."

I knew this meant I should ask him how he knew to ask this, but I couldn't. Even the thought of it made me feel sick. The truth was, I was afraid that I'd want to get away from him.

"Why did you lie?" I asked, instead.

Sam's hand twitched against my own. "Because I'd already broken enough rules… and I didn't want to scare you. I knew if I told you *how* I knew, I'd never see you again…"

I braced myself for what I didn't want to hear and found myself closing my eyes as if I could shut it out.

"I wanted to know you, and maybe you'll hate me for

saying this, but I'm glad I lied. If I hadn't, I don't think I would have got to feel what I feel now."

I opened my eyes.

"I haven't felt what I do for you, for a long time. I haven't let myself feel *anything* in a long time," he said, slipping his hand into mine. I gripped back as if letting go meant I'd lose him forever.

"I tried to walk away from you, but I couldn't. I had to keep seeing you even though I knew it was dangerous for both of us." He gave a grim laugh. "Someone like me pining after you… It was hopeless from the start, but it was like it was beyond my control. I think I could have managed to stay away if it hadn't been for Zac."

I swallowed nervously.

"I saw him kiss you and…" His eyes glowed. "…It just lit some fire inside me that I haven't felt in decades and I—"

"Wait. What?" I gasped, sitting up. "Decades?"

Sam looked awkward beyond recognition, but he soon gained back his composure and looked me in the eye. He nodded. "I'm a little older than you, I guess," he said.

"You don't say." I blew out a breath and waited for him to continue speaking. It seemed that now he'd opened the flood gates, he couldn't stop, and I didn't want to stop him either.

"I just… That night, something snapped, and I had to take back what I'd said to you, even at the risk of you finding out more about me."

"So…" I took a deep breath and readied myself for an answer I was scared to hear. "*What* are you?"

Sam looked at me for a long moment and even I

could see that his face clouded with a thousand thoughts and memories. He swallowed nervously. “I’m Sam,” he whispered.

In that moment, I knew that’s all he could say, and I was okay with that. He wasn’t ready. He’d shared a lot more than I ever expected him to, and the raw emotion that punctured his face was agony to look at. Whatever he was, he clearly hated himself for it, but I needed to know one more thing.

“Sam… Do they want me dead?”

A shadow passed over his face and his silence was answer enough.

After a few minutes, Sam shifted uncomfortably on the sofa. He was quite obviously still in a lot of pain.

“That’s why they did this to you…” I whispered, realisation pinning me in place.

Sam shifted to rest his head on the arm of the sofa. He didn’t open his eyes as he answered. “I broke the law. I deserved everything I got.”

I shook my head in distaste. How could he possibly think that? Was his opinion so low of himself that he truly thought he deserved this kind of treatment? Getting to my feet, I made for the door without a word.

“Where are you going?”

I looked back and Sam’s eyes were still closed. “I’ll be back in a second,” I said, creeping out of the room towards the bathroom.

I filled a small basin with lukewarm water and hunted down some cotton wool, which I carried back to the lounge. When Sam opened his eyes a fraction and saw what I had collected, he looked at me apprehensively.

“Don’t look so worried,” I said, laughing to myself.

"Anyone would think I'd just brought you a vile of poison." I knew this was probably useless, but it eased my guilt. Sam wouldn't be in this state if I'd just stayed away.

Kneeling on the floor beside the sofa, I leant over him and gently wiped away the blood from his face and underneath his jaw. All the while, Sam's eyes remained on mine. I knew he was watching my every move, but I knew he'd never hurt me. I trusted him, so I continued until the water had turned a pinkish hue and Sam's face was clean. When I was finally satisfied, I looked up to find that his eyes were closed and his lips slightly parted.

The gash beneath his eye remained and his hair was still caked with blood, but at least all the blood on his face and neck was gone. I finally felt my guilt ease and I yawned as tiredness swelled up inside me. I hadn't realised how exhausted I was until now. Sitting carefully beside Sam and resting my head on the back of the sofa, I closed my eyes and let myself fall into a deep sleep.

CHAPTER *Nineteen*

I awoke from a dreamless sleep with a jump, as something nearby moved. As soon as my eyes adjusted and I worked out where I was, it all came rushing back to me with renewed clarity.

"Hi," Sam said.

I turned and blinked at him blearily. He was grinning at me and he looked better. The glint was back in his eyes and the gash had gone completely. Only a few dried smears of blood remained in his hair. Rubbing the sleep from my eyes, I sat upright on the sofa and looked about, getting my bearings, and saw it was already light. Panic rose in my chest—Dad. I quickly got to my feet, feeling a blanket drop to the floor.

"Don't worry. Your dad called last night," Sam said, picking up the blanket and draping it on the arm of the sofa. "Seline said you were sleeping on the sofa," he grinned mischievously. "Which, technically, is true…"

"Was he okay?" I asked apprehensively, my voice croaky.

"Yeah," Sam said. "Seline told him she'd make sure

you went home after lunch. It's still early now."

I nodded and stared at him. I was amazed by how quickly he had healed, but his greyish skin tone remained, and as I looked at him seriously, he stood and took my wrists gently in his hands.

"I'm fine," he reassured me. He scanned my face before opening his mouth to speak, but something stopped him and he closed it again. I looked at him steadily so he knew I needed the truth. His jaw clenched and he sighed just as I heard Seline enter the room.

"Does she know?" Her tone held a mixture of intrigue and pride, and as she stood in the doorway, her eyes flicked between the two of us.

"Not yet," Sam said with a grim determination. Turning to me apprehensively, he knelt down in front of me. His eyes were still deep black, but his gaze was kind. "Is there any way you can make this easier for her?" he asked Seline. She shook her head.

I felt my heart beat erratically against my ribs. This was it. What had I got myself into? I watched as Sam unzipped his hoody and threw it on the winged chair before turning to me with a look of inner turmoil stretched across his face. He reached to his sleeve and pulled it up revealing the intricate black hourglass tattoo that I'd come so close to touching.

"You wanted to know," he warned. I glanced at him nervously. "Well this is me, right here on my arm." I frowned. "This is all the time I have left…before I turn to dust."

I felt my head shake in confusion and when I opened

my mouth; my throat was like sandpaper. “Dust?” I whispered.

“I didn’t say it would be easy to understand,” said Sam. I looked into his eyes and knew what he was saying must be true. I would never have believed it if I hadn’t already discovered that Seline was a witch. A whole new parallel world was being exposed to me and I was expected to just believe it.

“When you say *‘all the time you have left,’* what does that mean?” I croaked, feeling my throat constrict further as I dreaded the answer.

“It’s a curse, Ava. It shows what time I have left.” He watched me for a moment. “When it runs out, I… I’ll turn to dust. I’ll die.” He spoke the last bit quickly as if saying it faster released some of the pain of telling me the truth.

“Die?” I whispered. I felt like I’d been punched in the stomach. “Can you stop it?” I asked. I couldn’t quite believe I was having this conversation and my hands trembled. Sam leant forwards and put his hands over my own.

“Yes,” he said, avoiding my gaze and I wondered what I was missing.

“How?”

Sam looked up at me and I could tell he was trying to gauge how I was going to react. “It’s complicated,” he said.

“I’m listening,” I said, pulling my hands away from his and staring at him intently.

“Um—” He huffed and ran a hand through his hair.

"Look, it's not something that you—"

"Sam," I said, interrupting him. I wasn't going to back down.

He sighed. "It's time. I need time," he said, watching me cautiously as he fumbled on. "Seline—she helps. She makes time for me."

He glanced in Seline's direction and I saw a look pass between them. There was still something they weren't telling me. "Seline—please don't let her run."

My eyes shot up to Sam, and I tried to swallow down the sensation of rising water in my chest as Seline left the room, leaving me alone with Sam. What was I doing? I wanted to confess how scared I really felt, but I couldn't move. I couldn't even allow my lips to utter a single word.

"Okay…" he began nervously, looking directly in my eyes. "Do you really want to know who I am—*what* I am?"

"Yes," I said, gently. I recalled last night and how he'd appeared so vulnerable when he'd said, '*I'm Sam'*. Now, he was offering to tell me. He felt confident enough, I supposed, as I hadn't run when he'd told me everything else. I couldn't back off now. Sam was putting himself on the line for me. I clasped my hands together hard and listened. His expression was resigned as he inched even closer to me, easing his arm up towards me.

"You see the black sand inside the outline? I want you to press your fingers to it and think of Zac." *Zac*. I raised my hand tentatively to his arm and he flinched away. "But before you do—please let me explain…

before you run."

I stared at him for a moment and his eyes pleaded with me. "Okay," I promised, wondering whether the truth would be that bad. He rested his arm on my knees and closed his eyes. He was trusting me and whatever he was trusting me with, I felt the need to reciprocate the feeling. He looked so peaceful with his lips closed and his eyelashes fanned over his cheek bones. He really was beautiful. I glanced down to his arm and took a breath, before dubiously reaching out a shaky hand and pressing my fingers to the tattoo.

I immediately felt like I was touching fire and Sam cried out in agony, making me retract my hand in fright. He opened his eyes and stared at me uncertainly.

"I'm hurting you," I faltered.

"Again," he demanded, thrusting his arm towards me with a dark, determined expression. I studied his face and saw that it no longer looked peaceful, but tortured. I needed to make this quick. As I touched the mark again, I forced myself to ignore the screams and focus on the colours and sounds I was experiencing. Images flashed wildly in my mind and it was a struggle to focus on any one thing. As I squinted into the blur, things came into focus and I was back in the sports hall at college. It wasn't what I had expected and I looked about wildly, wondering if Sam was here too, but he wasn't.

I suddenly became aware of hot bodies pressing in at me as I felt myself jumping along with the music, but had I danced to this band's music? I couldn't remember. Hearing someone squeal in excitement next to me, I turned to see Louisa. She was grinning from ear to ear as she bobbed up and down to the music, then she leant in close to me.

"Not to knock Fortitude, but this band is *amazing!"*

I felt myself laugh as I watched Louisa.

"I can't believe Ava's missing this one," she shouted over the music.

Frowning, I glanced down at myself. I was wearing clothes just like Zac's. In fact, I *was* wearing Zac's clothes—the same clothes he'd been wearing when he'd died. I *was* Zac from *that* night.

The beat of the music picked up as the drums intensified, rising into a brilliant solo. I felt my heart rate increase, but it wasn't my heart rate—it was Zac's. The sweet smell of the stage smoke filled my nose and the streaming of different coloured lights saturated my vision—but I felt amazing. My body buzzed with everything happening in the room and I felt alive.

A girl with long blonde hair that I recognised from English swept over to me and I felt my eyes widen. Her blue eyes gleamed as she grinned at me, making me smile, but something made me move away from her and push my way through the crowd towards the front.

Stumbling through the jumbled bodies, feeling the trickle of sweat down my forehead, I was hot, but my back was cold. My mouth was parched. The drum beat was quickening further still as the guitarist played a melody of higher notes. He was on his knees at the front of the stage and his movements started to blur as if the heat in the room was melting him. I tripped over my own feet.

"Loser," echoed in my mind. I turned to face the slight figure I'd fallen into and her face slipped and swayed. I stumbled onto the floor, hurting my knees. My hands were on the cool, hard floor. It swayed nearer as my stomach convulsed and my back arched. Sharp pain grabbed at my side, and then I was on my back, my entire body shaking and my senses mixing into a dizzying cocktail of colour, sound and smell.

Colour. Black eyes. Hands on my shoulders. *His* hands. Jealousy invaded my already clouded mind. *Ava*. He was no good for her. Black eyes burned into my brain. They were too black. Something in them glinted hungrily and my vision swayed. I saw panic fill his eyes as fear filled my own.

A pain was gripping my body, one muscle at a time as sickness filled my throat. I couldn't breathe. All I could see was black and the sensation of grips on my shoulders as something wet trickled from the side of my mouth. My body jerked hard, constricting my lungs. I was choking. I couldn't breathe. Then all sensation left my body.

The next thing I knew, the images and sounds around me started to distort as if someone was pinching them away from me, and I fell back on the sofa in Seline's house. Gasping for breath and gripping at my clothes, I was relieved to see that I was myself again, but I was even more relieved to be back and safe.

Sam was slumped on the floor next to me, breathing heavily, sweat dripping from his pale face; my mind was swimming from what I'd just seen. Zac's death had just replayed in my own head. In fact, I'd experienced what he had. It was painful and frightening and I felt for Zac. Tears brimmed at my eyes and a lump filled my throat as I wished I'd been there for him.

"You okay?" Sam gasped, a pained expression still taught on his face. I nodded silently through my tears, though I wasn't okay at all.

"Did you see?" came Sam's voice quietly.

I was in shock. "How did you do that?" I gasped. "I just saw… I mean I *was* Zac and he…he…"

Sam watched me in silence. "He overdosed, but by the time I realised, it was too late."

"But you…your eyes. I saw your eyes and I knew… How did he know?" My breathing became ragged and my head swam—then I felt a cool hand cover my eyes and I smelt a strong scent of mixed herbs.

CHAPTER *Twenty*

A potent stench of antiseptic filled my nose, immediately making me wretch. The smell was stronger than normal, and my eyes watered, blurring my vision. Flashes of insipid green and blue flew past me, and when I squinted hard, I saw the doctors and nurses that had attended to my mum. They were working faster than normal and it was hard to focus on them. I wiped furiously at my eyes, but my vision wouldn't clear, and as I listened, I realised I couldn't understand a word they were saying either. It wasn't that they were speaking another language, but it was like someone had put distortion effects on their voices so that their cool professional tones sounded deep and slow.

I hurried down the corridor towards the usual double doors of the operating theatre, but the faster I ran, the further away the doors stretched. I halted and stared at the doors, but they only started to grow bigger, taller, larger until they loomed straight ahead of me and I thought they'd never stop. I squeezed my eyes shut and braced myself for the force of the doors to slam into me, but nothing came.

I opened my eyes and the huge operating lights glinted through the windows in front of me. The doors were within reaching distance, my heart started to beat faster, and I wondered if this could be the moment. I could find out what was behind those doors. I reached out my hand towards the silver handle, but just as my fingertips grazed the cold metal, a hand on my shoulder stopped me. Turning around, my vision filled with those endless black eyes that had become so familiar to me. They were so black, it was hard to look at them, but I couldn't look away either. They were drawing me in, deeper and deeper into oblivion, further away from the doors that held the answers I sought. Then in a flash, light filled my senses, startling and warming me all at the same time, and I felt the weight of my body, laying on something soft.

I opened my eyes blearily and squinted as sunlight filled my vision. As I awoke, I was met with other sensations, like the warmth of the sun in the room and the heaviness of my head on a cushion and the smell of bacon. I reached up to run my hands over my face and gazed around the room groggily.

It was Seline's lounge and I could see from the clock on the mantelpiece that it was only just eleven. I'd only slept for a few hours, but it felt like longer with the dreams. Then realisation crashed into me…

Pulling myself upright, I tried to focus. Had Sam really shown me Zac's death through the black inked marks on his arm? A lot had happened, but I had no recollection of falling asleep.

"Morning… again…" came Sam's hesitant voice.

I turned my head, shocked to find out that I wasn't alone. Sam was sitting on the arm of the sofa just behind me. He was wearing a fresh t-shirt and the blood was gone from his hair. I looked at him anxiously, but his black eyes reminded me of the dream, and I had to look away again. It seemed weird that only hours ago I would have felt safer in Sam's presence than anywhere else, and now I couldn't even look at him.

"Hi," I muttered, feeling the weight of unease between us.

"You alright?" he asked, gazing at me with a curious expression on his face.

When I answered with silence, he nodded to himself.

Knowing what Sam could do was a lot to take in, and I was beginning to wonder if I'd bitten off more than I could chew. Maybe Dad was right—even after our heart to heart last night. Maybe Mum was a lot stronger than me. Then again, she'd been dealing with drug addiction and depression, not death cults.

"I should phone my dad," I muttered. I reached into the back pocket of my jeans, but my phone wasn't there. I moved aside to look down the side of the sofa just as Sam held it out for me. I looked at him questioningly, but he looked away sheepishly. I took it silently. Thankfully there were no unread messages from Dad, but it looked as though Sam had sent one.

"You went through my messages?" I said, feeling more than a little violated.

"No," he said, carefully. "I sent one to your dad to let him know you were staying for lunch and he could join us if he wanted. I knew he'd worry."

"Looks like you had quite the conversation," I said, scrolling through the messages. Dad had asked how he was and then moved on to question him about me. I sighed and put my phone into my pocket before facing Sam. "Well, thanks, I guess. I think I'll give lunch a miss though," I said. "It's Saturday and I have college work to do." I knew this sentence sounded ridiculous after what I'd just experienced, but I didn't feel much like staying here any longer. I needed some space and it was a good excuse to leave. Then something occurred to me and I turned to face Sam.

"Do you have my keys, too?" I asked, knowing full well he'd already taken them.

"You're leaving?" he asked, the predator in him surfacing. "Don't you want to talk about everything?" His pupils dilated and fixed on me and I could practically see an animalistic part of him rearing its ugly head. I knew he wouldn't hurt me, but I also knew for certain now, that he wasn't your regular human.

"Well, how long do you expect to hold me captive here?" I asked, gently, raising an eyebrow. There *were* a thousand more questions running through my head, but I knew if I stayed, I would ignore them. I'd just pretend everything was okay. What I needed was time to think about what to say to Sam. I needed time to think about how I really felt about him.

After studying my face for a fractionally longer time than was normal, Sam got to his feet and stretched out a hand to pull me up. I hesitated, but sighing in defeat, I reached for him and clambered off the sofa with his help. I regretted standing almost instantly, as a wave of sickness filled my stomach and I had to take a steadying breath.

"It's Seline's magic. It can make you feel lightheaded."

I stared at him open-mouthed. "She put a spell on me?" I didn't like that someone could control me like that, but I knew why she'd done it; Sam had asked her to so I didn't run.

"It was mostly herbal; just to help you calm down," he said. "I didn't want you driving home in that state." He reached up to stroke my cheek with his thumb. I flinched. Ignoring my reaction, he slid his hand into mine again. "Come on, you need some food inside you and you'll feel better afterwards."

"I'm not hungry," I said. The last thing I wanted was to eat, but as Sam guided me gently into the hallway, aromas of bacon hit my nose and my mouth instantly started to water.

Seline looked up from the sizzling stove as we came into the kitchen. "Hello, Ava. I've made brunch as it's still a little early. Take a seat." She smiled at me kindly and I nodded politely in return.

"Thanks," I muttered to Seline as Sam pulled a chair out at the kitchen table and placed his hands on my shoulders to get me to sit down.

"I knew you wouldn't be able to say no to Seline," he murmured, sitting down next to me with a smirk on his face. Despite everything, that smile made my heart rate peak, but I tore my gaze from his. I had the truth now and it was all coming together in my mind. Sam could see death coming. He was cursed. And Seline—she was a witch and was helping somehow. Sam had said she made time for him. I didn't entirely understand that part, but I guessed it was because of the hourglass on his arm. It must have been part of the curse.

As I looked around the room, I felt a little disconcerted with my current company, and I could feel my hands clamming up; maybe that was the spell. Maybe that's why my dream had been so bizarre. It could explain the distortion in everything, and maybe even why Sam's eyes had appeared, holding me back from the door.

"You okay?" Sam said, staring at me with concern, but his eyes were too much and I looked away quickly. "Ava?"

"Yeah, fine," I mumbled, the burn of Sam's eyes on me still. "It's just a bad dream I had." I tried to act casual, but I felt Sam's hand creep onto my arm and when I looked at him, he was serious.

"What kind of dream?"

"Nothing…just about my mum's death. It's the same dream I always have, but it was just weird this time." I shrugged. I wasn't really in the mood to talk. But then those eyes flashed in my mind and an image of Sam standing in the barn came rushing towards me. *Have you remembered how she died yet?* echoed from my memory. I turned to Sam. I felt like the wind had been knocked out of me. I stared at him in utter shock.

"You know how she died, don't you?" I said, feeling the blood drain from my face. A look of guilt momentarily crossed his face, then it was replaced with sympathy. He nodded. Tears brimmed in my eyes. "Excuse me," I mumbled, scraping my chair back from the table and marching from the kitchen. I had to get away from him. It was all beginning to make sense. Sam knew how my mum had died. He'd practically told me so the first time we'd met, but I'd put it to the back of my mind and forgotten. I could ask him to show me, but the thought terrified me and I wasn't sure I could handle the truth. Reaching the front door, I fumbled on the coat hooks for my jacket.

"Ava?"

Sam's voice stopped me in my tracks and I turned to face him, wiping the tears from my cheeks. He stood in the doorway of the kitchen, his hands hanging at his sides. His face looked pained. "I'm sorry. I didn't think you'd want me to show you," he said.

"I don't," I managed, wiping again at the tears now streaming down my face. "Can I have my things please? I want to go home." I needed to be away from Sam. I was flying too close to the sun and I was beginning to burn.

"Ava…" Sam's voice was uncertain as he approached me.

I took a step back and stared hard at him through my tear dropped lashes.

He stopped, a look of sadness crossing his face. He feared I'd not come back, but I needed to be selfish now—for my *own* self-preservation. I waited patiently, without saying a word as his eyes bored into me pleadingly, desperately, terrified.

Finally, he reached into his pocket and produced my keys, but as I moved to take them, his hand closed around my fist, sending warmth through my arm. I gasped. When I met his eyes, he looked back at me with such grief that it made me want to rewind time and forget everything I'd just learnt—but I couldn't. I had to go, even though I knew walking away from him now would crush him.

"I need to be alone," I muttered.

After a fraction of a second, his gaze dropped and his grasp loosened on my hand. I could breathe again. Turning on my heel, I headed for the door without looking back. I couldn't look him in the eyes. If I did, I'd only go back and I needed to be strong. I needed space to think. If I turned around now, it might just destroy me.

I thought about what he'd said: '*I didn't think you'd want me to show you*'. I knew in that instant, if I touched his hourglass and thought of her, I would experience her death. I wasn't sure if this was something I could ever endure, let alone months after she'd gone. Could I ever be around Sam again, knowing he knew the truth when I didn't?

After fumbling to get the key in the lock, I climbed in my car and started driving away from Seline's—away from Sam. Had I really just got to the bottom of all the mystery surrounding him? Was it true that he'd be gone forever once the hourglass ran out of time? How much could Seline hold off his curse? I pictured the intricate mark on his arm and as far as I could recall, there had been only miniscule amounts of time left. Could it be possible that this meant he only had a matter of weeks, or even days left? It was then that his words—'*I'll turn to dust. I'll die*'—echoed in my head, and I started to regret not saying goodbye to Sam; whatever he might be; whatever he may have done.

CHAPTER *Twenty-One*

How long did he have left? This same question echoed in my mind and stretched life into one thought. I couldn't sleep; I couldn't eat; I couldn't concentrate at college even though there were only a few days left until the holidays. I had no idea how much time had passed. *Time*.

"You need to eat, love," my dad said, placing yet another plate of food in front of me. I didn't bother looking to see what it was. I wasn't hungry…

Day passed into night. Night passed into day. Messages came. Sam. Sam. Louisa. Sam. Louisa. Voicemails blinked. I'd turned my phone off eventually. Then that voice was there…

"I need to see her. Please, Pete. I just want to talk."

"I don't think that's a good idea."

I felt exhausted…of everything; of life. I was frozen. I just couldn't find the will to do this anymore. I'd been through too much and I needed to breathe.

"Ava? Your dad asked me to come and see you. We should make the most of our time off. Do you want to go out?"

"No, thanks," I mumbled, watching as Louisa got up

and left again.

His voice.

"Ava, please! Just let me in. I need to talk to you."

A glimpse of his face before my Dad swept him out again.

Weeks passed, then it all stopped. No more messages. No more voicemails. No more visits. No more of those eyes. No more of that voice. No more Sam. My insides screamed in agony, but the fact was I didn't have the energy to do anything about it. I was tired of fighting, and what if…what if seeing him made it all real? What if I was too late? What if I'd already lost him? How long ago had I found out the truth? My heart ached when I thought of his horrified gaze as I'd left without a word. I couldn't even begin to imagine how he felt now. All I knew, was how terrible I felt.

"Ava?"

I was huddled under the bus stop watching the rain. It was the first day back after two weeks of holiday. It hadn't really registered with me, but now I was back. I should have been in English, but half way there, I'd found myself changing direction. Instead, I'd walked to the bus stop, in spite of the dreadful weather. I couldn't face people, my dad included. I'd decided to wait here until it was time to leave.

"Ava, honey?" came the voice again.

I looked up into luminous green eyes.

"Ava…"

"Seline?" I uttered, confused.

"Yes," she said, smiling kindly and placing a hand on my shoulder.

"Seline," I whispered. Seline was here and relief swept over me. Without warning, everything I'd felt over the last weeks crumbled inside me as a sob escaped my lips. She encircled me in her arms, just as my mum would have done if she'd still been here. My face was pressed into her woollen coat and I clung to her as if my life depended on it. I was sure I caught a lingering aroma of Sam, which only made me sob louder.

"Seline. I'm sorry," I said, sniffing, "I just can't… I couldn't…"

"Come on," she whispered, putting an arm around my shoulder and walking me down the road. I didn't know where we were going, but I didn't care—then I stopped in my tracks, fear suddenly gripping me. I had to know.

"Seline. Sam…" I hadn't uttered his name in weeks and it caught in my throat.

"He's alive," she said. I breathed a sigh of relief and watched her walk towards a small red car, which was parked on the side of the road. "Get in," she said. I climbed in after her without a word, but as we began to drive, something felt wrong. Seline was too quiet and her eyes seemed too fixed on the road ahead.

"Seline?"

"Yes?" She was avoiding my eye contact and the relief that had come so easily only moments before, disappeared.

"Seline. What's wrong?" I watched as her lips pursed and she looked almost on the brink of tears. "Seline!"

She glanced at me. "He's not well, Ava… and not like last time. He won't recover from this if it gets worse, and he's refusing everything I can do for him." His time was running out. I felt sick with anger.

"Why? Why is he refusing?" I demanded, already knowing the truth. Seline glanced in my direction, but she didn't elaborate. I already knew why he was refusing her help. "I'll make him then," I said resolvedly.

How long had it been? Was there enough time left to save him?

The rest of the journey was silent and fixed on the destination. As we reached the tiny farmhouse, all I could think was that I wouldn't let Sam die, especially because of me.

Following Seline inside the tiny cottage, the cool air hit me and I had to pull my coat around me. Seline nodded towards the tiny front room, and as I watched her go to the kitchen, I turned and opened the door. The room was dimly lit with the curtains closed, and when I saw Sam, I had to stifle a gasp. He was slouched on the sofa with his head lolling in front of him, only half conscious, and I could see that his hands were cracked like stone, crumbling at the ends.

I went to him and sat down as gently as I could. His head heaved up to look at me, but my blood ran cold at his gaze. His complexion was flecked grey like rock, and it was almost as if the whites of his eyes had leaked into his pupils. They had turned a pale grey colour, and I strained to see the glint I was used to; I found nothing. It was as if I was staring into a stranger's eyes. There was no recognition in them, and I felt a wave of fear rush over me. He didn't know me. It was as if he was gone already, and when his head lolled forwards again, I felt tears prick at my eyes.

"Sam," I whispered, hoping that he was still there enough to know who I was, but he simply rested his head on the back of the sofa and closed his eyes. Panic bubbled inside me. I had done this. I needed to help, but I didn't know how. Looking to the door in hope that Seline would come back soon, I felt myself flinch. Sam's ice-cold hand had curled around my own, sending goosebumps prickling up my arm.

"Sam," I gasped, relief flooding through my veins as I curled my hand round his fingers as gently as I could.

"I'm sorry," I said, tears slipping from my eyes as I turned his delicate hand over in mine. "You're so cold." It felt as if he'd been outside for hours, and I wondered if he could even feel the pressure of my hand in his.

Looking around the room, I noticed a blanket draped across the side of the sofa. Pulling it over, I proceeded to lay it across Sam's body, making him strain his eyes to look at me.

"No," he grumbled, as if speaking through gravel and pushed the blanket off onto the floor. I began to feel useless. I was out of my depth and I wondered why Seline thought I could help. My presence didn't appear to be making any difference and I doubted he even knew it was me. He was a ghost of the Sam I knew and, perhaps, he'd made this decision regardless of my opinion of him. Maybe he wanted to die. At this thought, my earlier resolve slipped, and I wondered if I was doing the right thing. If Sam wanted to die, who was I to stop him? Getting up from the sofa, I tiptoed from the room and down the hallway to the kitchen.

I found Seline leaning over something at the stove, her back to me. "Seline?" I whispered, trying to hold back the tears threatening to bubble over again, but feeling the ache of a lump in my throat. "I know he's dying." I didn't know how to put what I thought into words, but before I could even attempt it, Seline whipped around to face me.

"Over here," she commanded, turning back to the stove. "You're going to help me give this to him, okay?" Her tone was stern and I knew in that moment that she'd never accept what I had to say.

Walking over to her, I looked into the pot on the stove as she chucked in what looked like beef jerky. I had a sneaking suspicion it was something much grizzlier than that. As she stirred it in, the brown broth turning into thick black tar, the smell hit me and I coughed unexpectedly. The concoction smelt like a mix between petrol, liquorice and soil.

"What *is* that?" I croaked.

"This—" Seline said, ladling a thick dollop into a small basin, "is what's keeping his clock ticking." She held the bowl out to me. I looked down to its contents without taking it. "This is a much stronger dose than normal. He hasn't had any in…a while." I knew she meant since I had avoided him. Taking a deep breath, I reached to take the bowl carefully between my hands and was surprised by how cool it was.

"Be careful, though. It holds a lot of magic, which, strictly speaking, I shouldn't be using," said Seline, marching from the kitchen towards the front room. As I followed her through the tiny house, I began to feel apprehensive about what was in store for Sam and how much pain he would have to endure. Selfishly, I also wondered how much of his pain I would be able to endure myself. I didn't like the idea of having to sit on the sidelines and watch him suffer.

Entering the tiny front room, I glanced at Sam and wondered if it was possible for him to have worsened since I had left the room five minutes ago. He looked a darker grey colour and his chest heaved up and down as he took huge, difficult breaths. Sweat trickled down his stony face and his jaw was set, concealing his pain. His discomfort made me feel helpless, and I didn't understand how I could possibly make him see sense. As Seline took over however, I dared to hope. She moved to hold her hand just above his chest, not quite touching him, but deciding something as she turned to me expectantly.

"Where do you want this?" I asked, aware that I was still holding what was effectively a bowl of dark magic, but she simply looked me up and down with intent. She was different tonight, on edge, and I couldn't work out why. When I placed the bowl on the floor where she pointed, she turned to me and placed her hands on my shoulders.

"Ava," she said, looking me in the eyes, "you have to do this."

I stared at her in shock and began shaking my head. "Seline, I—I can't—" I stammered, but Sam's gruff voice interrupted me.

"Ava—" He opened his eyes to meet mine. His eyes were glazed in grey, but his expression was level as he took a deep rattling breath and managed to speak.

"Please, Ava. I trust you." I stared at him apprehensively, panic setting in as the enormity of what Sam was asking dawned on me. I glanced at Seline skeptically, but she looked back at me with as much unease as I felt. She held out a small cloth and started to explain.

"Just apply the ointment to the black marks," she said. "It sounds straight forward, but you have to understand that this is black magic and black magic isn't kind to its users." Pushing the cloth into my hand and giving me a stiff, encouraging smile. "If you need me, I'll be right outside," she whispered in a hushed tone, then brushed past me and closed the door behind her, leaving me looking down at the cloth in my hand.

I turned to Sam whose muscles tensed and relaxed with every breath. He was getting worse by the second. Straining to open his eyes, he stared at me through the fog of pain. He was asking me to do it now.

I could feel my hands clamming up as I started towards him, but I needed to do this. Moving the bowl around to the other side of his legs, I sat gently on the sofa next to him and was reminded of the motions I had gone through last time I'd sat here with him, wiping the blood from his skin. That had been a useless exercise, but now, I was attempting to save his life. You can do this, I told myself, you need to do this for Sam—or you lose him.

Taking a deep breath, I thought about where I should start. I knew that he had the marks on his arms and chest, and I'd noticed a small glint on his back before. I sighed, resining myself to the fact that I would probably have to undress him.

"Sam?" I said nervously. "Seline said I have to put the ointment on your marks, okay?" I waited, but all I got as a reply was a groan that sounded so guttural, I was sure I could feel his pain. Hesitantly, I reached for his shoulders and heaved him forwards. He was broad shouldered, muscular and not easy the move, but I just managed to lean him against my chest. His stared at me irritably as I tugged at the hem of his t-shirt.

"Sorry, I need to take off your shirt," I whispered, feeling the heat in my cheeks. As Sam simply glared at me, I took the bottom hem and pulled it up and over his head, revealing his bare tattooed torso. I'd seen the tattoos once before, but they were usually a vibrant black, like pure ink. Today they were lighter, like white burn scars on grey crumbling rock, and I couldn't stop myself from reaching out to touch his skin. It felt rough and cold and lifeless.

It was then that I noticed that the marks were all words, intertwined and nonsensical, as if someone had dropped the words from a book straight onto his chest. Some were large and some words were tiny, but they were all there, as if being shouted out onto the night air: *I should have, I never, I could have, he never knew.* It came rushing at me like an enormous gust of wind. They were wishes—wishes of the deceased; voices forever etched on Sam's skin. In an instant, I wanted to read all of them and search for any signs of my mum or Zac, but I bit back the temptation. A strained noise echoed through the tiny room and Sam's back arched off of the sofa, unable to contain the agony any longer. It was time.

Leaning down, I dipped the cloth into the bowl of tar,

making sure that it didn't touch my own skin, and brought it hesitantly to Sam's chest. I didn't know what his reaction would be to the magic, but I took a breath and pressed the cloth onto the marks with purpose.

As soon as it touched his skin, his eyes flicked open and filled with fierce agonizing pain. He growled at me in anger and breathed fiercely through the torment. I kept a steady eye contact with him, watching the grey of his eyes ripple as if something had landed in a deep pool. His body went taught with anger as his eyes began to flicker, but he wasn't looking at me. Something was revealing itself to him, which I couldn't see. What was this magic doing to him? What did it make him see? Taking the cloth away and watching his face soften again, I knew that the magic was affecting him in ways I couldn't even imagine—I wasn't sure I could bring myself to continue inflicting this pain on him.

Waveringly reaching down, I dipped the cloth in the tar again and looked to Sam's chest where I had dabbed the ointment. I frowned. It had seeped into his skin and disappeared completely, but the marks were becoming stronger again. It was like ink, darkening the marks on his body. The magic was revitalizing Sam and giving him life—giving him time. This was what Seline had concocted to help him. Was this how they were trying to break the curse? Could it even be broken, or would Sam be forced to endure this every time he needed more time? I felt sick in the pit of my stomach. Sam couldn't be the bad guy. I knew that however tough this became, I had to carry on.

Meeting his gaze apologetically, I pushed the cloth

onto the next patch of embellished skin and clenched my own teeth as another rumble of pain issued from his lips. His eyes became fire again, and he stared at me with loathing as I stared back at him with resolve. No matter how much he despised me for inflicting this pain on him, I was determined to force my own feelings back at him. I loved him and I wanted him to know. I hadn't realised until this moment, but it was true, and it had taken me to the brink of losing him to figure it out. I was completely and desperately in love with him.

Again and again, I forced the black magic into his body, and each time his pain became more intense, but I knew that this was saving his life and giving him more time. I thought hard about my feelings and at points, I almost felt as if he could see my thoughts. I hoped he could and I hoped that, somehow, they would make this horrible process more bearable.

After what seemed like hours, I began struggling to keep my eyes open, and I knew that it must be getting late. I looked at my phone and saw that it was only nine though and thankfully I'd had the insight to message Dad earlier. I'd told him I was staying at Louisa's for a study night. I knew it was wrong to lie to him, but when I'd been in the car with Seline earlier today, I'd known it was going to be a long night. I'd been right.

I was emotionally and mentally exhausted, and Sam's breathing had become even more labored. He looked exhausted to the point of passing out, but his skin had far more colour and the cracks on his hands had slithered away. Whatever I was administering was working, but we weren't done yet. There was still around a quarter of the tar left.

"Almost there," I offered, forcing a small smile onto my face, but he looked back despondently. The colour had returned to his eyes, but the shadows remained. I just hoped Sam was still in there somewhere. It was clear that the dark magic was torturing him, and I wondered what demons he was being forced to face. I knew I had to push on. I needed to finish the task and I needed to be strong about it.

"I have to do your back," I said as confidently as I could, blinking furiously against my own exhaustion. I expected a groan of impatience, but he stared back at me as if remembering something. It was the first sign of humanity he had shown all night. I allowed a glimmer of hope to ignite inside me, but the feeling was short lived, taken over instead by a sense of impending doom.

"There's a mark…on my back…you haven't seen before…" he said with some effort. His voice was quiet and strained, but it no longer sounded like he was talking through a throat made from shards of rock. As he heaved himself up into a sitting position, he looked at me with fear.

"It's okay." I sighed, feeling drained of all emotion. In the last month, I'd experienced my friend's death, discovered witches existed and I'd found out that Sam could see death coming. Surely, he could give me a little credit? "Just turn around," I said, resigning myself to the fact that it would be something bad.

He hesitated. "Please… don't leave again," he pleaded, fixing me with that obsidian stare. Then he turned to face the door, revealing the marks I'd not seen before.

An ancient clock face marked with roman numerals stretched across Sam's entire back and encircled a figure cloaked entirely in black material that flowed and entwined around the clock hands, rippling across Sam's shoulder blades as he moved. Around the outside of the clock there swirled various faces and as I moved closer, I could just make out that they all held varying expressions: grief, terror, sadness and even peace. It was an intricate design and I couldn't help but marvel at it.

"It's stunning," I breathed, running my finger across a silver blade that followed the curve of the clock, then dropped down to the small of Sam's back.

"No, Ava," came Sam's wearied voice. "It's the mark of the cursed." I frowned in confusion and stared at the image embroidered on his back. As I did so, things came together in my mind, like someone pulling a thread that weaved two halves together. Everything snapped into place and I stared in terrified disbelief.

The blade that the figure was holding was a scythe and the hand holding it was pale and bony. This wasn't just any figure. This was a figure used and known throughout different cultures; the figure that stretched back into history. This was the figure that haunted the living and the dead alike: the representation of death in living form. This was the Grim Reaper.

As if he heard my brain figure it all out, Sam slowly turned to face me with a stoic look in his eyes. I shook my head as I struggled to accept this horrifying truth. He gave a faint nod, confirming what he was, and I gasped as my heart fluttered uneasily in my chest. I immediately shuffled back on the sofa.

"You come for people," I whispered as he continued to stare at me. "You come for people when they're about to die?" The silence was deafening and seemed to stretch on forever as I waited for him to answer.

"Yes," he whispered.

I held back a sob. "Did you come for Zac?"

"Yes."

I looked at him, frozen to the spot. I needed to ask another question; a question that I almost couldn't bring myself to ask for fear of what the answer would be. "Did you come for my mum?"

He stared at me for a long while and the tension stretched out between us, then he nodded silently. I held my breath and took in this information, but it was too much and my eyes pooled with tears. I shivered in the cool of the cottage and felt the rising waters of panic in my chest. My whole body was trembling in fear. He'd taken my mum. *That* was how he got time. I was unable to speak. Sam was *death*; the thing that had haunted my nightmares and tortured me for months; the thing that had altered my very soul and changed me into a person I thought I'd never become.

I couldn't look him in the eyes. He moved towards me slowly and cautiously, as if I were a wild animal that he needed to be careful not to scare, but I couldn't have moved if I'd tried. I was frozen to the spot, incapacitated by shock. As he placed his hands gently on my shoulders, I felt the tears well over my eyes and run down my cheeks. Now, my unexplainable unease around Sam from day one made sense, but I'd never imagined it could be this. I'd debated cults and super powers, but never an infamous figure from throughout the ages. I stared down at my twisted hands.

"Ava?" His voice seemed unsure and as his hand brushed my cheek, I felt a rush of panic. I'd been so stupid. I'd sensed Sam was someone to avoid, but I'd pushed the feelings deep down inside of me. Now I was facing it head on, watching in horror as this scenario played out in front of me, unable to stop it.

Standing up suddenly, I dropped the cloth on the floor and walked from the room, all the while feeling his eyes on me. I needed to get away from him. I marched through the tiny dark hallway and my skin crawled with guilt. I'd trusted him. I loved him; but he'd killed my mum.

CHAPTER Twenty-Two

My hands slammed into the back door and I stumbled out onto the patio at the back of the house, gasping in the chilly air. Evening mist had settled, and as I searched the immediate area, my heart raced. I hoped Seline had been true to her word and stayed home. I needed to see her. Maybe she'd tell me this was all a cruel joke.

"Seline?" I shouted. My vision was blurred with tears as I scrambled up the grass verge onto the damp lawn. My shoes slipped and I was sure my jeans must be covered in green stains, but I didn't look back. I staggered upright and brushed past the ferns where I had hidden only a few nights ago. It all came flooding back to me, and I wondered if *that* Sam would have taken my life had Seline given him the chance.

Rounding the huge lolloping branches, I breathed a sigh of relief. A small wooden sun house came into view, dotted with fairy lights, and I could just see Seline inside, dozing in a chair. As I approached and stepped up onto the decking, I knocked gently on the window.

"Seline?" I said, watching as my breath cast white puffs into the air. Her eyes flickered open and when she saw my tear stained face, she hurried to the door, concern etched on her face.

"What is it?" she said, ushering me inside. "Did he hurt you? Are you okay?" She held my face in both her hands and searched my eyes, but all I could do was nod as tears continued to stream down my face.

"Ava? What happened?" I opened and closed my mouth as I tried to think of something coherent to say. "I knew this was a bad idea…" she began.

"I know—" I managed to stammer.

"It was a stupid idea! I'm so sorry, Ava, honey," she said, stopping and standing up straight. "What state is he in? Do I need to use magic?" She stared at me with a kind of feared anticipation.

I shook my head. "No, he's fine. I'm fine. I just—I found out," I sniffed. "I found out what he is, Seline. He showed me the rest of the markings on his back. I know he came for my mum." I broke down into full blown sobs, my vision blurring completely. Seline pulled me into a tight embrace, and I cried until her cardigan was damp with my tears and I had nothing left to give. I couldn't believe I'd been so stupid. It seemed so obvious now that I knew the truth, but it had suddenly made everything more complicated. I was beginning to realise why Sam had held off telling me. I was in deep now, and even if I'd wanted to leave, I wasn't sure that I could.

"He's wanted to tell you from day one," Seline said with sympathy, pulling me to sit down on the tiny cushioned bench beside her. I was exhausted and as I flopped down beside her, I wasn't sure I had the energy or the space left for empathy.

"He still took my mum," I uttered. I thought about all the times I'd let him comfort me, and I felt like I'd wronged my mum. He'd taken her *life.* What was I doing? He was the Grim Reaper.

"I know, Ava," said Seline, "but he's also risking his existence to be with you. He knows what he's done and he's known all along that when you found out who he was, you'd probably walk away."

"Then why bother?" I said, watching as Seline flinched at my words. "What's the point if he knew I'd walk away all along?"

"People can be very selfish with their own feelings," she said, a wistful smile spreading onto her face, "especially people like Sam."

"What do you mean?" I huffed.

"Imagine only ever feeling the things those feel in their last moments of life… Now imagine what love must feel like in comparison to those feelings." Seline's eyes were wide with wonder as she gazed at me, then she looked towards the door.

I followed her gaze to Sam, standing at the end of the dark lawn, watching us. Even as he stood further than fifteen feet away, I could feel his eyes boring into my own. Only moments before, I had stared into those same eyes, forcing my thoughts into his head. Little had I known that those same eyes had stared into my mum's as she had taken her last breaths. All I could think was that he knew how she felt when she died. Goosebumps trickled along my arms, and I forced myself to tear my eyes away from his.

"I imagine you can empathise with Sam more than

most," said Seline. I swallowed at the lump in my throat but it wouldn't budge. I was so confused. I was sure that I loved Sam, but those feelings were in conflict with the part of me that just wanted to scream at him.

I looked back up at him, but all I could see was the conflict in my own eyes as my reflection in the window pane stared back at me. I didn't know what to do, but the decision was taken out of my hands as Seline got up and opened the tiny wood framed door. Sam paced forwards and my heart started beating faster and faster until I thought it might break a rib. Squeezing past Seline into the tiny shed, Sam gazed at me apprehensively. I felt cautious in his presence as if he was a stranger. Fear of the unknown.

Lowering my eyes, I edged across the bench, allowing him space to sit down, but leaving space between us. I shivered. Although the tiny door was open, I knew it wasn't the cold making me react like this. Sam sat down next to me, but, as if he'd known what I was thinking, he left a small space between us.

"I'll leave you to talk," Seline muttered, giving me one last encouraging smile before leaving.

At that moment, Sam stood up and towered over me. I immediately withdrew, but as he sat back down, he produced a blanket, which he proceeded to drape around my shoulders. A peace offering. The blanket settled around my shoulders and as we sat in silence, listening to the pitter patter of mist droplets on the roof, I started to relax.

I met his gaze and was knocked back by what I saw. His eyes reflected everything I felt: fear, anxiety, wonder and love, but they held something else, too—patience. I knew in that moment that he'd wait for me, however long it took, to understand and accept him. I watched as his eyes searched my face for something other than hate.

"I don't hate you, if that's what you think," I whispered, feeling the heat rise in my face. I hated having to explain my feelings. I knew that I didn't hate Sam. I knew it as soon I saw the turmoil he was in. He knew he'd done something potentially unforgiveable, but I also knew that he cared for me.

"I can deal with hate. I expect you to hate me," he said certainly. "I just don't know what I'd do if you were afraid…" He trailed off and watched me.

"I am afraid," I admitted.

Sam's whole demeanor immediately changed, and I watched as all hope left his face. His shoulders dropped, along with his gaze, and he let his head fall forwards. He sighed, running his hands over his face.

"But that doesn't mean I'm going to walk away," I said. Sam's head snapped up, his eyes all over my face. "My mum always taught me to face my fears," I said simply, staring back at him. "And if that means facing you and letting you know how I really feel, then that's what I'll do."

"Now I'm afraid," he said, shifting to face me apprehensively, waiting for the onslaught. I took a deep breath and readied myself to voice my thoughts. My hands were already sweating and I had to rub them on my jeans.

"I don't hate you…" I mumbled, thinking of how to word everything in my head. "I don't hate you because, somehow, I trust that you would do the right thing."

Sam opened his mouth to speak, but I held up a hand, silencing him. It was hard to talk about my mum and even harder when Sam was watching me with such intensity. The lump grew in my throat, but I was determined to speak my mind.

"But I do need to know what happened and how all of this works because I think you're still trying to protect me and I need to know the truth. I can handle it, Sam," I said, feeling more confident as I spoke. "I feel like I've betrayed my own mum. I feel like I've been stupid for trusting you, and now the guilt is eating me up inside. It's unbearable."

I stopped and took a breath to compose myself, and as Sam continued to watch me, I couldn't stop the flip in my stomach as his eyes met mine. Tearing my gaze away, I continued with determination, closing my eyes in concentration.

"I'm angry with you for keeping so many secrets from me and I'm angry with you for believing that I would just walk away from you—after everything that's happened." The tears started rolling down my cheeks and I breathed angrily through them. I had so many feelings bursting inside me and it was hard to sort through them all. As I opened my eyes and looked at Sam, I became aware of something else I needed to say.

"And I'm mad with you for making me feel the way you do. I'm mad at you because it feels completely fine even after you took away my mum." I gasped for breath and wiped away my tears in frustration. "I'm just mad at you because I never imagined this is how I'd fall in love."

I finished, shocked at myself. The words had tumbled from my mouth before I could stop them; it was like I'd opened the flood gates to all my feelings and I no longer had control over what came out.

Sam's breathing quickening as he looked wildly over my face in shock. As I watched him, I realised the enormity of what I had just said to him. The heat rose in my face as I waited for him to respond. I began to worry that he didn't feel the same way about me. Before I could think any more about it, he kissed me hard on the lips with a hunger so desperate it scared me.

I'd never been kissed that way before and I kissed him back hesitantly at first. As his strong arms circle around my back, a warmth spread through my lungs and I felt safe in his arms. I allowed myself to revel in the feelings inside me, pushing away the feelings of unease. I kissed him back with just as much need, but was disappointed when he broke away from the kiss and put his lips to my ear.

"I love you too, Ava—more than I can explain." His voice was unsteady and breathy as he proceeded to slowly plant more kisses along my jaw to my lips, where I eagerly kissed him back again. The night's events were suddenly thrown from my mind, as if someone had tossed a black sheet over them and all I could see was Sam.

All the feelings inside me were exploding like thousands of tiny bombs all going off at once. As he continued to kiss me, he moved even closer, pressing his body against mine. His warmth radiated through his t-shirt and I breathed deeply, wanting to inhale that smell of Sam. Leaning over me further, I felt my resolve slip as

I let him press me back on the cushions. My own hands were instantly in his hair, pulling him closer. I could feel the weight of his upper body on me and the uneven rhythm of his chest matching my own breathing, but it still wasn't enough. I'd never felt this all-consuming rush inside me before—then he pulled away, sitting up.

I stared at him wide eyed, as I sat up too, still breathless and a little embarrassed. He met my gaze with a dark, hazy stare. "Sorry," he muttered. I smiled coyly as he planted another lingering kiss on my lips. "I'm not used to these kind of feelings," he said and for the first time, he looked almost as awkward as I did.

Blushing furiously at his words, I fiddled with the hem of my t-shirt. "Me neither," I mumbled, feeling light headed.

"Ava." Sam's face was serious as I looked up at him. "We will talk," he said, taking my hands in his. "When you want to know about your mum, I'll tell you whatever you want to know. You're right—you need the truth."

When I looked at him, his expression held more than any words could ever convey and I knew in that moment: if it took a lifetime for me to forgive him, he'd spend a lifetime waiting.

It was then I felt that already overwhelming feeling inside me swell and become something akin to fear and pain and joy all at once.

CHAPTER *Twenty-Three*

The following morning, I awoke with a start and found Sam standing above me, holding a mug of tea. I blinked up at him.

"Morning, beautiful," he chimed, sitting down on the side of the bed with a grin on his face. "I like you in my bed."

I was in Sam's bed? I sat up and looked around the room. Clothes were strewn across the back of a desk chair and books were piled in the corner of the room on a shelf. I'd only been in his room once before, when he'd been ill that time. Now, I knew better than that. I breathed in and a deep, warming aroma filled my nose. It was the same smell that knocked me senseless every time Sam was near. He held out the thick hand pottered mug in his hand, the steam escaping into the air.

"Thanks," I muttered and took it from him. I was suddenly very aware of the tiny camisole I was wearing, making me feel naked. I always felt aware of every inch of my skin around Sam. As I hugged the duvet to my chest, I blew on the tea and let my mind wander. A jolt of embarrassment ran through me and I looked warily at

Sam.

"Where did you sleep?" I asked with what I hoped sounded like casual curiosity. I vaguely remembered ascending the stairs to bed, but I couldn't remember where Sam had slept. I jumped at the thought that I might have slept next to him. He ran a hand through his scruffy bed hair with a look of deep amusement on his face.

"Don't worry, you didn't corrupt me. I slept on the sofa." He laughed quietly to himself and I watched him, amused too.

I shuffled upright to drink my tea and it was just cool enough not to burn my mouth. It immediately warmed me, making me feel more awake. I needed to be alert around Sam. I knew what I felt for him was real, but I still needed a few details. I'd never thought of the Grim Reaper having any kind of humanity before yesterday. In fact, before yesterday, I'd never really given the Grim Reaper much thought at all.

Having realised I hadn't spoken in a good few minutes, I looked up at Sam, but he appeared to be lost in thought too. He was staring mildly at the duvet on my knees, and I immediately wanted to know what he was thinking. I wondered if he was thinking about me, but decided not to broach that subject. Instead, I decided to find out what had happened last night after our kiss. I remembered talking for a while and feeling completely exhausted. Sam had wrapped the blanket around us and I must have fallen asleep.

"So…" I whispered, cupping my hands around the mug and pulling my knees up to my chest. "Why did you sleep on the sofa?" I wasn't sure why I was asking. I was glad that he had, but I still wanted to know why. A small smile crept onto his face and I knew he was weighing whether to tease me further.

"I slept on the sofa…" he said, "because you fell asleep in Seline's garden room. I brought you up here to bed and you sprawled out. You were completely out of it."

"Oh," I muttered, a little abashed. I couldn't remember as much, but I did vaguely remember feeling exhausted. I still felt groggy and if truth be told, a little tetchy.

I tucked another stray lock of hair behind my ear. The window was open a crack and a breeze kept blowing strands of hair around me, making me feel like Medusa.

"You're funny in the morning—kind of like a grumpy dwarf," said Sam.

I cocked an eyebrow at him. "And you're far too happy in the morning," I said. He laughed. I couldn't help but smile back, despite how I felt. I'd slept through the whole night, but it felt like I hadn't slept at all. My eyelids were heavy and my head was muzzy with tiredness.

I leant over to place my mug on Sam's bedside table and became unpleasantly aware of how much my body ached, as if I'd used muscles I never knew I had. I'd only ever felt like this once before, when my mum had forced me to do a kettlebell gym class with her, but now I wondered if I was coming down with something. Putting my hand to my forehead, I briefly wondered if I'd be able to convince my teacher to send me home.

"You okay?" Sam asked. He'd been watching my

every move.

"Yeah," I mumbled, looking at him, "I just ache. I think it must be adrenaline."

"Well, I do have that effect on women," he said, smirking, and lifted the duvet covers to slide in next to me. I immediately felt the warmth of his body against my bare legs, making me blush. I slid over, careful to avoid any further body contact, but it didn't go unnoticed. He shifted next to me, his eyebrows raised in question.

"What?" I said with an air of confident innocence, but was knocked back by his expression. A tiny, soft smile crept onto his face and his eyes crinkled the way boy's eyes do when they like you.

"I make you nervous," he stated, his eyes still smiling.

"I make *you* nervous," I said, feeling tiny explosions going off in the depths of my stomach. I was nervous, but not because of what he was. What was more thrilling, was that I knew I made him nervous too.

"You're not wrong," he said, but his demeanor changed as he searched my face, his expression turning serious. "You know… you don't look all that good actually."

"Ouch," I said, with sarcasm.

"No. You look peaky."

"Wow, you really know how to make a girl feel good."

"You would know…" he said, amusement flooding his face. I knew he was winding me up again, but I still felt the tiny jump of nerves inside me. Being in such close proximity to Sam when he was being this flirtatious had to be bad for you. I glanced sidelong at him as I recalled the way he'd kissed me last night. There had been such a vulnerable human side to him yesterday, but now, he seemed to be back to his normal, confident self. In fact, I was sure he felt better than me today, and I felt a selfish bout of pride envelop me. *I* had helped him. The fact that he would never have been in that state if I'd only spoken to him before, however, was a fact I was willing to push aside for—oh, I don't know—the rest of my life.

Sam's car was a far smoother ride than my own car. I wasn't sure how he was achieving this feat on these roads, which seemed to be littered with pot holes and huge gaping puddles covering half of the road. It had rained most of the night, not that I had been aware of this. I still couldn't quite believe how fuzzy my memory was, and I was beginning to think Seline's magic had something to do with it.

I'd raced home this morning for a shower and a change of clothes before college, but only to Sam's insistence that he drive me there. When I'd gone upstairs, I'd left a very tired looking Dad behind with Sam. "Good Luck," I'd muttered under my breath, but as a small smile played about Sam's lips, I knew he'd heard.

When I'd emerged from the bathroom fifteen minutes later feeling clean, but still a little out of sorts, I'd heard them talking. I knew I shouldn't have, but I moved closer to the stairs.

"So, these friends of yours… they don't sound like a

good bunch."

"They're okay, but I crossed a line."

"We all make our fair share of mistakes in this life, son, but what they did to you wasn't right. You understand?" I couldn't help but smile. If only he knew how much more life experience Sam probably had compared to him.

"Yes, sir," said Sam and I could tell he was smiling too. I held my towel around me as I moved away from the stairs, then I heard Sam's voice again.

"I just hope you don't think your daughter is making a mistake with me." I heard my dad grunt in response and I cringed.

"My daughter is a clever girl," he said with a long sigh, "but she's been through a lot, and she's a little different to the Ava I knew. She's changed, and I know she's finding her feet in a new world; one without her mum."

A new world.

"I understand," said Sam.

"I know you do..." Then there was silence, but it wasn't awkward; they'd come to an understanding. When I'd appeared ten minutes later, they had both been smiling. It had made me smile too, looking at these two men who cared more about me than anything or anyone else.

As Sam's car splashed through settled water, the memory of that conversation made me smile, and I rested my head back and watched as the spray threw itself into the hedge. I began to recall the journey I'd made here only months ago. I'd been dreading the move to Willow

Farm. I'd still been living in the depths of grief and I'd been certain that I wasn't ready to move on. It felt wrong somehow, to try to start afresh when I hadn't had closure from the past. But then, life seemed to have a strange way of righting itself. I'd come to the conclusion over the last few months that whatever came your way was what was supposed to be.

So much had happened since that day, yet, it all seemed right, and I was beginning to remember what it was to feel normal. I wasn't quite there, but it was like a crack in the curtains in the depths of night – you were rewarded with a small glimpse of daylight. It wasn't quite enough to get up for, but enough to be reminded that another day would come.

Glancing over at Sam, I saw the irony in death himself making me feel more alive than anything or anyone else. I'd barely even noticed that I'd begun to emerge from the mist, and although I knew it would hang over my head for a while, at least now I could see through it. Maybe there was hope. I knew there was no chance of returning to who I once was. No amount of anything could leave a soul unchanged, but maybe I would emerge as if from a chrysalis, an altered soul ready for a different way of living. After all, I had no desire to return to the girl I was before my mum had died. That girl was strong, but not as strong as the girl I was now. I felt like I'd lived now, and I was glad for the pain I'd come through; there was no going back.

I needed to live my life and make the most of the present, but right now I was exhausted. So much had happened, and my body ached. I shuffled in my seat to try to get comfy, but to no avail, and I was beginning to seriously reconsider college.

As I glanced over at Sam, I couldn't help but feel a little put out. His eyes were alert, his complexion was clear and he practically radiated energy. I couldn't help but wonder at how he had transformed in only a matter of hours. He'd been so close to death last night, if that's what you would call ceasing to exist; I wasn't entirely sure it was the same thing anymore.

Catching my reflection in the wing mirror, I thought *I* looked closer to turning to dust than he did. What on earth had Seline's magic done to me? I looked horrendous. Turning to Sam, I opened my mouth to speak, but closed it again when I saw the look on his face. He seemed lost in thought as he looked hard at the road, but for once, his thoughts didn't cast shadows under his eyes. He looked almost content. I could tell it had been a huge weight off his shoulders, revealing the truth last night. I knew in that moment I'd done the right thing by telling him how I felt. I still had questions, but for today they could wait.

As I watched him drive, I saw his demeanor change fractionally. You might not have noticed it, had you not known him, but I was becoming obsessively tuned in with his every move. I couldn't help myself. Sam's brow had furrowed marginally, giving his discontent away, and I could see the muscles in his upper arms were taught, as if ready to react. What was he aware of that I wasn't?

"Sam?" I asked hesitantly, eyeing his fingers, which gripped the steering wheel until they had turned white at the ends. Something was bothering him, but he ignored me, glancing briefly into the mirror at my side. Without warning, he turned left, slamming me into the side of the car. Pain lanced up the side of my arm. "Sam, what—"

"We're being followed," he said, his voice thick. I turned to look behind us and felt stupid for not noticing before. We were being followed by a slim silver car with blacked out windows. It wasn't a familiar car, but the way it tailed us made a shiver run through me.

I watched the side mirror with scrutiny as Sam drove us along a straight country road with open fields on either side. I half expected the silver car to turn off at some point, allowing us both to laugh at our overreaction, but as we drove on, that possibility became more and more unlikely. Sam had disregarded the route to Meadow Hill and had taken several random turns; tests to see if they followed. They followed each and every one without hesitation.

Glancing sideways, I could see that Sam's jaw was set in a hard line. Hurt showed in his face and it was then that I dared to ask the question that pounded in my mind. "Is it them?"

"Yes," replied Sam without a beat. He glanced in the wing mirror again as he breezed past the hedgerows. He'd rammed the gear into fifth and we were picking up speed fast, but the other car, smaller and faster, had gained headway. Sam swore under his breath as the tiny sports car inched to the edge of the road in an attempt to undertake us.

I looked at Sam apprehensively and gripped the edges of my seat, feeling the weight of the speed in my stomach. We must have climbed to over eighty miles per hour on the tiny road, and as I glanced in the wing mirror, I could just make out a male figure in the silver convertible. As it neared, Sam spoke. "Hold on."

Without further warning, he punched on the brakes sending the sports car racing beyond us as we took a sudden right. Hedgerows stretched above our heads on either side of the car and Sam put his foot down on the accelerator again, sending the cars suspension into overdrive as we bounced over several uneven mounds in the road. I grasped hold of the overhead handle.

"What do they want?" I said, glancing at Sam's tense shape in the driver's seat as I awaited the answer I already knew would come my way.

"You," he stated simply. I'd thought as much, but I still felt like the wind had been punched out of my lungs. I stared at Sam and he looked back so fiercely that I felt confident he'd do anything to stop them getting to me.

His eyes remained fixed ahead as we sped onwards, the only sound being the outstretched branches of nearby hedges brushing the side of the car. It was as if each whip of a branch was a thought passing through my mind. What did they want with me? Did they want Sam too? Did they want both of us? Was it my time to die? If it wasn't, why did they want me dead? Goosebumps raised on my arms as I thought about how they might do it, or would they make Sam do it? I already knew it was a possibility. Would it be quick? Would it be painless? As if reading my mind, Sam glanced briefly in my direction and spoke.

"I won't hurt you," he said, "and neither will they." The ferocity with which he said those words punched me in the lungs. I couldn't reply. I could speak even as we sped on, towards a junction.

"Ava?"

The junction was closing in. I closed my eyes in suspense and Sam swore loudly, punching on the brakes and jolting the car to the side. There was the tinge of pain in my ears as a forceful metallic scraping sound erupted around us and then I felt my sense of gravity flip in my stomach, pressure filling my head like a water balloon. My head hit the side of the car, sending ringing into my ears and blurred colour into my vision. My body whipped from side to side like a ragdoll, my seatbelt pinched my ribs, and I quickly realised the car was upside down, rolling and scraping along the road. Gravel and glass sprayed up into my face, making me scrunch up my eyes. It seemed fitting that this would be my end—then it all seemed to slow as the car tumbled across grass and came to a stop.

My ears were ringing and my heart was beating fast in my chest as I blinked dust from my eyes. I coughed. Something was hissing inside the car's engine, but all I could see was the foot-well below me. We were upside down in the car, but I was strapped in by my seatbelt, which was now cutting into my chest.

Through a crushed window to my side, I could see that we were lying on grass. I lifted the lead weight of my own head to look further out, but feet came into my view. Desperation lead me to force my arm up to undo my seatbelt with a click, allowing my body to crumple in on itself in the sea of glass and metal. Exhaust fumes filled my nose and I felt the car shift under me.

"Take my hand," came a familiar male voice, just as a strong arm appeared at my side. Without thinking, I took it and was pulled through the broken window.

I staggered up-right, pain lancing through my whole body, but as I looked at the overturned hunk of metal that had been Sam's car, I froze. In front of me stood Blake, Franco, Jules and one more, older male figure—Mr Jenson, whose hand was still on mine. I pulled my hand back and stared. Jules and Franco yanked Sam from the car and held him by the arms. He strained against their grip, but Jules swung his clenched fist into Sam's stomach, making him double over in pain and gasp for air.

"Sam!" I screamed, but as I tried to run, Blake moved fast and grabbed my waist. He pulled me backwards and wrapped his arms around me. The smell of fuel and cigarettes filled my nose as he gripped me hard to his chest.

"Get *off* me!" I screamed, trying to punch my way free, but he tightened his grip, crushing my already bruised and aching body. "You're hurting me," I whimpered, looking to Sam, who met my eyes from the floor. They were filled with apology.

"Boss? Where do you want the girl?" Blake called, huffing as he held his grip on me. Mr Jenson's eyes glinted as he took a step towards me. Tears brimmed at my eyes and my body began to shake involuntarily.

"Miss Blume…" His professional teacher voice had disappeared to be replaced by a lingering drawl which clung to my ears. "I hate to see you so distressed," he said, reaching for a strand of my hair and twisting it behind my ear. I wanted to scream at him to leave me alone, but I couldn't bring myself to take a breath to speak. All I could do was look into Mr Jenson's cold expression.

"You're a beautiful young woman." He tutted and shook his head dramatically. "I can see why he wants to keep you, but you see, Ava—he's been an insolent child and now he needs to be punished." He looked me up and down as if I were a specimen to be studied.

"What do you want with me?" I whispered. My voice was quieter than I'd expected and I kicked myself for sounding weak in front of him.

He smiled at me. "You don't know?" he spoke quietly, an edge of humour to his voice. I shook my head, wincing as pain shot through my neck. "Well, well, he *has* kept you in the dark, hasn't he?"

I glanced at Sam, but he was still slumped on his knees, his head hanging. I couldn't tell if he was hurt or ashamed. I kept my eyes fixed on him as Mr Jenson took a few paces back.

"You know, Ava," he mused, as if he were still in the classroom, "you're an amazing young woman. You're strong, intelligent, full of life. I see exactly why Sam has acted as he has, but he doesn't *deserve* you."

Mr Jenson turned to face me, but my eyes were still on Sam. He hadn't moved an inch and it was beginning to unnerve me. Amongst these men, he seemed so compliant, and I couldn't understand why. It wasn't him. He was so confident.

"My father used to tell me a story when I was young...about a boy who was sent to fetch a hen from the coop so his mother could use it in a stew." My eyes unwillingly slid to rest on the man in front of me. I raised an eyebrow at him, but he ignored it. Was he really going to roll into a story? Who was this man? The Mr Jenson from my English lessons had clearly all been an act.

"Yes, I remember it well. I think you'll like it, Sam," he said, glancing back at him. Sam's shoulder blades flexed as he heaved an agonizingly deep breath.

"You see, when the boy reached the coop, he saw how beautiful the creatures really were and he couldn't bring himself to take it to his mother for the chop, no matter how hungry he was. Instead, he hid the hens away and told his father that they had escaped." Mr Jenson leant his gangly frame over and pinched a blade of grass from the floor. He twisted it around his fingers.

"But, of course, his father knew that hens were not the brightest of creatures, and in no instance would they be able to escape. He took it upon himself to *find* the hens. He knew his son had hidden them somewhere as he knew his son well. He was soft, like his mother. So, at midnight, he went to bed as normal, an hour after his wife and son said goodnight—but he stayed awake. When he heard the click of his son's door, he followed him downstairs and out into the farm lands and beyond. From behind a tree he saw his foolish son feeding the now plump brown hens. He had kept them hidden in an old, long ago abandoned barn."

Blake coughed in what could have been humour, but his arms tightened around me, making me wince in pain. Mr Jenson looked at him disapproving as if he was merely a nuisance interrupting his teaching.

"When the boy was helping his mother the next day, his father crept into the barn and mixed rat poison into the hen's feed. Over the coming days, he watched as his son became downcast. He knew the hens must be dying. When the last one died, his son finally came to him and told him what had happened. The boy's father nodded and explained that this was simply the natural order of things. He owned up to poisoning the hens to teach him a lesson. He said man and animals cannot co-exist like this. He said that in life, there is a hierarchy whether we like it or not, and it is easier to accept it now." Mr Jenson stopped and turned to me. His expression was inquisitive and he obviously expected me to have something to say.

"So, you're teaching Sam a lesson because he made a mistake…" I mumbled, sarcastically, taking shallow breaths against the pain Blake was inflicting on me. "Where do I fit in?"

"My sweet Ava…" he said, moving even closer to me so I could feel his hot breath on my face, "*you* are both the mistake and the lesson." Before I could say another word, he whipped around and walked towards Sam. Fear penetrated my chest. This was it. Sam was right. They wanted me dead, but not because of something I had done, but because of Sam's feelings for me. They wanted to punish him for feeling something for me. I looked over at Sam, but as he lifted his head, Mr Jenson stood in front of him, concealing him from me.

"Take her to the car, Blake," he called over his shoulder. "Bind her wrists." Blake swiftly turned me, lifting me off the ground and slinging me over his broad shoulder.

"Put me down!" I screamed, kicking out hard, but his grip was strong and my efforts had no effect on him. I gave up, instead twisting my neck to try to see Sam, but I could only see Mr Jenson's tall frame over the grass verge. Suddenly, Blake loosened his grip so that I slid down his muscular frame. My feet came back down on the ground with a thud, and I was face to face with Blake. He held my wrists tight to his chest as I continued to struggle.

"Let me go," I whimpered, pushing him hard in the chest with little to no effect. The smell of leather and cigarettes penetrated my nostrils and I pushed harder against his chest, but that only increased his amusement. Reaching into his back pocket, he produced a length of rope and proceeded to tie it around my wrists. I strained against him and winced. Something in my hand hurt, but before I could think any more about it, Sam's voice reverberated through the landscape.

"Ava—" A sickening thud interrupted his cry.

"Sam!" My head whipped around. "What are they doing to him?" I asked, desperately struggling against the restraints Blake was applying to my wrists. He said nothing as he pushed me towards a four-by-four with blacked out windows.

I came into contact with leather as I was thrown inside the vehicle, the door shut behind me with a thud and everything became silent. It was as if I was in a bubble. All I could hear was my unsteady breathing and the ringing in my ears from the crash. Looking down at my tied hands, I noticed a trickle of red on the inside of my wrist, along with a pinching sensation. I turned my hands over. I could see a small shard of glass in a cut on my palm, but the pain was like welcome relief compared to the agonizing space opening in my chest. I could do nothing to stop that pain. I wasn't sure I believed in a god, but I found myself closing my eyes and wishing to an unknown entity for Sam. *Please let him be okay.* I felt the car move as the back door opened and Jules and Franco heaved a bloodied, unconscious Sam into the boot.

"Sam!" I cried, relief and terror sweeping through my body in one. "What did you do to him?!" I screamed, sitting up in my seat to see over into the boot. Sam lay sprawled on the carpeted floor, lifeless and still. His face showed no signs of damage, but I'd seen Jules punch him hard in the stomach. The boot closed with a thud and silence stretched out in the car once more.

"Sam? Can you hear me?" My voice sounded breathy. The other doors opened and Blake and Jules climbed in the front, followed by Franco who slid in next to me as a passenger. I glanced in his direction but he kept his eyes facing forward as if looking at me might weaken his resolve. "What did you do to him?" I demanded. "Franco? Please… He's your friend." I stared hard at him and he shifted uncomfortably in his seat.

"Franco…" Blake's tone was a warning. Franco turned to me and lifted an arm, his sleeve slipping down, allowing me to glimpse the same tattoo on his forearm as Sam. I opened my mouth to plead with him again, but before I could utter a word, he blew something from his olive-skinned hand into my eyes, sending me into a whirl of soundless colour.

CHAPTER Twenty-Four

Bile flooded my mouth and my temples throbbed. I spat it out on the dirt floor where my head stuck to the grit and dust. Without moving, I could see that I was no longer in the car but in some kind of abandoned building. I strained to raise my head off the ground, but it produced more pain and I flopped back onto the ground, taking deep measured breaths to stop my stomach from overturning itself.

When I looked down at my hands I saw that my wrists were still bound with rope, which was now stained with my blood. That's when I became aware of the constant searing pain in my hand where the small shard of glass had wedged itself. Pushing my wrists to the floor, I attempted to push myself to a sitting position, but I winced loudly at the pain, signaling the others that I had woken up.

"Ava!" Sam's deep voice echoed through what looked like a derelict car park. The space was lined with enormous concrete pillars, stained with different coloured graffiti. Directly in front of me, a long wall was patterned with many tiny green windows that looked like they hadn't seen the light of day in years due to the amount of moss and ivy growing on them.

"Ava?" Sam's voice was strained this time, but as I attempted to sit up again, I was immediately pushed back down to the floor by a strong hand. I shrieked in pain as my hands hit the ground, forcing the glass further into the wound. Tears sprung to my eyes.

"Don't touch her!" Sam roared, his voice bouncing off the hollow insides of the building. I breathed deeply and looked down at my trembling hands. My whole body ached and I was exhausted. The pain was becoming too much. What had they done to me? Glancing behind me, I eyed Jules, who glared down at me. "Please," I pleaded with him, tears brimming at my eyes. "I just need to clean out my hands."

"You don't need to worry about that where you're going," he grumbled shortly. His eyes widened as he looked behind me and I turned, coming face to face with Mr Jenson. His blonde hair had curled at the ends in the damp of the building, and his face held something like pity as he gazed upon me before turning to Jules.

"I'll take her, Jules," he said, pulling me up by the knot at my wrists, sending shooting pains through my arms.

"Ow—you're hurting me," I complained, feeling my legs struggle to stand on the hard floor. A voice in my head was telling me I should fight, but I didn't have any fight left in me. It was as if my muscles refused to be of any use as he dragged me, tripping and stumbling, through the long concrete building. When we finally reached an opening, he let go of me and I fell on the floor. I landed on my front and searing pain shot through my arms yet again, but this time, I didn't scream. I stayed sprawled on the floor as Sam erupted with anger, his growls ripping through the building.

"Stop hurting her!" he bellowed.

I looked up wearily towards his voice and could see that he was bound by two long metal chains that stretched out between two concrete posts. His chest was bare and red bruises stretched out over his torso where the other men had beaten him into submission. I was vaguely amazed that he was still standing after the beating he'd endured, but there was still a great deal I didn't know about Sam. He must have had some kind of healing abilities, but if that was true, then it hadn't been Seline's magic that had healed him when he'd been hurt before. I watched his chest heave frantically and as my eyes met his, I felt the overwhelming urge to cry. His eyes bored into me, telling me to stay strong, then he turned away to look behind me.

"Ben, please…" he whispered, sending my brain into a field of fog. Mr Jenson stepped forward, I knew that that must be his name.

"Well, well," he drawled, kneeling down next to me. "I've never known a reaper to care so much about a human life before. It's quite captivating." He glanced at Sam. "Sure, I've known a few swift, disappointing romances, but *love*—no, I've never seen a reaper love before." His shoes scraped on the floor as he stood up and walked over to Sam.

Sam stared at Ben through hooded brows, but didn't say a word as Ben gripped his chin and turned his head from one side to the other, examining his face. "I think it's time to test how strong your love really is," he purred.

"What do you think, boys?" A smile crept onto his face as he turned to Jules who stood just to the right of me. "Jules? Franco?" Jules nodded with a sneer on his face, but Franco continued to lean casually against a distant wall. He didn't nod. Ben continued regardless. "Jules…"

Jules moved towards me and pulled me to my feet. I stumbled slightly, but managed to right myself. Jules took my injured hand and stretched it out in front of me, reaching for the glass in my hand. For a split second, I thought he might remove it, but the pain burned into me as he pushed hard. I tried to stay strong to begin with, but as the shard of glass sliced through more and more flesh, tears welled in my eyes. I breathed hard, determined not to scream, but the pain was too much.

"Please—" I cried, my knees buckling underneath me, but Jules continued. I watched the blood run down my arm and drip onto the dusty floor. I pulled hard away from Jules as the pain became too much.

"Enough!" Ben's voice echoed through the building. I collapsed onto the floor, cradling my damaged hand and letting the tears run down my face as I sobbed. I looked to Sam and saw how angry he was. Ben turned to face him, his head cocked to one side, and I knew that this was just the beginning.

"Oh, how disappointing. Perhaps Sam isn't in love after all?" He raised an eyebrow as if daring Sam to speak. Sam's eyes flicked to mine and back. I could tell he was trying to act disinterested, but it was too obvious. Even I could see the pain in his expression.

"Or perhaps you need a little more encouragement to show your love?" Ben turned to me and held out a hand towards me. I stayed frozen on the floor, but two strong hands lifted me from the ground again and both Franco and Jules pushed me forwards. I shivered, partly from the cold and partly from nervousness. All I could do was stare hard into Sam's black eyes. I was only a few meters away from him and I began to hope that he had some kind of powers.

"Okay, Ava…I'm going to show you what the lovely Sam is really like." Reaching into the back of his jeans, he produced a knife. My breathing hitched.

"Hands," he demanded and Jules thrust my bound hands forwards. I shut my eyes tight, unable to watch. I felt a pinch and the rope fell from my wrists just as I felt the glass being removed too. I opened my eyes again in surprise and watched as Ben tossed the shard of glass to the floor. "You need your hands free, Ava."

Ben took my hands and gently placed my fingertips on his temples, making my flesh crawl. Then it hit me. The sensation rising into my fingers and spreading through my arm was like fire. I tried to pull away, but Ben's hands clamped down onto mine, holding me still. The heat burned right into my neck and chest. As it hit my face, my vision changed and colours and sounds whipped past me.

When the sensation ceased, I found myself in a road lined with trees, and the sound of tyres skidding on tarmac immediately filled my ears. I whipped my head to the left just in time to see the car coming right at me, sending shooting pains throughout my entire body. The pain was intense and I screamed, but my own voice was whipped away from me as the colours blurred again.

This time, I found myself in a nightclub. I felt a little woozy as I sipped on a drink, but when I turned on my bar stool, something hit me hard in the head. The pain was unbearable and throbbed through every nerve. As something cold started running down my forehead, the colours began to whip fast around me again.

I came to a halt in a bedroom, and I became aware that I was lying under a soft duvet. I heard a shuffle and looked up only to see a pillow coming down on my face. I held my breath, trying to push the pillow away in panic, but my body strained for more air and my lungs burnt. I was suffocating. I couldn't breathe. The colours whipped around me again.

I was crawling in a hot, smoky room with the roar of fire in my ears and a screaming child in a far room. I tried hard to see my way through the smoke and managed to find the door, but as I stood and wrenched it open, heat hit me hard in the chest. I fell backwards and the heat disappeared just as quickly.

I was marching fast along a pavement in inner city London, my heeled shoes clacking underneath me. I glanced over my shoulder to see a man wearing a grey hoody with a black scarf pulled over his face. Something sharp plunged hard into my ribs and the colours whipped again. Just as I felt myself coming to another agonizing scene, a male's scream broke through my vision. It was long and hard and pulled me out of the scene with the speed of a whip. I fell hard on the dusty floor of the carpark and Sam was standing over Ben, trembling and breathing hard. The chains were still hanging from his wrists.

"Ava—get out of here," he demanded, keeping his focus on the ground. There was something he was holding at bay, something he was trying to control: that part of him I'd seen that night at Seline's. "Ava," he growled with warning. I looked around me and Jules and Franco were nowhere to be seen. How had he done that? "Ava! Now!" he roared at me, his obsidian eyes flashing.

I clambered to my aching feet and, somehow, found the energy to start running along the grimy floor to the end of the carpark. As I reached the exit, a force hit me hard in the chest and held me in place. I stretched out my arms, but I couldn't move any further, like I was trapped in a glass box. I pressed my hands out onto what felt like a cool window pane.

"Sam?" My voice echoed next to me inside the box as I banged against the invisible force. "Sam!"

Footsteps echoed out in the carpark, and I felt a desperate sinking feeling deep inside my gut as Ben sauntered towards me, a knowing smirk on his face. He nodded appreciatively and began to clap.

"Bravo, Ava, my dear. You put on quite a show for dear Sam back there. He's quite distraught, you know." He looked pleased with himself. I looked back in confusion as I pressed my undamaged hand upon the glass. "Oh…the boys have got him safely trussed up again, though, so not to worry."

"You pig!" I screamed. "What the hell is wrong with you? He's not a toy!"

"No, but he *is* a reaper," he said matter of fact. "It's really a shame that you weren't mentally present to see the show. He's quite a magnificent beast when he lets his real powers show."

I frowned at him.

"Oh? He hasn't shared that with you either? A reaper in love *and* trying to live a human life. How demeaning…" I stared hard at him and pursed my lips. "What *is* it darling?"

I shook my head and stared at the ground forcefully. I wouldn't give him anything else to laugh about or have an opinion on. The less I said, the better for both of us. He knew that Sam hadn't told me the whole story yet and he was picking away at the loose threads inside me. I wouldn't let him succeed in making me change my mind about Sam. I was going to win this battle of minds.

"Tell me, Ava—how is it that you came to meet the alluring Samael?" *Samael*? Was that his real name?

"My dad's farm," I answered shortly. "He was helping over the summer before I arrived." Ben blinked at me, suppressing a grin. As he gave me a pitying look, I felt sick. This wasn't how I had met Sam. It was obvious now. How had I not seen it? As I thought more about it, clues seemed to jump out at me. My memory of meeting Sam was on the farm. He had asked me if I remembered how my mum died, but I'd never had the nerve to ask how he knew to ask. I didn't like where this was going… Had I been a complete fool?

I glanced down the row of pillars, half expecting Sam to call out to me and beg me not to believe this man standing in front of me. When only silence came, I suddenly felt alone. Ben's voice, however, was clear.

"I think it's time for you to find out the whole truth, Miss Blume. Come with me."

CHAPTER *Twenty-Five*

Ben held out his hand, and I stretched my own bloody hands out, glad to find I was no longer encased in the transparent holding cell. I took a cautious step forward, wobbling on my feet, but Ben grasped my wrist before I could fall. I winced at the pain in my hand, but righted myself, taking my arm back from his grip. I didn't want to touch him any longer than I had to.

"Come…" he said, as if coaxing a small child. Glancing behind me, I knew there was no point in running. If they could trap me in a glass box and tame Sam in a matter of seconds, what chance did I have? As if he knew what I was thinking, he spoke. "You know you can't outrun us, Ava. Come…" He held out an arm as if holding open a door for me.

I could feel the weight of his stare on me as I stepped towards him, my achy muscles protesting with every step. I only just managed to stay on my feet as I fumbled my way forwards through the fog of pain in my head.

As I rounded the corner, I saw Sam slumped in the chains, breathing heavily with a large, raw slash across his middle. Deep red blood seeped out from the wound and dribbled down his stomach.

"Sam," I whispered, stumbling towards him. I was surprised when I felt the dull warmth of his skin under my palms. Nobody had stopped me. Without hesitation, I pressed my good hand to his wounded torso feeling his muscles relax under my touch.

"It's not healing," he whispered.

"It's a mild poison," Ben mused out loud, "…thanks to Franco. He is especially gifted."

"Ava," Sam rasped in between taking ragged breaths. "You have to get out of here." He was trying to say goodbye.

"Not without you," I countered, determined, but he simply shook his head.

"How touching," said Ben, oozing with sarcasm as he sidled up next to me and gazed at Sam. "Ava and I have just been having a little heart to heart and we have concluded that it's time for you to come clean." Sam's eyes flickered and I frowned as the black in them rippled.

Ben stepped in front of him. "Give me your hand, Ava, dear."

I shook my head, slowly, with purpose. "No," I said quietly, "I don't need the truth." If Sam didn't want me to know, then I didn't need to know. He'd protected me so far.

"Give me your hand, or I will slice it off and command it myself." Swallowing nervously, I hesitantly offered Ben my unhurt hand. In an instant, he jerked it forward to make contact with Sam's hourglass mark. My ears filled with the sound of Sam's screams and I heard Ben's voice as if from the end of a tunnel.

"Think of your mother, Ava." I did. It wasn't hard.

As Sam's shrieks filled my head, the fire burned in my arm, only for a second this time, and I found myself transported to the inside of a car. It felt familiar, but it didn't smell like my car, or look like it for that matter. The seats were navy and rough on my legs as I shifted uncomfortably, the smell of fresh cotton air freshener flooded my senses. I was in my mum's car. As I looked down, I found that I was driving, my hands clasped on the wheel. *I* was driving—not Mum. Her voice echoed in my ear.

"You looked lovely in that dress today, Ava, sweetheart." My eyes whipped around to glance at her. Her dark hair curled behind her ears where she was wearing her usual pearl earrings. Her hazel eyes glowed as she smiled at me, and I felt my mouth twitch into a smile. "We'll have to get you some shoes to match."

My glance revolved back round to the road. The motorway was relatively clear, and I was enjoying the feel of driving Mum's new car. It was so smooth compared to any of the cars I'd driven in lessons. I heard my own voice in the car.

"Thanks for today, Mum. I love the dress." I began to wonder what other girls would be wearing to the end of year prom and I hoped that nobody had a dress like mine. Turning briefly back to my mum, I smiled again, but her face turned wild and her hands stretched out in a brace on the dashboard. I flipped my head around a second too late and the car spiraled headlong into the car in front, spinning us around and crushing my chest into my locked seatbelt. I applied the brakes and the car came to a gradual stop with a gentle bump against the barrier.

There wasn't time to breathe a sigh of a relief, however, as we came face to face with bright headlights and the deep sound of a horn. A lorry ploughed straight into us at full speed, unable to stop. There was a huge crashing jolt, tipping the car and skidding it along the ground with an ear-piercing screech. Pain wrenched through my torso, into my head and through my lungs. My leg cracked and I felt breath go from my lungs as I screamed.

As my eyes opened, I saw my own bloodied, lifeless body hanging from the seatbelt below me in the car. I felt my mouth move and heard my mum's traumatized voice scream. I looked down at my body—I was my mum.

"Ava! Not my baby girl! Ava!" My head was throbbing and a hand enclosed over my shoulder. I turned and it was Sam, but he was different, like a mirage. Black shadows swirled around him like a living cloak and his eyes—his eyes were exquisite and terrifying at the same time. They were black and shining and full of life—and hungry. He looked beyond my mum to my lifeless body. He reached a hand out, but a scream issued from my mouth – my mum's mouth.

"No, please—not my girl! Please…take me instead." He paused and his eyes, which were both full of life and lifeless, looked deep into my mum's. I swallowed back my terror as I stared into his face.

"It's my time. It's not hers," I heard myself say. Was

this really what my mum had said? This piqued Sam's interest and he looked into my mum's eyes with renewed hunger.

"Please take me, not her. Look how beautiful she is." My mum's voice was soft and full of love. "She's so young; she has her whole life ahead of her."

Sam stared coldly into my mum's soul. The look was so lifeless that it caught my breath. Slowly, he turned his gaze towards my body again. In that moment, it was as if he saw what my mother saw and his eyes widened. Something human flickered in his gaze and he retracted his hand. Instead, with a flick of his arm, he placed his hand to my mum's forehead. I felt cold spread into my face and quickly take over my entire body until I felt weightless.

Colours whipped past me in a blur, all the sensation leaving my body as I fell back down on the dirty concrete floor. I was back in the abandoned carpark. Crying and gasping for breath, I looked up into Sam's eyes. The same eyes that had looked into my mum's and taken away her soul; the same eyes that had looked so hungrily down on my limp lifeless body; the same eyes that had looked into mine and declared their love.

Guilt racked me as I gasped for breath. It should have been me. I killed my own mum. It should have been me that died. All that suffering was my own fault. I deserved it. I looked down at my bloodied hands. Ben's earlier story suddenly made sense. The boy had been foolish to save the beautiful hens. I had been foolish. Sam had been foolish. My time had come despite trying to avoid it. My mum had died in vain. My hands shook as guilt and anger grew inside me like a demon taking possession.

"Why didn't you tell me?!" I screamed. My voice was raw and desperate and hurt. I stared hard at Sam, shivering involuntarily at the memory of his cold hand touching my skin—my mum's skin.

"Ava, I…" His eyes pleaded with me and I noticed that they held humanity in them unlike in the memory. "I had to take her—to save you. It's the balance. At the time, I didn't know—"

I shook my head at him furiously as more tears spilled over the brim of my eyes. "You should have taken me," I muttered. "It was my fault. It was my time." I looked at him coldly. Sam stared back at me for a long while, his expression pained.

Ben clamped a hand on my shoulder as he bent down beside me and anxiety swept over Sam's already broken expression.

"But that's not all, is it Samael? Are you going to tell her, or should I?" he asked innocently. There was more? I looked at Ben and he gazed at me with a kind smile. "Why do you think he's still here, Ava?"

I saw the last grain of hope leave Sam's eyes. Guilt swallowed him up and he looked down, but I couldn't tear my eyes away from him. When he finally looked up again, anger swamped his face with the same black hunger in his pupils. I knew his anger was directed at the man crouched beside me, but I gasped anyway. This was the real Sam. This was the Sam that he'd been hiding from me—the Sam that I had sensed all along, but pushed out of my thoughts. He wasn't human. He wasn't animal. He was the Grim Reaper. He was dangerous. In a split second, all the pieces came flying together like birds in formation.

"That's why you got the job at the farm." I watched as he fixed his eyes hard on me. "And why you're all here…because of me?" He didn't say a word, but he didn't have to.

"Samael…she deserves the truth," came Ben's fake scholarly tone.

I continued to stare at Sam as I spoke. "You wanted me, too?" I whispered.

His gaze softened as he looked at me sorrowfully. "Yes."

The cold crept up my spine and I felt my gut twist in horror. He'd been following me all along, waiting for an opportune moment. Had all of this been him playing me?

"But the more I watched you, the more humanity affected me. I started *feeling,* Ava—something not familiar to me. You—you drove me mad." His eyes blazed. "You were being so *stupid.* I've never known a human to be so free with life before. You should have died at that rave!"

I flinched at his tone and stared at him. "Then why didn't you do it then—at the rave?"

Sam was breathing fast now and I could see the turmoil he was in.

"You could have left me to die. You could have taken my soul. Why didn't you?"

"I don't know," he whispered. His eyes darted from

one direction to another, lost in confusion. "I couldn't... The pull to you was addictive. I'd never felt anything like it before. It made me want to rip out your soul and kill anyone who touched you all at once."

I stared at him, this creature I'd driven to distraction. He'd made the wrong decision to keep me alive and was suffering now because my own stupidity had driven him mad. I needed to fix this. I shouldn't even be here. This was all wrong. It wasn't love he felt for me. Maybe it never had been. What he felt was hunger—for my soul. That magnetic pull between us—that was Sam calling me to my destiny. It was time for me to go. Getting to my feet, I turned purposefully to Ben and he looked at me inquisitively.

"Take me," I murmured.

Sam's head flicked up and stared at me, horrified. "Ava, no!" Sam's face was frantic and he pulled wildly at the chains, sending crashing sounds echoing through the concrete chamber, but I didn't look at him. Ben was right—Sam was *acting* human. I'd seen the real Sam now, and he was just killing himself trying to be something that he wasn't; I knew what that was like. This was the easiest way.

"Ava!" His voice bellowed strong with anger, but I ignored him. I was going to save him. Sam couldn't bring himself to end my life so I'd do it for him. I was supposed to be gone. I stared into Ben's face with determination.

"Do it," I whispered.

He raised his eyebrows in surprise and admiration as he turned to Blake. "Would you do the honors, Blake?"

he said. Without hesitation, Blake sauntered towards me, his eyes rippling with hunger, but I found I wasn't afraid. I stepped towards him, my head held high.

"NO! Ava, don't be stupid!" Sam strained fiercely at the chains, ripping one from the concrete post. Franco stepped forward and touched his arm, sending him into a fit of pain. I turned to look at him to tell him that it was okay, but his expression was menacing and full of rage.

"Quickly," I said to Blake, closing my eyes. In a second I heard Sam's desperate plea tear through me as the cold entered my body. All at once, every sensation stopped and I was weightless. All exhaustion, searing pain, grief and intoxicating longing for Sam lost to impenetrable, white silence. I was floating.

My hand stretched out to the familiar operating theatre doors and to my surprise, they opened. Light threw itself around me, and I felt myself being pulled in by an invisible force. A smile crept onto my face as my mum stood waiting for me, her hazel eyes, just like my own, shining. I knew I'd done the right thing, and I let out a long breath. Finally, I was free. I was gone.

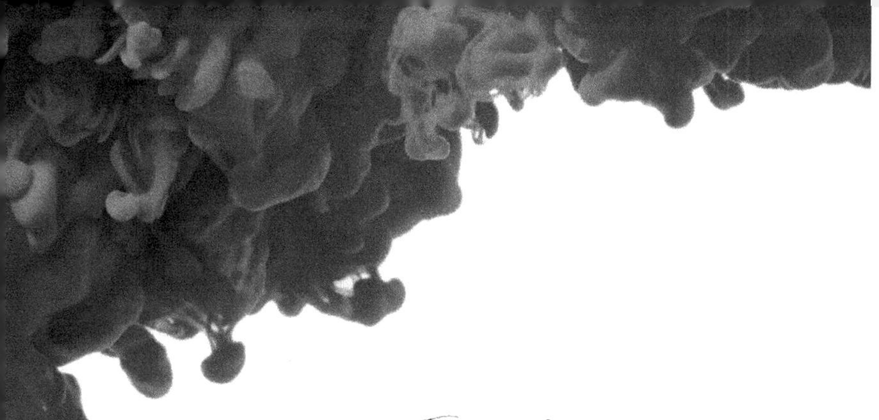

CHAPTER *Twenty-Six*

Sam

Her body crumbles to the floor. Pain punches me in the chest. It isn't physical pain—but something human. I hear myself shout at the top of my lungs and feel it reverberate through my chest. Blake's hand drops to his side.

"The job is done. No harm done, Samael."

Anger surges through me. Ben's lucky I'm in these chains and weakened by this damned humanity coursing in my blood. Franco appears in front of me. *Of all the people.* I stare at him, betrayed. He's holding a shadowed blade; the same one he struck me with earlier. What the hell? What is this thing? Nothing should be able to injure me like this. What kind of magic is this? I can still feel searing pain in my abdomen like I've never felt before.

"It would never have worked out, Sam. Your path is set…" Blake says. I look at him and my blood boils. I've never wanted to destroy another reaper more than I do right now. The only girl I've ever loved in this Gods-damned existence is lifeless on the concrete.

I start trembling from anger, from fear, from the gaping hole left inside me. Power floods into me from a deep, forgotten place inside me, and I tear the chains from the concrete, releasing my arms once more. I lunge at Blake's throat before he can react, but physical pain sears into my abdomen again and I buckle. I gasp as my knees thud to the floor, and I retch as the blade crunches against my ribs. The pain is agonizing, and I can taste iron in my mouth. When I look into Franco's eyes, choking on my own blood, he simply stares down at me – hard. Then I fall forwards as my friend pulls the blade from me. Spitting metallic blood onto the floor, I curse violently.

Black blood.

I'm bleeding black, metallic blood.

Reapers don't bleed black blood, unless—

Fire burns in my throat and I open my mouth to gasp, but nothing happens. My eyes flick wide to see a blaze of red, and I slip through the air. I am falling. My heart catches in my mouth. I hit the ragged ground with a thud, but no pain comes. I don't know where I am. I squeeze my eyes shut and open them again, but I'm blind. I strain hard into the sheet of nothing in front of me. Nothing. Where am I? I don't recognise this place. I look down to see if I'm still bleeding, but I find that I have no body. What the—?

I can feel myself, though. Is this the same place I bring the damned souls? Is this how it ends? Is this limbo? It must be. There's nothing. Nothing at all. I don't even feel tired. I'm just a thing in this desert of nothingness. All there is, is an endless horizon of red… there's not a thing to see. Nobody. Am I to be lost here for eternity? Maybe eternity has already passed. How much time *has* passed? Is time even a currency here? I need to block this blinding, endless vision out.

I focus hard to block it out. I focus so hard, but… nothing. My vision doesn't blur. I have no eyes. My heart doesn't thrum. I have no heart. I'm not even sure I have a soul. If I do, it must be ugly and dark—like me. I am a demon of death. I *was* a demon of death. What am I now? Maybe I'm not that cursed thing anymore. I don't know what I am. Time passes, and all I can see and all I am is endless red. Red blending eternally into red.

Something black glints in the distance and I fix on it as if it's magnetic. It's the first thing I've seen in… days? Maybe my time in Limbo is up. Maybe it's my soul, come to collect me. It flickers and glints on my horizon and I stare hard at it. I will it closer. I have no body. I have no legs, but as I think about it, I am closer to it. I think about it again and I find myself wishing I had arms. I want to grab it, but it moves out of my reach. It's taunting me. I stare down at where my body should be, but there is just infuriating, blinding red.

I try speaking, but I don't know why. I know I have no voice. I have no body. Is this where I must reside for eternity? Do I have to endure an eternity of *this*? I know the answer to that. This is where I belong—trapped in a world of nothing, away from real living souls. Away from her. I should have stayed away from her. I should have been stronger.

Something hits me hard in the side and it sends me spiraling out of control, whirling like a pinwheel through the red canvas, away from the black glint. I'm not afraid. Then I jolt to a stop. I look for my point of reference: the black glint, but it is completely gone. There is just red now. I stare out into the nothing and I don't feel a thing.

Then she's in front of me. She's beautiful. Her hazel eyes stare into me and her hair falls down her front. She walks towards me, smiling, but her eyes are so terribly sad. I want to touch her. I want to feel her in my arms. I want to hold her. I want to feel her warmth in my cold, soulless chest. She stops just in front of me and I try to reach out, but I have no damned arms. Now, her expression has changed and she's walking away. *No. Come back.*

What was that? A vision?

The red stretches out in front of me, behind me, above me and below me and there is no time. I exist only in thought. I need to get out of here.

Who was that girl?

Something glittery starts to rain down and I stare at a spec as it floats directly in front of me and past where my body should be—beyond into oblivion. What is it?

More of it floats down, piece by piece. It begins to conceal the canvas of red. It falls heavier until there is just silver and it runs like a river below where my feet should be. It begins to rise higher and higher, and I feel its warmth. It's rushing now like a rapid and it rises fast. It's hot and it's suffocating me. I look down again and can see that it's sand.

It's *time*.

I am aware of a swelling feeling inside, drawing something cool through me. The sensation builds and it becomes hard to focus. Suddenly, I feel breath. I look down and I have a chest. I gasp for breath and the red is gone, replaced by black. My eyes move in my head and as if using them for the first time, I peel them open. I am staring into dull, green human eyes.

My stomach lurches and I find myself overwhelmed by hunger. I need time. I need to reap. I launch myself forward and grasp the blonde-haired woman's throat. It burns as if her skin is on fire, but I need her time. She gasps for air as my grip tightens on her throat. Her eyes are wide with terror as I raise my hand to her head.

"Sam—" she croaks. Ignoring her, I press my hand to her head and close my eyes, inhaling deeply, concentrating. The woman tears at my hands with her nails as I focus in on her soul. I see it. It's mine. I reach out to close my hand around it, but the woman croaks out her last words.

"She's inside you." I pause. What strange, nonsensical words these humans utter in their last moments. Shaking my head, I refocus. I see her soul again and as I reach out to grasp it, something inside me jolts hard and blinds me. I see her—a young human with deep hazel eyes and flowing brown hair.

I flinch back from the blonde woman, freeing her soul. She extends her own palm towards me and sends waves of searing pain through me. I cry out in torment and stumble backwards into the wall, hearing a clatter of ceramic as I knock something to the floor. The pain is agonizing, and I feel my hands pressing into my temples to try and release the tension building underneath. How is she doing this? I try to focus on finding my own surge of power, but there is none. I'm empty. It immediately reminds me of how helpless I was before the curse claimed me.

I manage to open my eyes and growl at her in fury, but she remains focused. The pain is constricting, burning inside my head, behind my eyes, inside my chest. I can feel myself slipping down to the floor, weakened by this unstoppable force put upon me. Then it hits me. I've felt this pain before. I've felt this pain in this house. This woman has inflicted this on me before. I stare hard at her. It rushes back to me. I know her.

"Seline—" I manage to croak, as the searing pain throbs in my mind. I'm sure the blood vessels in my head must be popping and I see silver, but then she drops her hands and I hit the tile floor. My airways are tight and I have to suck air back into my lungs. *Seline.* I know this woman—this witch. I look up at her as I remain on all fours. She stares wildly back at me, her hands still out in front of her, ready to defend her soul. I remember now, this is not a woman to toy with.

"Seline." My voice is hoarse. She nods, eyeing me sternly. "I remember you now."

She lowers her hands and stares at me. "Good," she says, moving to the kitchen table and pulling a chair back. "Sit down," she orders. I'm shocked at first, but a small voice in the back of my head reminds me that this witch is powerful; more powerful than me. I climb off the floor and sit where she has directed me. She purses her lips and regards me with interest.

"Do you remember her?" she asks. She is being cautious.

"Do I remember who?" I watch as she shifts uncomfortably in her seat.

"The hazel-eyed girl."

I stare at her and think of the girl with flowing brown hair. "No," I say simply. It's true, but why do I feel uncomfortable? I see something like panic cross the witch's face. "Who is she?" I ask.

The witch regards me for a moment. I can see sympathy in her eyes. "Someone important to you," she says quietly. I raise an eyebrow. I'm a reaper. We tend not to care much of others. It comes with the territory. I don't understand what this woman is suggesting.

"Try to remember, Sam." *Sam*. She knows my name. I stare back at her blankly and it's clear that she's not going to give up. I have no idea what this woman is talking about, though. Irritated, I scrape my chair back from the table.

"I'm leaving." I turn to walk out of the house and I'm surprised to find that I know the way through the tiny farmhouse to the front porch. I open the door forcefully and march across the gravel, but I hear the witch's footsteps on the driveway behind me.

"You loved her, Sam," she calls out. I pause.

"Love?" I can't help but laugh at her. "I'm a reaper. Reapers don't love. We take life." I stare at her, incredulous. I'd really like to take *her* life. I can feel her power and it makes me hungry, but I turn away before I'm tempted. It's not her time; not that Ben would object to my straying from the balance.

"You wouldn't take hers," the witch continues purposely. "You were supposed to, but you didn't. You would have done anything for her, Sam. You took her mother instead of her and right now, she's laying in my house waiting for you to give her her life back."

That's it. I turn and march angrily towards the woman and grasp her throat. I'm tempted to try and take her soul again. She needs to be careful. "I don't—*love*. I'm a reaper." I hesitate for a moment. I can feel her pulse underneath my fingers, but I've experienced the pain she can inflict on me. *Walk away*, I tell myself. Unfurling my fingers, I do—I walk away. Cursing under my breath, I begin to understand why the other coven members succumb to temptation on a regular basis. It would be so easy, but I'm not stupid enough to try again with her.

CHAPTER *Twenty-Seven*

I pick up my drink and down it in one. It burns the back of my throat, but doesn't ease the disquiet inside me. I feel eyes on me. A girl with rippling blonde hair and killer blue eyes smiles at me from across the bar. I don't smile back, but my throat constricts as I inhale her scent. I admit that I'm tempted, but I see the shock register in her face as my eyes ripple. Stupid move. It's too open here and too busy.

I do want time though. I've never wanted it more. It's as if being so close to my own demise has elevated my need to reap souls. I'm hungry and I need to devour humanity. Leaving a wad of notes on the bar, I leave without a glance at the girl. I want to tell her she's got lucky tonight in ways she couldn't even imagine.

It's dark outside and there are plenty of people partying tonight. There's bound to be someone I can take. I've definitcly comc to the right place. I can feel my throat rattle in anticipation as my mark burns under my sleeve. It's never burned so much before and I pull my sleeve up to inspect the damage. I frown. The hourglass is full. But that can't be right. What has that witch done to me?

I glance at my phone. It's almost two in the morning, which means a few unsuspecting, vulnerable souls will be wandering the streets soon. *No.* It's not the balance. I shouldn't upset the balance, but then I've never felt like this before. *It wouldn't be the first time.* I curse under my breath and grip my throat hard. This hunger is beginning to consume me. *I need time.* I shouldn't bend reality to my own advantage, but—*once more. Just once more.*

I wander across the road and conceal myself in a shop doorway. There's a grey-fronted nightclub right across the street. The neon blue sign flanking the front reads *Edge*. Its windows are boarded up with wooden boards plastered in old posters, and the peeling emulsion on the brickwork suggests it isn't the most eloquent of public houses.

I watch as two bouncers mill about in front of the double doors, conversing. They are both heavily built; nothing I couldn't contend with, even with my power depleted—but then a girl stumbles from the doors. I stand up straight and watch as she reaches into her bag and takes out a pack of cigarettes and a lighter. She glances either way down the street and then stumbles aimlessly along the side of the building to the corner, obscuring herself in an alleyway. *This is your chance, Samael.* I move.

I saunter across the road towards her. She clocks me immediately.

"Hey." I use my best boy-next-door voice to lure her in, and I watch her pupils dilate when she looks at me. "Where's your friend?" I ask. *I hope she doesn't have anyone with her. It will make this easier.* She shrugs and smiles at me. She must be in her mid-thirties judging by the lines at the edge of her eyes and the decade of clothes she wears. *She's alone right now. It's enough.* I smile back. "Come, I'll walk you to the taxi rank." I take her hand as I walk her along the high-street.

"Thanks," she mumbles, leaning on me for support. "I should call Leanne and let her know I'm leaving." *She is with someone. Too late now. You've made your move. Just do it.*

Her breath has the fresh fumes of alcohol on it, but I can feel the pulse in her wrist and the life emanating from her. My chest burns. I know I shouldn't be doing this. It's against the code, but I've never felt like this before. *I need time.* I need *her* time; it's right there for me to grasp.

The mark on my arm throbs painfully as if sensing how close I am to the kill. I make a quick decision and push her against the nearest wall by her shoulders, sweeping her red hair back from her face. She gasps and fear flickers for a moment before she looks into my eyes. Now, she's looking at me with desire. She thinks I'm going to kiss her, but as my eyes glint and darken, her expression changes.

This isn't right. *Do it,* a voice calls out in my mind, and I listen to it because my throat is on fire and the pain is blinding me. Guilt flickers inside me, but I can't bear my raging appetite any longer and I press my hand against her forehead. I find her soul and grasp my hand around it, clinging to it. The life fades from her eyes and her muscles relax to become a dead weight against me.

But then *she's* there, like a tidal wave in my mind—

the girl with hazel eyes. Her brown hair whips around her face and she glares at me with a fierce understanding—and *love*. I see her hand move towards my face and feel it's cool pressure on my forehead. Then I am thrown from my reverie and find myself back in the darkened street.

The breath catches in my burning throat.

Burning.

Still.

Growling in desperate fury, I let the dead girl slip down my body and crumple on the floor in a heap.

What is this magic? The witch is responsible for this. I turn and stalk out into the night.

CHAPTER Twenty-Eight

I hammer on the farmhouse door with my fist. It rattles on its hinges and I'm half tempted to kick it down. "Wake up, witch!" I hear my own voice bellow into the night. It's three in the morning, but there's no way I'm dealing with this any longer. What the hell has she done to me?

The door swings open and she regards me with caution. "You look like you've seen a ghost," she says, her eyes attempting to hide her mirth, but I'm not laughing. Fuming, I push the door wide and march past her into the tiny hallway, bracing myself against the doorframe of the kitchen. The burning is still there, only quenched for mere seconds when I reaped the girl.

Turning to face the witch, I stare at her from under hooded brows. She radiates life, and I have to swallow back my appetite once more. Not her. I need her.

"What is this, Seline?" I try for a calm and human approach.

"Oh, we're back on first name terms?" She says, eyeing me mercilessly. She's pushing her luck, but I need her to take this curse off me. I need time. I need the burning to stop.

"Get her out of me," I spit.

She narrows her eyes at me.

"I saw her." I don't want to explain how.

"Follow me," she says and walks towards the stairs leading to the upper level of the farmhouse—to the girl. I follow her and she turns into a small bedroom.

I feel like I've been here before; the space feels familiar. The room is lit by a small bedside lamp, which throws shadows onto the uneven white-washed walls. The curtains are closed, but flutter in the night breeze coming from the window. Under the window, laying on the bed, is a petit brown-haired girl. Her eyes are closed, but I know who she is: *the hazel-eyed girl*; the girl in my head—lifeless, though.

"I'll be right back." The witch leaves, closing the door behind her.

I turn back to the room. It feels familiar, but unease settles in me. I am alone with the girl. Who is she? I move to the edge of the bed and stare down at her. Her complexion is pale and her eyes are closed. She looks peaceful but something about that feels wrong. Her hair lays across the pillows and flows down over her shoulders. *Ava.* Is that her name?

Her skin looks so soft. I want to touch it. I reach out and trace my hand along her hairline and down the side of her face. The witch said I loved her, but reapers don't love. How could I love her? Reapers are devoid of emotion—devoid of humanity. I can't deny that this particular human is beautiful—inside and out. I can sense a darkness inside her that shimmers like black onyx. She is no normal human.

The witch reenters, and I take my hand away from the girl, but I'm too late. The witch sees. Something surges in my chest as she comes towards me and the girl, and I reposition myself so I am between the two of them. The witch pauses and assesses me.

"Do you recognise the room?" Her tone is cool and inquiring.

"No."

"Do you recognise the girl?" The witch nods towards the girl. *Ava.* I look at her again and, this time, something inside me twists uncomfortably. I look away again.

"No."

"Do you know she willingly died so you could continue?" She smiles.

I frown deeply at her. She isn't telling the truth. No human would do that. It doesn't make sense. Why would a human die to save a soulless entity that causes death?

"She loved you, Sam," the witch says, as if she can hear my thoughts. I narrow my eyes at her.

"I put a spell on you both," she says cautiously. I know she's debating whether to go further. Her heart beat is fluttering unevenly in her chest. She knows I'm as much a danger to her as she is to me. Taking a step towards me, she continues to explain.

"After you broke away from the coven, I knew they'd come for you both. I've been watching you very carefully over the past months…" She stops and licks her lips. She's unsure.

"Go on..." I say, through clenched teeth. I need this girl's soul out of me. *Just go along with the witch,* I tell myself.

"You were afraid of her to begin with. She produced feelings in you that you didn't understand, and you came to me for help. Luckily for you, you came to exactly the right person, and I knew how to help." She cocks her head to the side to monitor the girl, and when she looks back at me, her gaze is steady and her heartbeat slows.

"When you showed her who you are, she left and that's when I think you realised what she meant to you. I think that must have been when you realised what it was you felt. So, I vowed I wouldn't let them harm you. I used some of the darkest magic I've ever used, so that if she died, her life would be preserved inside you."

"That's not how it works…" I mutter darkly.

"I bent the rules." She glances at the girl again. "She lives in the very marks on your body, Sam. If you want her out of you, you need to gift her her soul."

I've never heard of anything like this before and I look at her with suspicion. "How do I know I can trust you?"

"If I'm lying," the witch says with certainty, "you can take my soul." I stare at her in amazement. No witch would ever give up their soul willingly. Turning back to the girl, I know I should try. If it's a trick, I'll sense it quickly enough to take the witches soul. If it's not a trick, then hell, I could kiss the damned witch if she can make this burning stop. It's driving me mad. There's no way I can live with it forever, so I bite the bullet and place a hand to the girl's forehead.

There's not time to think. The pain is immediate and radiates all over my body. It is excruciating as if the girl's spirit is trying to expel itself from my very pores. I choke on my own vocal chords as I gasp for breath—then something tickles the inside of my throat. I try to cough, but I lose my breath and end up retching as the tickling turns to scratching. Fire ignites in my mouth and I think I'm going to be sick.

My whole body heaves, and a tiny black glint, like a firefly, momentarily hovers in the forefront of my mind.

It's teasing me, and I want to grasp it back, but it begins to spin and glow. It becomes brighter as it swirls and, in an instant, expands – blinding me. I am knocked off of my feet and find myself staring at a thousand thoughts and memories: the girl standing in a barn screaming, grief filling my ears and my eyes, suffocating me; the girl dancing amidst coloured lights, kissing a boy; the same boy dying in a whirl of panic and pain; gushes of wind on a mountain top—I'm kissing the girl and her hazel eyes gaze at me; I am lying on a sofa with fire burning inside me whilst she presses warmth and pain to my skin.

I gasp and shuffle backwards, away from the swirl of memories. I'm breathing fast. Shock. I stare at the body on the bed as the memories fade away.

I wait…

She stirs and her eyes flicker open. Overcome by some desperate longing deep inside me, I scramble upright to see into them; and I'm astounded at their beauty. They are so full of sorrow and pain and grief and life—and *love*.

I stare at her. I can feel something rising in my chest and it's not pleasant. Something in my throat is choking me. What is this? What magic is this? The excruciating, burning sensation from before has gone, but something else is rising inside me. It's squeezing my insides. I can't breathe.

Stumbling back onto the floor, away from the girl, I turn angrily to the witch, but she only smiles at me triumphantly.

CHAPTER *Twenty-Nine*

Ava

My eyes ached as I blinked against the light. I felt like I hadn't opened them in days and I raised my hands to rub at them. Goosebumps prickled my arms as curtains blew around me, and when I managed to focus on them, I realised I wasn't in my room; I was in Sam's. I must have slept here again. My dad was going to be *really* mad.

Pulling the blanket further up my body, I breathed in the familiar scent in the room. With a crashing overload of memory, I remembered that I shouldn't be here. How was I alive? I gave away my life. Was this heaven? The last thing I could remember was the light, the weightlessness, Ben and Blake and Sam. Sam had screamed my name as I'd let them take my soul. *Sam.*

Something moved in the corner of the room and I turned my head towards the door. Seline was standing a distance away, but she wasn't looking at me. She was smiling at the floor – and then I saw him. Sam was climbing to his feet, moving towards her, but the muscles in his back were tense. He was angry.

"Sam?" My voice was quiet and he froze, the

muscles in his back heaved a deep breath.

"Sam?" I tried again, uncertainly. I could feel the panic rising in my chest as emotion took over. He was standing facing Seline, unmoving. The lump grew in my throat as I tried to swallow back tears. I knew I'd gone too far. I'd pushed him away. He couldn't even face me.

"Seline?" I tried, fearing nobody could hear me. Her body turned to me, but her gaze remained on Sam.

"Sam…" she said, her voice raw and full of power.

"What did you do to me?" Sam growled at Seline. I couldn't understand what was wrong.

"That feeling inside your chest…" Seline said tentatively, moving towards him.

"What magic is it? You said it would stop. I returned her soul." His voice was strained and full of rage.

"It's no magic I could conjure," she replied simply, placing her hands on his shoulders. "It's what's already inside you." Her face was serious.

Sam's body trembled and he took a step back from Seline. "Seline, I'm warning you…"

"It's not magic, Sam. It's what you fear is true… what you won't believe. But it's real. Just turn around and look at her." Seline spoke softly to Sam.

What had I done to him? Nervously, I pushed hard against the bed to try hauling myself into a sitting position. My body had never felt so dull and heavy and it hurt to move, but I needed to make him see I was sorry.

"Turn around, Sam," Seline said again in a measured tone. "See for yourself. It's not magic…"

I managed to sit up and heave my legs out of bed, but my head spun furiously, making me dizzy. The sensation sent spots in front of my eyes, and I gripped the side of the bed. I felt Sam's hands on my arms, holding me steady. I looked into his eyes. Confusion and fear were all rolled into one.

"Sam…" I whispered. His eyes bored into mine but he still didn't say a word. Would he be able to forgive me for what I did? "I'm sorry. I doubted you and I thought you just wanted to take my soul, but I was stupid. I know how you feel because I feel it too. It didn't go away when I died. I just—I had to see her. I convinced myself that you—I just—I knew you'd never be able to do it…" I knew I was blathering on and he probably hated me for everything I'd done, but he needed to know.

"…and the others, well—" I stopped and swallowed hard at the lump in my throat. I could see the agony in his eyes, and I just wanted to erase what I had done to him. The tears brimmed and I sobbed. "I just made a decision and I thought I was doing the right thing." I looked at Seline, but she simply nodded and left the room.

"Please don't hate me," I whispered, searching his eyes. He still hadn't said anything, but as he continued to stare at me, I saw his expression change. His shoulders stiffened and his brow furrowed marginally. It was if he was seeing me for the first time.

"I don't hate you," he uttered. It was as if he was telling himself this fact more than me. His disquiet was unnerving me, and I wondered how I could right it—and then he spoke.

"God…" he whispered, "…the witch was right."

"What?" I searched his face, but he gave a small shake of his head. A tiny confused smile crept onto his mouth and reaching up, he ran trembling fingertips down my cheek, through my tears.

Relief spread through me as I felt the warmth of his palm against my cheek. I turned my head and breathed him in. All tension left my body. It felt so good to be back with Sam, despite everything I had found out. Sam shifted to sit next to me, but he kept his hand on my face, and I allowed myself to revel in the sensation of him touching me. I had the impression he felt just the same.

When I did finally look at him, I was met with those deep black eyes, gazing at me more intently than they ever had before. I could see the deep sea of emotion in them, making my chest constrict and expand all in one. I wanted to take away all the pain I'd caused him. I moved to touch his face, but he took my hand in his. I couldn't help but feel a small stab of disappointment.

"No…" His face was still and the blood rushed in my ears as I sensed what he was about to do. "Ava, I've never felt more alive than I have since meeting you, but I'm a reaper—"

"I don't care," I said with certainty.

"You do. If you don't now, you will someday when I have to take someone you love." His eyes burned as he looked at me. "I took your mum, Ava…" I felt his hand slide out from underneath mine. "I've hurt you enough."

"No," I whispered, leaning towards him. Was this really happening? Was he trying to leave? The cold spread through me. "No… I won't let you walk away."

"I've been selfish, Ava." His voice was strong and he stood up from the bed.

"No," I said more forcefully, making him look up.

"You have not been selfish." I stood directly in front of him, suddenly finding the strength in my legs to stand. "If you have, then I've been just as selfish."

Sam gazed at me curiously.

"You've tried to protect me all along, Sam. You tried pushing me away before, but you couldn't do it. You said so yourself '*I have a better chance of leaving you alone than you do of leaving me alone.*' Well, you're wrong," I said, moving closer to him. I ran my hands up his shirt sleeves and felt pride glow in my chest as he tensed under my touch.

"Ava…"

"Sam… I didn't give up my soul to a reaper for nothing," I whispered. Sam's eyes blazed with anger, recalling the moment when Blake took my soul.

"That was a stupid move," he growled.

"I'd do it all over again." My voice was strong – confident.

"I know," he said, a glint returning to his eyes. "That's what concerns me. I'm not sure I have the *time* to keep you out of trouble."

"Then I guess you better get to work…*reaper*."

A small smile crept onto his face as he looked into my eyes. "Don't tempt me…"

CHAPTER *thirty*

Louisa gazed at me from across the kitchen table, her hands wrapped tightly around the mug in her hand and her eyes fathoming something in the distant recesses of her mind. "Who's Blake?" she said, raising her eyebrows at the three of us.

I shifted in my seat. The guilt was eating away my insides, and I was already beginning to wonder if I'd done the right thing.

"No one of consequence," uttered Seline, breaking the tension by acting as if none of what had just happened had happened. "Just an acquaintance. We just thought we'd let you know that he left town today."

"Okay…" she said, a look of pure confusion crossing her face. She got up from the table, and all I could do was give her a half measured smile. "I'll see you at college, Ava," she said, glancing briefly in Sam's direction as she headed for the front door. "Don't do anything I wouldn't!" A small smile crept onto my face as I heard her call out in the hallway. At least she was still in there.

"You had to…" came Sam's soft voice in my ear.

I turned to him. "I know," I said, "but I feel so guilty.

It feels wrong to just delete him from her mind." Sam nodded silently.

Seline had asked my permission to use magic on those necessary to keep them safe. The reapers thought Sam and I were dead. Both Sam and Seline thought this was what had allowed them to move on from the area, which could only be a good thing. The only downside was that Louisa would never get to say goodbye to Blake.

There was also the small issue, now that I knew the truth about Sam, that I was expected to keep the secret and not share it with anyone—including Louisa. I'd reasoned with myself that simply withholding information wasn't lying. I wasn't entirely convinced that wiping her memory of Blake's existence was the right thing to do, but I needed to remind myself that it would keep her safe as well as protect her from unnecessary heartbreak.

The same had gone for my dad, who now believed I'd gone to stay with my aunt for a few days to visit Mum's grave. Nothing more was needed as he'd been kept in the dark anyway, and I was more than relieved that I hadn't shared more with him over the past months. Plus, how on earth did you explain to your dad that your reaper-boyfriend's reaper-friend killed you and then your witch-friend helped to bring you back to life? I thought this was one stone better left unturned.

As for everyone at college, all they would know was that I had gone missing, driven to distraction from grief. This meant that I would have to be the weird girl whose mum had died, but that was okay. Maybe I *was* the weird girl whose mum had died. I'd made my peace with that and was stronger for it. After all, if it hadn't been for her,

I wouldn't be here.

I smiled and tentatively brushed my hand along Sam's arm. He'd seemed distracted since it had all happened, and it was beginning to unnerve me. "Are you okay?" I asked. "You seem distracted."

I wondered if he was already missing being amongst his own. It must be a lonely existence being a reaper and being with others that bore the same curse must have eased the suffering to some degree. He had explained to me that he'd need to find some reapers sometime as it was a requirement to travel with a Watchman; which was what Ben was. I realised this was why Ben hadn't had the markings like everyone else.

Sam had explained that Ben didn't take life. Instead, it was his job to ensure that the reapers kept the natural order and the balance. As a Watchman, he had to report back to a higher power, but Sam explained that Ben craved the power and had lost all moral judgement a long time ago. He'd often disregarded the reapers' behavior when it came to taking souls that weren't ripe. Despite telling me all of this though, I could tell that it pained Sam to break from his coven.

Sam looked into my eyes, but I could tell his mind was somewhere else. "I'm fine," he mumbled, but I wasn't convinced.

"Tell me."

He took a deep breath and shifted, looking serious. He wasn't going to let this go, was he? He obviously thought I was better off without him. "Sam, if this is about—"

"I reaped a girl's soul the other night," he said. Despite the tension in his shoulders, I couldn't help but notice his pupils shimmer with life. This was Sam.

My mouth formed the a small "*O*" as I understood what was playing on his mind. This was about *that*. I gave a small nod to indicate that I understood. I wasn't sure how else to proceed. Clearly, he wasn't too sure either as his eyes dropped to the floor.

"I screwed up," he said with a frown.

"No," I whispered, inching closer to him and resting my forehead on his. "It's okay." He broke away from me almost immediately.

"No, Ava, you don't understand. It wasn't her time," he said, his voice raising. "I took her soul. I just took it because I felt like it." I let the information sink in, but I knew there was no point in fighting it. Sam wasn't human. He was here for a purpose and he needed to fulfill that.

"It's okay," I began tentatively. "It's what you have to do," I said, looking him straight in the eyes. "You keep the natural order." I spoke quietly in an attempt to calm him down, but it seemed to infuriate him more.

"But it wasn't her time," he growled, turning on me.

Standing up in front of him, I looked him hard in the eyes. "Maybe it was…" I said, raising my eyebrows at him. "You didn't force her to go with you." I watched as he realised what I was saying, and his mouth dropped open in shock.

"How—you were there? You saw?" he stammered.

I'd seen everything that had happened from Sam's point of view. I'd seen the girl in the bar and felt his hunger as he gazed at her. I'd felt the unbearable fire in his chest and the piercing burn on his forearm. I'd even felt the blinding pleasure of taking the girl's soul in the street and I'd never felt so alive.

"Yes," I said.

Sam's expression turned from shock to horrified wonder. "When Seline said you were inside me, I thought she was lying. I thought it was just a trick to get me to bring back your soul. I never..."

I smiled in amusement. It was strange to see such a powerful creature so undone at the seams. He seemed to be lost for words.

"I saw you," he said, faltering over his words. "Your hair. Your eyes..." he swallowed hard. "But for you to be aware, to see what I was doing... God, Ava."

Seline had trapped my soul inside a vessel of immense power—Sam. On the night when I'd applied the black magic to his markings, I'd inadvertently been transferring my own soul into him, leaving only a morsel for the other reapers to take when they came for my soul. Seline had known all along that the natural order would have to be kept and, somehow, she'd known what I'd do if I was faced with the truth.

The fact was, I understood Sam's nature more than he realised, and although the truth seemed grizzly, I knew it was a certainty of life that I had to accept. Everyone had to die at some point, and if I had to die again, I hoped Sam would be the one to take away my spark. After all, he already had a firm grasp on my heart.

That night, I didn't find myself in a hallway full of doctors and nurses with the stench of disinfectant stinging my throat. My mind had finally put that dream to rest. I had the truth now. As painful as it was that I had to live with the knowledge that I had been driving when the car crashed, I wouldn't change a thing. In death, my mum had given me a gift. All I could do now, was make the most of the time she had given me.

Now, my dreams were peaceful, and I found myself walking hand in hand with Sam down a long, cobbled, moonlit street. The wind was chilly and the air cool, but I could feel the heat and life radiating from Sam. My heart buzzed with joy as he turned and slid his arms around my waist, pulling me close enough to feel his breath on my hair. A warm glow spread through my bones as I relaxed in his grasp. I knew I was in the arms of death, but I also knew I was exactly where I should be. He might be a reaper, but we'd been brought together for a reason and I loved him incorrigibly.

I gazed into his profound, unfathomable black eyes and inched myself forward on my tiptoes to brush my lips against his. His mouth was soft and his breath intoxicating. I curled my arms around his neck, sliding my fingers into his soft curls at the base of his neck. This was it—this was how I felt most alive—in the arms of death.

Breathing a sigh of contentment, I leant forward to utter those three little words that I knew Sam longed to hear, but something glimmered in my peripherals. My breath froze and my heart stopped beating. There, on my forearm, emblazoned on my skin in rich black silk, was the intricate design of an hourglass.

Epilogue

Franco

We headed north on the soul-thread Blake followed, and I hoped all had gone to plan. I hoped my friend had not guessed what I'd done. His powers had been weakened since he'd allowed humanity into his soul, but I hoped this would work in my favour. He could not find out—not yet. If he found out now, it could be catastrophic. I was taking a big risk in helping the witch. I had known Sam was the one the moment he'd refused to kill the girl. Seline Archibald had only confirmed this as she'd told me of how she'd watched them fall in love.

The reaper in love.

That's why she'd fixed the shadow sword, so it would keep him from the eternal depths of hell.

The witch was powerful; one of the ancient Waterhouse line. I knew I could leave her to fix them both, no matter how long it took. We had already waited centuries for the prophesy to deliver. What was a few more years?

"Franco! Andiamo!"

I glowered at Blake. I just hoped the time would pass

quickly. Sam's weakened state had allowed for Blake to take control over the coven's senses. He was powerful, but not as Sam had been. Ben was not happy about the exchange. He'd been able to cover up our anarchic lifestyle when Sam was our dominant. But now, who knew what he'd face as Watchman? Who knew what we'd all face in the age of the prophesy?

As I walked into the dark alley, in the shadow of Blake's power and the absence of my brother, Samael, I sent my friend a silent thought: "Perdonami amico." *Forgive me, friend.*

THE END

Acknowledgments

When I started writing this, I dared myself to write a few words each day to see what would happen. Well, it was like finding a whole new part of myself that I always knew was there, but I'd never allowed out. Months down the line and Ava and Sam became very real people to me, looking over my shoulder, tutting at me when I wasn't working on their story. They were quite persistent in fact, that I had no choice but to finish the book.

Well here it is and I have a lot of people to thank!

Tim, at the beginning, the middle and the end, the tough times, the fun times and the moments of utter madness, you pushed me on. You dared me. You reminded me 'What if?' You knew exactly how to appeal to my competitive side and what to say to get me fired up and ready to write. Thank you for your enthusiasm, patience and love. Thank you for winding me up something rotten!

Thank you to Mum and Dad for always telling me to strive for more and dream big. You're some of the hardest working people I know and your encouragement, creativity and eccentric nuances have shaped who I am today and I couldn't be more proud to say that I am your daughter.

To my big sister Katy, whose lust for life and

compassionate words have been like a beacon and whose love for adventure is what made me do some of the best things I've ever done.

To my big brother Tom, for all those times you chased me around the kitchen table on my plastic tractor, but also for being the best and quirkiest big brother I could have wished for.

Thank you both for cheering on your mad little sister!

To Lina, my best friend, my partner in crime (ok, only rice-crispy related crime) and my second sister in everything but blood. You read every (and I mean EVERY) draft and you were honest from the beginning, whilst also loving Ava and Sam as much as I do. You're one of the most selfless and compassionate people I know and I'll be forever grateful that we were placed in the same flat at uni all those years back!

To Laura and Kathy. You didn't disown me when I moved to the country, buried my head in a pile of books and writing and became despicably terrible at communication. They say best friends are the ones you can go for months without seeing, but when you do, they bring a flask of wine. They do say that, right? You guys are the best!

To '*The Rejected*'. You know who you are and we all parted ways, but thank you for being some of the most awesome school friends and for accepting my peculiar ways. Sadly, two of you passed away far too early. You will be missed by all of those who knew you, but know that a little piece of each of you will forever live on in this story.

To Jill, for being the most honest and hilarious editor I could have wished for. You always have me in tears of laughter, keeping me positive, but keeping me real. You always ask the right questions and now I write with your voice in my head! Thank you for taking the time to know my characters, to understand them and to love them.

Bring on book two, and more tears of laughter.

To everyone at Oftomes who welcomed me into this bookish family. You've all been so supportive and I love how everyone cheers each other on.

To Claire and Chris at Eight Little Pages. Thank you for creating such a stunning cover for Saving Death. You've done Ava and Sam proud!

To all my wonderful followers on social media. You've had a wait for this book, but you've stuck with me, so thank you.

Lastly, to Benjamin Alderson. It all started with a live Instagram feed and a plee. 'Please read my book!' Well of course, you read it and I'll always remember receiving your request for the whole manuscript (the request that had me running about my work place in glee)! Thank you for listening, thank you for reading and thank you for loving Ava and Sam; but mostly, thank you for believing in me.

Rosy was born in Reading into a wildly creative and eccentric family, where she was always encouraged to be herself. It was in this environment that she learnt the importance of creativity and it is where she first began compiling all of her ideas, which she still has squirrelled away in a secret location. Her wild imagination and dreams would often give her inspiration and even today, she keeps a dream diary, but it was only when she took Creative Writing and Drama at university that she really began to share her writing with people. However, she has a small group of friends that she always shares her work with first!

Rosy now lives in a small and very old cottage in Somerset with her partner and her cat, Pepper. When she is not writing, she teaches at a local primary school, reads, runs and enjoys cooking.

www.rosyendean.com

Lightning Source UK Ltd.
Milton Keynes UK
UKHW01f2013060718
325340UK00001B/45/P

9 781999 963378